TAKE*OFF*

TAKEOFF

JOSEPH REID

THOMAS & MERCER

Text copyright © 2018 by Joseph Patrick Reid
All rights reserved.

Published by Thomas & Mercer, Seattle

www.apub.com

Amazon, the Amazon logo, and Thomas & Mercer are trademarks of Amazon.com, Inc., or its affiliates.

ISBN-13: 9781503949133 (hardcover)
ISBN-10: 1503949133 (hardcover)
ISBN-13: 9781503949126 (paperback)
ISBN-10: 1503949125 (paperback)

Cover design by Damon Freeman

Printed in the United States of America

First Edition

TAKEOFF

CHAPTER 1

Wednesday, July 15

Everything changed when the blood struck my right cheek.

Prior to that moment, the cross-country flight had been completely routine. Well, other than having a sixteen-year-old girl in tow. As a federal air marshal, I always traveled alone. Of course, she was the reason for my trip that day. And, technically, I wasn't an air marshal anymore.

At least, not like before.

Exiting baggage claim at LAX had felt, as always, like approaching the mouth of a tremendous cave. Out past the lanes of traffic, where the overhanging ceiling stops short of the parking garage, golden sunshine trickled down to a few stunted palms. Their fronds danced weakly back and forth—likely more from the passing cars than anything else, but enough to tantalize with the possibility of fresh air and a breeze.

Stuck back by the doors, though, we were still bathed in shadow, overhead fluorescents providing the same dim light they'd emit at midnight. The concrete beneath our feet, stained sooty brown, couldn't help but give you ideas about what the cloud of acrid exhaust trapped beneath the overhang was doing as it filled your nostrils.

It was good to be home.

At least for a second.

The girl and I had only taken two steps out the door when the suits started toward us from their van idling at the edge of the curb. Five guys, bulky with muscle and the vests you could see beneath their clothes.

They'd been waiting for us.

But they weren't the only ones. While no one paid it any attention at first, a black SUV pulled in just behind the FBI van.

As the lead suit drew up to us, he raised a badge and announced himself as Special Agent John Moore. "You must be Walker."

"How'd you guess?" I asked.

Moore chuckled. "Tattoos, shaved head. Dressed like you just flew in from Cancún. Franklin told me to look for the guy I'd want to frisk for drugs." Then he turned to the girl. "Which means you must be Max."

Her name was the last word Moore ever spoke.

The blood that struck me wasn't a remarkably large amount. Just a few drops, really. But the way the spatter erupted from Moore's throat, it had the same effect as a left hook thrown by one of those cage fighters you see on TV: it turned my head, drove me down. I fought to keep my eyes forward, trained on the girl and the bright flashes from the black SUV, but everything blurred.

Understand, I'm no stranger to guns. I grew up with them, and the past few years, the Sig Sauer P229 on my hip has been my steadiest travel companion. Until recently, I'd put at least a hundred rounds on target every other day, and that was on top of the paintball simulations we ran in a mocked-up aircraft cabin once a week.

But here's the thing about all that: I'm used to being the one slinging bullets in the opposite direction, not dropping to dodge a hail of screaming metal. In fact, before this particular day, I'd only ever been shot at once: six weeks prior, by a crazy woman in a lightning storm. A single shooter, at night, one semiautomatic pistol to worry about in limited visibility.

Nothing at all like facing three submachine guns, point-blank in broad daylight.

As my body followed my cheek around and down, I reached for the girl, who'd moved slightly ahead of me on the way to the FBI vehicle. My fingers found fabric somehow, and I dragged it with me. Turned out to be Max's hoodie. She landed on top of me in a heap, then rolled off sideways.

I glanced over, worried she might try to stand, but she stayed put. Flattened herself on her stomach.

Good girl. Smartest move she'd made all day.

Max looked at me, eyes wide. The gunfire had managed to wipe clean all the attitude and superiority she'd shown since we'd met eight hours earlier. Those wide eyes, normally a crisp, cornflower blue, had faded to the color of well-worn jeans, her skin china white against the brown cement.

Rolling to my back, I drew the Sig and pointed it past my toes, toward the black SUV. The gunfire had paused momentarily, and now I saw why: Moore's team was scattered across the sidewalk, all lying still or writhing weakly.

The rear door of the SUV popped open, and a man slid out. Tattoos everywhere, up his neck, onto his face. I've got plenty of ink, but this dude put me to shame. He even had black-and-red swirls etched on his cheeks and forehead. A machine gun dangled from his muscular arm, until he brought it around and finished one of the writhers with a short burst to the head.

When he started toward Max and me, I pretended the swirl on his forehead was a bull's-eye.

As his body slumped to the ground, I realized that wouldn't buy us more than a couple of seconds.

Flipping over onto my feet, I grabbed Max's hand and dragged her into a crouching run back into the terminal. The glass of the doors, broken inward by the gunmen's first barrage, crunched beneath our shoes. Another hail of fire rang out. As those shots pinged around us, I noticed the firing positions changing.

Whoever had remained in the SUV was now following.

Inside, travelers who'd been too stunned to move after the first volley of shots were now running, their screams mixing with the sound of ricocheting lead.

No way to help them now except by continuing to run, drawing the fire away from them . . . not that we weren't already doing a masterful job of that.

The nearest baggage carousel was empty but turning, its silver plates sliding endlessly counterclockwise. I forced Max up onto it, then jumped on behind her. When three bullets sounded against the plate by my left shoulder, I spun and spotted the nearest pursuer coming through the doors: another muscular mass of tattoos, gun raised.

I fired twice, center mass, and dropped him.

Behind me, Max was crawling away along the curve of the carousel. That wouldn't help us once it circled back around. I grabbed her hood again and steered her up onto the carpeted platform above the carousel.

Some airport carousels feed suitcases up from below. Not LAX. Here, the bags tumble down ramps from darkened holes in the ceiling. Fortunately, the ramps point toward the rear of the building, rather than the front.

Squatting behind Max and keeping my eyes on the doors, I herded her forward to the foot of the ramp. When I gave her ass one last shove, she got the idea.

With the conveyor belt moving down toward us, it was slow going—she looked more like a kid than ever, clumsily crab-walking her way up the metal chute. While she fought the belt, I fired two more shots toward the door and hoped Max wouldn't tumble back down at me, rammed by some giant suitcase.

Above me, her second pink Chuck Taylor disappeared into the black square overhead. Quickly as I could, I climbed after her.

CHAPTER 2

Monday, July 13

Two days before I met Max was my first day back in the office after a six-week break. Although I hadn't been working, it wasn't exactly what you'd call a vacation. Not unless you're partial to hospitals and doctors, shitty hotel beds and takeout food, funeral homes and grieving parents full of scorn.

Oh, and bills. Lots and lots of bills.

Like I said, not exactly a vacation.

So while I would have preferred to spend that Monday surfing or tinkering on one of my circuit projects, returning to work after an early-morning errand actually felt almost normal. A relief.

Despite being only two blocks from LAX, the Federal Air Marshal Service's LA field office sits on a relatively quiet street lined with nearly identical glass office buildings. Because we're considered undercover agents, our building's signs all say "Questar Express." Someday, I'd like to meet the guy in DC who gets paid to come up with the names for corporate fronts—that's gotta be some kind of job.

When I got to Vince Lavorgna's top-floor corner office, he was stuck nose deep in paperwork. Holding the results of my errand in one hand, I rapped on the door frame with the other. "Got a second, sir?"

Lavorgna's black beard twisted up into a half smile when his eyes met mine. "Come in, Seth. Shut the damn door." He stood and reached across the desk to pump my hand before I could reach the guest chair or set the plastic bag on the floor. His grip was as strong as ever—Lavorgna's built like an NFL linebacker—but his voice sounded softer, gentler than usual. After settling back into his chair, he looked me up and down. "How are you—"

"All due respect, sir, can we skip it?"

"Sure," he said after a moment. "I just—"

"Thanks for the flowers, sir. I know they came from you, and from Loretta, and I—"

"The whole office contributed."

I shot him a look, but he just nodded.

"Really."

"Well, I appreciated them. Sarah's family did, too. But I think the best thing now for everyone—for me—is if we can just skip past the whole pity-party stage. I've got this new job, let's start working it."

Lavorgna stroked the tip of his beard between two fingers while his eyes scanned over me. It felt a bit like playing poker, something I didn't ever want to do with Lavorgna. "I get that. And I've been there, believe me."

Most times, when someone starts to give me an "I been there" speech, I have to resist throwing up in my mouth. You're not me, never gonna be me, so spare me, you know? But I reminded myself that Lavorgna wasn't that guy. Until recently, I'd always wondered what mysterious job had generated all the plaques and pictures decorating his office. Then an FBI friend of mine told me Lavorgna had done some superdeep undercover narcotics work. Serious shit, so from him, I'd take the lecture.

"This is no pity party. You've been through a lot. What that Berkeley woman did to you and Sarah? That's a lot of weight to carry around. People want to help you with that, if you'll let them." He raised his eyebrows and tilted his head, but I didn't react. I was still hoping the usual edge would creep back into his Philadelphia accent. "Plus, there are procedures. You tell me you're ready, I'll take your word for it. But eventually, the docs are gonna have to get a look at you."

"Shrinks, you mean?"

He nodded. "Anybody involved in a shooting."

I shrugged. Should have expected that. And anyway, I had much bigger things to worry about than some psych exams: before our gunfight in the rainstorm, the crazy woman had done a whole lot of other damage, not the least of which was framing me for double murder and exposing my identity on TV. That last part might not sound like much, but for an air marshal, it's potentially career ending. Flying incognito was out of the question now, but since I'd tracked the woman down, the Service thought I might still have some value as a "liaison to law enforcement," whatever the hell that meant. "What do I do in the meantime?"

"The bosses in DC are still toying with ideas for how best to use you in this new role."

So, apparently the bosses didn't even know themselves.

"But," Lavorgna continued, "they've come up with an easy one for your first time out."

I raised my eyebrows and winced, waiting for it.

"Don't worry. It's not that bad. Just babysitting a celebrity on a cross-country flight."

"Who?"

"Some teenybopper with a hit on the radio, a takeoff on some old song. I've never heard of her." Lavorgna glanced down at a paper on his desk. "Max . . . Magic? Can't be her real name."

My godkids in Texas probably knew her—it'd give me an excuse to call them. I was trying to do that more these days. "Anyone tell you why she needs babysitting, sir?"

"Her father contacted the FBI about death threats. All celebs get them, but since she's so young, I guess he's extra anxious. Anyway, they'll escort her to JFK and hand her off to you. You fly with her, then pass her back to them at LAX."

"Why don't they just fly with her?"

"I think this is one of those . . . efforts at interagency cooperation." Lavorgna's beard compressed into a couched smile.

I nodded, but it still wasn't adding up. "If she's such a big star, why doesn't she have her own plane, her own pro detail? Why fly commercial?"

He shrugged. "All excellent questions, Mr. Law-Enforcement Liaison. I suggest you ask the people in the know."

"Loretta book me?"

"Believe so."

I scooped up the bag and got to my feet as quickly as I could—hanging around would only draw more questions about how I was doing. "All right, sir. I'll see you in a couple of days."

"Qualify downstairs before you leave. You been shooting?"

"Not the usual amount, but enough. I should be good."

Lavorgna rose, and stuck out his hand again. This time he looked me square in the eye. "It's good to have you back."

I wove through the maze of cubes outside Lavorgna's office until I reached Loretta's. Pecking away at her keyboard, she didn't see me coming.

"How's the prettiest girl in LA?"

I don't think I've ever seen her old bones move so quickly. Before I knew it, she'd spun around, hopped off her chair, and wrapped her spindly arms around my waist.

After a long moment, she reached a hand up to either side of my head and tilted it downward until my blue eyes were looking straight through her spectacles into her brown ones. Loretta's voice always had a certain warble to it, but I could swear it almost cracked as she asked, "How are you, dear?"

"I'm fine."

Her lips drew to a point, and she glared over the top of the glasses at me.

"Really, I swear."

"You know you can't lie to me, boy."

Loretta grilling me about how I was handling Sarah's death felt awfully ironic: One of the last romantic nights we'd had before . . . before everything had changed, we'd gotten into an argument over dinner about Loretta. Sarah couldn't understand why I was always ordering extra food on our dates—when she found out it was for a woman at the office, well, she'd stormed out of the restaurant, blue eyes blazing. Once I'd finally caught up to her outside and explained, things got better, but it had made for a nervous few minutes.

Now my heart raced the same way it had that night, and I had to look away from the pressure of Loretta's gaze. After somehow managing to swallow, I said, "I'm . . . sad. But that's natural, right? It'll fade eventually." I knew from experience that last part was a lie, but I hoped Loretta couldn't tell. I looked back down at her. "Right now, I'm just glad to be home."

"You beatin' yourself up? Blamin' yourself for what happened?"

"No, ma'am," I answered too quickly.

Still, she released me and sank back into her chair. "Good," was all she said.

As relieved as I was that she'd stopped asking questions, the way Loretta moved worried me. So did her skin. The color of dark chocolate, it always looked as thin as tissue paper, but today it appeared every bit as fragile.

I produced the plastic bag and set it in her lap. "You know, when I landed yesterday, I was so hungry I couldn't help myself. Headed up to Langer's for a sandwich, but my eyes were bigger than my stomach. With me going out of town now, you think you can finish the rest off for me? I'd hate for it to go to waste."

Loretta wrinkled her nose. She knew as well as I did that Langer's Deli wasn't open on Sundays. Besides, the heat from the brisket sandwich was still palpable through the plastic. We'd played this game for two years, but today none of the usual teasing came, no sharp rebukes. She simply turned and placed the package on her desk. That was worrisome, too.

"How've you been?" I asked. "How's Bob?"

"You know us. We're getting by."

I tried not to let her see me wince. *Getting by* was what she'd called it when I'd caught her early one morning in the office kitchen, making a ketchup sandwich from the communal bottle and a stolen slice of bread. The reason I'd been bringing her my "leftovers" ever since. "If you need money—"

Loretta's eyes darted at me. "That's enough, young man."

"Yes, ma'am." My chin dropped to my chest. Then I raised my eyes. "But how is he?"

"Weak," she said, turning back to her monitor. Her voice had dropped to a whisper. "It's tougher this time." After a moment, though, the warble came back into her voice. "Big trip to New York, huh? Gonna go see the bright lights, catch a show?"

"Something like that."

Although she booked all our travel, Loretta never seemed to distinguish between the neon-filled Times Square of her dreams and the airport-hotel reality we air marshals dwelled in. Truth was, I relished the idea of a little room service and a few uninterrupted hours to doodle and tinker.

Loretta turned in her chair and pressed a folder into my hand. I could see it was marked and tabbed the way she always did it. I'd long since abandoned the idea of asking her for electronic itineraries. "Thank you, ma'am."

"I'm just happy you're home," she said. "I missed you, boy. Make this trip quick."

◆ ◆ ◆

The New York airport hotel, as it turned out, didn't have room service. At the restaurant downstairs, I was able to order some chicken soup that wasn't horrible. Then, back in my room, I tried drawing some circuits but didn't get very far. In the moment, I blamed the uncomfortable desk chair; deep down, I knew that wasn't it. The room wasn't all that different from dozens of places I'd managed to work.

Truth was, since all the trouble, I hadn't been particularly creative.

Dan Shen, my friend and patent attorney, hadn't said anything about it yet. But I could tell from our phone calls he was wondering. Whenever I stared at the pad, none of the images that usually filled my head seemed to come. Instead of circuit boards and processors floating around my brain, it was all lab tests and medical procedures.

I switched the lights off and climbed into bed, but ended up staring at the ceiling, thinking about Loretta. I figured that was probably just as well—given the dreams I'd been having over the past few weeks, insomnia felt like an improvement.

Returning to the desk, I opened my laptop, queued up several podcasts from my favorite tech blogs, and loaded them onto the player that fed my earpiece. My brain has this weird condition where, if it's not being constantly stimulated by some kind of chatter or focused by adrenaline, it can go off-kilter. And I don't mean normal mind wandering or polite daydreaming. Thoughts keep multiplying inside my head, and if they get to the point where they go exponential, I can end up a twitching, drooling mess.

It's put me in the hospital before. It's not pretty.

Fortunately, I had plenty of content to choose from: The past few weeks, I hadn't listened to any of my usual electrical-engineering podcasts. Instead, struggling to keep up with what Sarah's doctors were saying, I'd been running articles about *cerebrospinal hypotension* and *acute anoxic encephalopathy* through the software I have that turns text into audio and listening to those through my earpiece.

Tonight, though, out of sheer curiosity I went onto the web and googled *Max Magic*. The links below her Wikipedia page mostly led to magazines, so I clicked a few. The photo spreads looked way more provocative than I'd expected. Two had the blonde youngster posing in bikinis, draped across a boat and sprawled on a beach. A third had her doing kicks in a tiny cheerleader uniform. The last one was the most suggestive: she was topless, mostly prone on a bearskin rug.

Backing out of that one, I scrolled down until I found some music sites. Her latest hit song proved easy to find—evidently it had held the top spot on the charts for three straight months. When I saw the title, I smiled and shook my head, surprised I hadn't heard about it somehow.

When I was growing up, my mother had never been much for music. But my dad loved his stereo. Every time we moved, which was often, that was the first thing he'd unpack, before any of my toys or the dishes or the silverware. Every evening, he'd blast rock and R & B records until Mom stormed in from the kitchen, demanding he turn the music down and open some moving boxes.

One of Dad's all-time favorites was "Be My Baby" by the Ronettes. In fact, I always got the sense that, while most guys his age had fantasized about Pam Grier as teenagers, Dad would've preferred a tryst with Ronnie Spector. "Be My Baby" was the first song on the first side of Dad's Ronettes record—to this day, he prefers vinyl, despite the CD player I bought him—and when I was a kid, he'd listen to it over and over. As the last chords of "Be My Baby" would fade, he'd jump from his chair to reach for the needle. I'd beg him to let it run, at first just for variety's sake. Eventually, though, I fell for the song that followed.

"Baby, I Love You."

The two songs are similar: a clicking cymbal or tambourine drives their beat as Phil Spector's orchestral "wall of sound" swells in the background. The Ronettes sing the chorus, while Ronnie Spector performs her *whoa-oo* flourishes over them. Both are classics, but "Be My Baby" always struck me as the rawer, more lust-driven song. It's an invitation to make out.

"Baby, I Love You" has a totally different vibe. A sweet song, it's a testimonial about being so in love with the boy she's singing to, the feeling moves her to tears. It's what every teenage boyfriend will never admit he wants his girlfriend to say about their relationship.

Flopping back onto the bed, I closed my eyes and hit "Play" on Max Magic's cover.

It was . . . interesting.

They'd added a loud, electronic backbeat and cranked up the bass. Max's voice wasn't raspy and throaty like Ronnie Spector's; it was clear and crisp, although I wondered how much she'd been Auto-Tuned during production. But really, the biggest difference was the emotion the lyrics carried. Where the original could convince you Ronnie might actually burst into tears at any moment, Max sounded like a little girl dreaming of how a love like that would feel.

If Max had put anything less into it, hers might have come off as cheap, or naive. But it didn't. The song still sounded heartfelt, only sung from a different place.

It gave me a glimmer of hope: maybe Max Magic wouldn't be so bad after all.

◆ ◆ ◆

Wednesday, July 15

Max and I were booked out of JFK's Terminal 8. Since it got a face-lift a few years ago, 8 isn't too bad. It could use better restaurants—the food court's abysmal—but otherwise it feels new and airy, with lots of chrome, windows, and high ceilings.

That's in the public spaces. Airports are kind of like Disneyland: there's a whole layer to them the public never sees.

Just inside security, the wall bears a series of unmarked doors. While they might as well be janitors' closets as far as travelers are concerned, one of them deposits you in a narrow hallway lined with industrial carpet and framed posters of old American Airlines ad campaigns. A string of offices sprouts off it, and a windowless conference room lies at the end.

That's where the FBI decided we should meet at noon.

With my doodling going nowhere and nothing else to do at the hotel, I arrived early and sat in the room alone. Despite the summer heat outside, I wore jeans in anticipation of the flight. A baggy, untucked resort shirt hid the bulge of the holster in my waistband while leaving my forearms bare. I didn't know how many people would recognize Max Magic by sight, but for this kind of job, I figured my tattoos might help scare some people off.

People are funny about ink. Those who don't have any immediately draw conclusions about those who do. Take me. While I'm not the biggest guy, I'm not the smallest, either—that, plus the shaved head and the tattoos get me all kinds of reactions. That I'm a biker. Or a banger. Never that I'm a federal agent and closet electrical engineer with fifteen patents to my name.

Folks who know tattoos, though, they get the complexity of it. Each of mine is a marker, a testament to something important.

Or someone.

Like the one I'd gotten just a couple of weeks before: the letters *S* and *A* inside a heart. I'd planned on getting it on my chest, close to my real heart. That's where it seemed to belong. Until I realized I'd only ever see it in the mirror with my shirt off, and written backward. I needed to be reminded more often than that. Eventually, I decided the inside of my right forearm, up by the wrist, would be better. There, it'd catch my eye every day.

I'd spent a lot of time staring at the new tattoo. I was doing it again when the FBI detail strode in.

Four guys in suits and ties, but no way you'd mistake them for lawyers or bankers. Jackets straining at the shoulders, not the waists.

Haircuts all high and tight. Walking with their weight forward, up on the balls of their feet, instead of back on their heels. They formed two pairs, one in front, one in back, bracketing a man and a girl.

The man couldn't have stood out more from the agents if he'd tried. His dark suit was fancier than theirs, made of a lighter fabric that seemed to sashay on its own as he moved. Instead of a collared shirt and tie, he wore a black T-shirt beneath the jacket. His face and hands had tanned to a deep copper, about the same as my complexion, but pale skin peeked out at his neck and wrists. His long, gray hair was styled and slicked into a large wave, cresting over his forehead, while his eyes darted restlessly between his smartphone and the room around us.

I put all the men over six feet, but Max Magic barely broke five. Still, she stood no risk of getting lost in the crowd. Cutoff jean shorts adorned with rhinestones bared virtually all of her long legs. A tank top matching her pink sneakers hung loosely from her shoulders, exposing her arms and the straps of a black bra working hard to make her breasts look even bigger than they were. White, plastic buttons resembling little candies were sewn onto the shirt, which bore the words *Sweet Tart*.

Sunglasses hid the girl's eyes but couldn't obscure how her face—all soft, childish curves—hadn't quite caught up to the rest of her. Still, if she feared whatever threat was supposedly dogging her, you wouldn't have known. Her expression was as loose and relaxed as the braid of streaky blonde hair draped down her shoulder.

One of the front pair of agents stepped forward, so I stood to shake his hand.

"Special Agent Gary Franklin," he said, flashing credentials at me. His voice had a slight drawl to it, like he'd been raised in the South but hadn't lived there in years.

"Seth Walker."

Turning, he gestured to the others. "With me are Agents Hayes, Lincoln, and Jackson—"

I smiled. "You guys are like a social studies test."

That earned me an eye roll. "—and allow me to introduce Gregory Drew and his daughter."

"Nice to meet you both," I said. "It's Max, right?"

The girl didn't react.

Drew, though, glanced up and locked his eyes on mine. "I just want to thank you in advance for taking care of my little girl. I can't tell you how much I appreciate it."

The intensity of Drew's gaze felt slightly unnerving. I nodded before addressing Franklin again. "What've we got here?"

"Mr. Drew approached us three months ago after receiving anonymous written threats against his daughter. Since then, we've been monitoring their mail, their incoming calls, providing light security—"

"Four agents is 'light'?"

"Usually we've been leaving just one consultant with them. But we felt that Max taking this flight alone might . . . expose her in some unique ways."

The way Franklin paused somehow didn't feel quite right. "She doesn't have her own private detail?"

"Yes. I mean, she did." Franklin's eyebrows rose as he nodded. "Single bodyguard, but he was former military and had done a fair amount of personal-protection work."

"Where's he now?"

"I caught him stealing," Drew said.

"Stealing," I said. "Okay. And you haven't replaced him?"

"I'm not going to trust my daughter's safety to just anyone, Mr. Walker. I was in the process of interviewing new bodyguards when all of this came about. Thankfully, the FBI has been taking good care of us since then."

Drew's lips spread into a smile that suggested he was extremely pleased my tax dollars were paying for his daughter's security detail.

"Why is Max flying alone? There a reason you have to stay here?"

"Max begins shooting on a . . . uh, movie in the next few days." From the way he shrugged as he said it, Drew apparently wasn't a big fan of the screenplay. Or something. "Meanwhile, I've got to stay here and wrap up work on some endorsement contracts. Those, and her recording career—they're the engine that makes this whole train run."

"Not for long," Max said. Her voice was flat, but not quiet.

Drew kept smiling at the agents and me. "We'll see, honey."

"Sure will."

He shrugged again but still didn't look at her.

"Are you a lawyer, Mr. Drew?" I asked. Except for Shen, lawyers have never been my favorite. And I was definitely starting to get that vibe from him.

"I started law school just before Max came along, but I stopped when Max's mom . . . well . . . I stopped. I'm Max's manager. I'm involved in all aspects of her brand."

In my peripheral vision, I noticed Max change the direction of space into which she was staring.

"I'm sorry for being behind on family history, but since you mentioned Max's mother, where is she?"

Drew's mouth opened, but the voice that rang out wasn't his. "She's gone. She was a junkie, and she left."

I glanced over at Max and could tell her eyes were blazing at me behind the shades. "I'm sorry to bring it up," I said. "I just wanted to understand the situation."

She turned away.

"Deborah left when Max was about six months old," Drew said. "Since then, it's been just the two of us."

I nodded. Because my godkids had lost their father, I knew a little about absentee-parent issues. "I'm guessing everyone has already asked you this, Mr. Drew, but just for my sake, do you have any idea who'd want to hurt Max?"

"I can only imagine it's someone jealous of her success, or someone who's patently deranged."

I turned to Franklin. "Bureau have any ideas? What about the ex–security guy?"

"We checked him out. Looks clean."

"Wouldn't it be safer to do this on some private plane?"

Franklin shook his head. "We're guessing this is some lone nut-case. Spends his time clipping letters out of the newspaper for his notes. Nobody knows she's taking this flight except us. She'll blend in a lot easier in a big crowd than she would at some rinky-dink private airport—you're not gonna have any problems."

"Oka-y," I said. If all that were true, Max wouldn't have needed a four-agent detail to escort her through the terminal. But since Franklin apparently thought I was stupid enough to believe it, I didn't see the point in pressing it further. "Sounds like this'll be a cakewalk, then."

The agents escorted Drew out, leaving me alone with Max. What, I wondered, did you talk about with a teenage pop star?

"So," I said. "You excited to get to California?"

She raised her hand and slowly twirled her index finger. "Yay."

"You know, I used to be an engineer, and I worked on a bunch of audio technology. When you're recording a song, do you get involved in all that?"

"No," she said, glancing off toward the door. "That's the sound engineer's job."

I waited a beat. "So, is Max your real name?"

Her head snapped back toward me. "Excuse me?"

"I mean, Magic's obviously not your real last name, right? So I was wondering, is Max your real first name?"

"That's my name." Her tone was that of telling a dog to sit for the fifth or sixth time in a row. "That's what everyone calls me now."

Since our getting-to-know-you chat was going so well, I checked the time on my phone and maneuvered my carry-on around the table. "We should get to the gate."

Instead of proceeding through the door, Max stepped to the side. When I continued to stare at her, she asked, "Aren't you going to get my bag?" A loud pink roll-aboard suitcase stood slightly behind her, where one of the FBI agents had left it.

I leaned down until my eyes were inches from her sunglasses. "I'm your protection. Not your handservant."

By the time we reached the gate, our airplane had already arrived and unloaded. I steered Max to the desk where, making it look like I was requesting an upgrade or something, I showed the agent my badge. She confirmed they were still cleaning from the previous flight, but took our tickets to allow us to preboard.

A lot of marshals I know like to get onto the plane early. The good ones figure it's best to check in with the crew and inspect the plane before any passengers come aboard. The bad ones, well, they just want to ensure themselves room in the overhead bins and get to their seat. I never liked preboarding—too noticeable. But today, given that people might already be ogling Max, getting her into a controlled environment as soon as possible seemed to make the most sense.

She followed me down the jetbridge and onto the plane, a 767. Maneuvering to the farther of the two aisles, I led us back to the last row of business class. Unsure if Max could reach the overhead, I stowed the rollaboard for her after she grabbed a few things out of it. Then I ushered her into the window seat.

As I eased myself down next to her, the cushions embraced my back more than I was used to, and my legs felt like they were swimming in space. I'd need to tease Loretta about getting me seats like this more often. Marshals get upgraded if a first-class seat goes unclaimed, but with fewer flights and all the elite programs, it's become an extreme rarity.

While I was still marveling at the luxury, a familiar female voice snapped me out of it. "Seth Walker, you keeping us safe today?"

I glanced up the aisle and saw Diane Carter approaching from the forward galley. A senior LA-based attendant with silver hair and a Brooklyn accent, Diane tended to fly cross-country routes. I'd flown with her maybe three dozen times over the years. "Not today. I'm on escort duty. Diane, meet Max." I turned, expecting her to be staring out the window at best, eye rolling or sneering at worst.

Instead, Max had her sunglasses off and wore a bright smile. It was the first time I'd gotten to see her eyes. "Pleasure to meet you," she said sweetly.

Diane blushed. "I'm sorry, I've flown with a lot of celebrities, but seeing you here is a real treat." She glanced up and down the aisle. "I don't mean to impose—I never do things like this, I swear—but my nephew is just about your biggest fan. Is there any chance—"

Max's smile grew even broader. "Do you have a pen?"

Diane scrambled off, then returned with a marker. Max drew the in-flight magazine from the seat pocket in front of her and began writing across the cover. "What's his name?" she asked without looking up.

"Steven. With a *v*."

Max filled almost the entire cover with handwriting before ending with a loopy, curvy signature that had two hearts next to it. She blew lightly across it, then handed it over.

Diane read the inscription quickly, then clutched the magazine to her chest. "Thank you so much! If there's anything I can do during the flight—"

Max's eyes sparkled. "Do you have any champagne?"

The question caught me sufficiently off guard that I didn't say anything, but rather looked to Diane. Her face, beaming just a moment ago, now dropped. "I—I'm sorry, I don't think I can do that." Without another word, she scurried back to the forward galley.

"Bitch."

I turned and saw that Max's expression had turned scornful again.

"Hey," I said, "watch it. You're not old enough to drink. You're only—" I realized I didn't actually know the answer. "How old are you, anyway?"

"I turn seventeen in three weeks."

"See, you're not even close—"

"I drink champagne all the time."

"You expect her to risk her job just so you can have a drink? Alcohol's a serious—"

Max released a large sigh. "In Europe, there's no drinking age, and they don't have half the problems with alcohol that we do. It's only here, where everyone's so uptight—"

"That's not true, and you'll get her in big trouble. Besides, it's not good for you."

She slipped the sunglasses back onto her face, midway up her nose, leaving her eyes exposed. "You're my protection, remember? Not my parent." Then she pushed the glasses up into place and turned toward the window.

Max continued staring silently outside, eventually donning headphones as boarding began in earnest. The aisle filled with passengers, and as those behind us took time getting settled, the line moved in fits and starts. I scanned everyone who passed, but none seemed to be paying Max any special attention.

Once boarding was complete, Diane and the other attendants moved about the cabin, prepping for takeoff. They ignored Max's headphones, and she remained lost in the world on the other side of the window. As we pushed back, she braced her foot on the frame of the seat in front of her and began bouncing it. She also twirled the tip of her braid between her fingers. Nervous or bored, I couldn't tell.

Since it didn't appear Max would be a great conversationalist, I started studying the passengers around us. The couple directly in front had needed wheelchair assistance and looked to be in their eighties—no threat there. Across the aisle, two business types were talking and laughing. They'd gotten cocktails while we'd been parked at the gate, and now it was impossible to tell if they were traveling together or just schmoozing. Both had big bellies, though, and didn't look like they'd last long in a fight. The rest of business class looked like it usually did—mostly white, older than average, all exhibiting some sign or another of wealth: fine clothes, jewelry, fancy tech devices. No one I'd finger as an immediate threat.

Maybe Franklin was right.

I pulled a pad and mechanical pencil from my bag and set the paper in my lap. I liked to doodle schematics on flights, so I figured I'd see if something came to me.

Nothing did.

After we'd leveled off, the seat-belt sign darkened with a chime. Max immediately clicked out of her belt, retrieved a small purse from the seat pocket, and stood.

I simply stared at her.

After a moment, she blew some air through her nose. "Excuse me."

"Where do you think you're going?"

"Uh, the little girls' room."

I nodded at the purse. "Anything in there I need to worry about?"

"Oh please."

"Seriously. Drugs, cigarettes, anything?"

Max spoke through clenched teeth. "I'm on the rag, okay?"

Not sure I'd ever heard it put quite that way, I slowly unbuckled and stood, releasing her into the aisle. While she strode quickly to the lav, I took my time sitting back down. No one appeared to be eyeing her. No one appeared to pay her any attention at all.

After several minutes, just as I was beginning to grow concerned, Max reemerged.

I rose and checked everyone along her route back while she moved in my peripheral vision. Her pace was slower this time, and the head of a balding white-haired guy in row four swiveled as she advanced up the aisle.

My right hand slid back toward my hip.

As Max drew within a row of him, the guy began gathering himself.

My hand closed around the grip of the Sig under my shirt, while the rest of my muscles tensed.

Max passed the man's seat before he moved. He stood, looked up and down the aisle, then headed for the lav she'd just vacated.

I let my hand drop to my side as Max reached our row. Her expression had softened considerably, and she gave me a weak half smile as she stepped inside.

I hoped things might be improving.

Twenty minutes later, Max said she was cold, and asked me politely to retrieve a hooded sweatshirt from her bag overhead. I obliged and saw Diane starting the food service. Soon we each had trays in front of us containing a vegetable omelet, fruit, and some kind of Danish with jelly in the middle. I wolfed the eggs, then turned back to the fruit. Glancing over, I noticed Max was using her fork to tease small chunks of mushroom out of the omelet.

"Aren't you hungry?"

"I don't eat eggs," she said.

"Allergic?"

She sighed. "Vegan."

"Then eat your fruit," I said in the most parental tone possible. "It's good for you."

Rolling her eyes, Max said, "I cannot wait to be rid of you."

CHAPTER 3

Wednesday, July 15

When I reached the top of the baggage chute, I braced my feet on either side of the conveyor.

The rectangular opening, barely wider than my shoulders, was surrounded on three sides by a metal screen extending up over my head. That served as a backstop: the fourth side was open and featured another conveyor belt, which, given where I was standing, pointed directly at my chest. But that was all I could see: bathed in the shaft of light shining upward from below, the remainder of the room seemed impenetrably dark. A droning, mechanical hum nearly drowned out the gunfire that still rang out.

Sensing movement ahead, I squinted against the blackness.

Max?

But as the motion continued, it seemed too regular. Too smooth and mechanical.

Quickly, an outline formed: straight lines, right angles.

A particularly large, hard-sided suitcase hurtled toward me on the oncoming belt.

I glanced around, but there was nowhere to go. Even on tiptoes, the top of the screen stood several inches above my fingertips.

There was only one option. I made the best jump I could with my legs splayed.

Somehow my fingers managed to grab the top of the backstop. Its upper edge sliced into my palms as I tried to get a solid handhold. Farther down, the smooth metal felt slick as ice beneath my feet as I struggled to scramble upward.

I'd just reached the top of the screen when the suitcase slammed into it. Vibration from the impact rippled through the metal, sending me toppling over the back side. I fell into the darkness until my hip struck something hard.

Rolling onto my back, my fingers found the floor beneath me. Smooth concrete.

As I sat up and took a breath, my eyes finally began to adjust. The ceiling hung extremely low, just a foot or two above the top of the metal I'd climbed over. Every few yards to my right and left, light shone up from another hole in the floor where another conveyor would send bags tumbling downward. The air smelled hot and musty, and the mechanical noise was even louder now, making the concrete rumble.

Following our conveyor belt backward with my eyes, I finally spotted Max huddled against a column several feet away, knees pulled up to her chest.

I started crawling toward her. When I got within two feet, she screamed.

The noise was masked by the conveyor's hum, but her open mouth and the look of terror on her face was unmistakable.

Then I realized: her eyes were focused behind me.

I dropped to the concrete, rolled onto my back again, and drew the Sig in one motion.

A head had poked up through our hole in the floor. Another tattooed face.

His eyes must've needed a moment, too, as they blinked several times before recognizing me. That's when my bullets hit him. His head dropped out of sight, leaving cascades of red splattered back against the silver metal of the collar.

Keeping the Sig trained on the hole, I shuffled backward to Max. She was huffing, hyperventilating, looking like she might vomit.

"This way," I yelled over the din. When she didn't budge, I got right up into her face, my eyes just inches from hers. "We can't stay here. C'mon!"

Finally, she moved, and we began following the luggage conveyor backward into the darkness.

Wide eyes and open mouths greeted us as we emerged from the maze of the luggage system onto the airport tarmac. The small group of baggage handlers pointed to several police cruisers approaching from the runways, flashers spinning.

Airport cops.

They didn't give me any great sense of relief. While it seemed like the tattooed bunch had given up on following us, I wasn't about to hang around to confirm that. I needed to get Max away from here. Now.

My Jeep was parked in the short-term garage wedged in the middle of the semicircular collection of terminals. We could access it from any of them.

Between my badge and gun, I managed to convince one of the handlers to ferry us to the next terminal in his cart and open the door for us with his key card. Leading Max inside, I studied her face. She hadn't said a word since the gunfire, and now her eyes were distant, almost catatonic. Although it was worrisome, I resigned myself to dealing with it later. "Just a little bit farther," I told her.

When we reached the garage, I quickened our pace to a trot. Pulling Max along with my left hand, I kept my right hooked beneath my shirt, just in case. We stuck to the walls and crossed in the middle of aisles instead of the ends, weaving between cars as we went.

The Jeep was waiting exactly where I'd left it on the third floor.

I spread one of the blankets I always keep in the back across the floor of the trunk for Max to lie on, then draped another one over her body. Once she was tucked in, I jumped behind the wheel and got us moving.

I guessed that the airport police had blocked up World Way, the loop circling through the middle of the airport, back by arrivals, as all five lanes were eerily empty when we emerged from the garage. Normally, I'd have jumped on Sepulveda and cruised down through the tunnel beneath the runways before turning for home. Today, though, I steered us out onto Century Boulevard instead.

As the airport slipped away in the mirrors, late-afternoon traffic swelled around us. With a couple of turns, I merged onto the 405, heading south. A lot of cars, but at least they were moving. Despite alternating speeds and changing lanes several times, I didn't see anything suspicious or consistent behind us. Finally, I slipped over into the fast lane and stayed there.

"I think we're clear now. You okay?"

No response.

I glanced back, but Max was facing away from me—no way to get a read on her. "I gotta call my boss. Hang tight back there. We'll figure this all out."

The silence continued, and I checked again. This time, I saw her side shift beneath the blanket. She was still breathing, and for now, I guessed that was enough.

I dialed Lavorgna, who answered instantly. "Oh, thank Christ," he said. "You all right? How's the girl?"

"I'm fine, sir. She's in shock, but otherwise intact."

"What the bloody blazes happened out there?"

I described the scene from the time we exited baggage claim. "You can tell Franklin, this is no lone psycho."

"The tattoos you saw. Sounds like something gang related. MS-13?"

"I thought of that, but these guys were . . . different. They looked foreign, somehow. And the symbols were more tribal than street, if that makes sense. What would a gang be doing trying to take down someone like Max, anyway?"

"Dunno," Lavorgna said. "But they never should have known when and where you two would be arriving. She do anything stupid, like text it out to all her friends?"

"Nope, I was watching her. The only time she was out of my sight, there wasn't any service."

"Then there must be a leak somewhere. I'll go back and squeeze the FBI to see what comes out. You just get the girl someplace safe."

"The media know she was here?"

"We've got the news on," Vince said. "They're reporting the shooting, but no mention of her as the target. Same on social media: folks talking about a shoot-out at LAX, but nothing about Max."

"Then I'm thinking my place." After the events of six weeks ago, I'd upgraded my security system. Significantly.

"You sure? If this gang expected you two at the airport, they may have done their homework."

I checked the sky, which was already starting to redden. "We won't stay long. But I'm worried about her—she's pretty out of it. Plus, I need supplies."

"Okay. I'll let Franklin and Drew know you're safe, but play dumb about where you're headed. When I know something, I'll call."

◆ ◆ ◆

I continued watching the mirrors but didn't see anything noteworthy. Still, rather than heading directly west, I took the 710 north, then jumped on Route 91 headed back toward the coast. I followed it all the way into Hermosa Beach, past Pacific Coast Highway, before pulling off onto a side street and reaching for my phone.

Finding your house broken into is a funny thing: it makes you paranoid. When the crazy lady got inside my place, she didn't take anything. The opposite, actually. But after spending hours scrubbing all the bloody presents she'd left off my floors and walls, I'd sworn that was never going to happen again.

Most of the security components I needed were available right off the shelf. Sensors on the doors and windows would detect if they were opened and warn me—by flashing a strobe light inside the house and by text on my phone—of the intrusion. No messages so far; that was a good sign. Meanwhile, webcams watched the yard, exterior, and interior, and I could access them from anywhere.

Like, say, from my phone on a side street in Hermosa Beach.

My house is a modern tri-level, the three stories each slightly offset from one another and connected by two separate sets of stairs. The ground floor has all three primary entrances: the garage, a side door leading out to the yard, and the front door out to the street. The middle floor contains the living room and kitchen, but it also has a balcony you can access from sliding glass doors. The top floor is the bedroom, which has its own walk-out balcony.

The cameras don't have the greatest field of vision—if the black SUV from LAX was parked across the alley from my garage, for example, I wouldn't necessarily see it. But as I toggled between the cameras, everything looked clear.

Tucking the phone away, I turned back toward Max, putting a hand on her shoulder. "You still with me back there?"

She didn't say anything, but her braid bobbed as her head slowly nodded.

"Okay, just five minutes more."

Tracking the coastline, I stole peeks at the water as we passed each successive block. Both the Strand—the concrete boardwalk running along the beach—and the sand beyond it were painted a Martian red by the final traces of crimson sunshine settling into the ocean. The water had grown a deep purple, but you could still see a line of clean breakers, crashing and rolling up the shore.

Good faces, maybe three feet.

I sighed over another day without surfing. At this rate, tomorrow was not looking too promising, either.

As we drew closer to the house, I began weaving up and down the cross streets, searching for the black SUV, or signs of anything else suspicious. My neighborhood in Manhattan Beach, known as the Sand Section, consists of pairs of paved streets and concrete paths leading up the hill from the Strand. The paved streets are barely wider than a car—they're essentially alleys providing garage access for the houses on either side. The houses themselves—every one done in a different style—face out onto the concrete paths, which locals call "walking streets." The streets and paths share numbers, with the paths confusingly designated as "streets," and the streets named "places." In this way, my front door opens onto 18th Street, while my garage opens onto 18th Place.

Mere steps from the ocean, land is at a premium. Lots are long and thin, yards can be measured in square inches, and the houses are packed together so tightly a bodybuilder would need to turn sideways to pass through the gaps between them. That said, people have found all kinds of ingenious ways of dealing with the cramped quarters. Most front "yards" on the walking streets are surrounded by some kind of low fence or wall and feature a sitting area, whether it's a wooden picnic table or a fancy stone fire pit. People have also made creative use of the breezeways between houses: some are completely filled with surfboards, kayaks, and other outdoor equipment, while others have been fenced off to create narrow gardens, outdoor showers, or just about anything else you can imagine putting in a narrow hallway. There are nooks and crannies in which to hide almost everywhere in the Sand Section. It's like a human rabbit warren.

As I cruised slowly from 15th Place up to 20th, I still didn't see anything abnormal. People driving home from work or dinner. Surfers trudging uphill with their boards, making me jealous. Lights starting to flick on against the onset of dusk.

Looping back to 18th, I triggered my garage door and pulled the Jeep in.

Max still lay on her side, eyes eerily open, and didn't react, even when I pulled off the blanket. "C'mon, Max," I said, "we're here." Slowly, she lowered her feet to the ground and started walking, as if in a trance. Grabbing her elbow with one hand, I shut the Jeep with the other, closed the garage door, and steered her inside.

Upstairs, I ushered her to the living area, where I spun the easy chair I normally use away from the windows and TV, back toward the coffee table and sofa. Max looked small as she sank into the plush leather seat.

I still couldn't get her to make eye contact, but her jaw was trembling. "You cold?" I asked. "Hungry?"

She nodded slightly. I retrieved a knit blanket my godkids' mother, Shirley, had sent two Christmases ago and wrapped it around Max's shoulders, then beelined to the kitchen. I usually don't keep much food in the house, but I found a package of ramen in the pantry, nuked it in the microwave, and brought the steaming liquid to her in a tall travel mug. Although it had to be seventy-five degrees out, the way she clutched the mug with both hands and slurped the soup, you'd have thought she'd just come in off the ski slopes.

"Take your time," I said. "Sip that down." After double-checking all the alarms and sensors, I sat on the couch across from her. Max's cheeks regained some of their pink hue as she drained the mug, and her eyes began roving around the house.

Finally, they settled on me.

"Thank you," she said softly.

I shrugged. "My job, remember?"

"The way they just pulled up at the curb and started shooting . . ." She pulled the blanket tighter around her and bit her bottom lip. Then her voice rose. "What was the FBI thinking, having us meet them outside?"

"I don't think they had any clue we'd be walking into something like that."

Max glared at me. "We could have been killed." But as quickly as her temper flared, her expression softened, and you could tell she'd begun replaying the images in her mind. "All those people . . ."

Her eyes found the floor again and stayed there for what seemed like several minutes.

My stomach knotted as I struggled to think of something to say to fill the silence. I wanted to reach out, to comfort her somehow, but the truth was, together we'd witnessed the worst carnage I had ever seen in person. Despite all my training, other than one crazy woman in Dallas, I'd never shot anyone before; today, I'd taken down at least three of our pursuers. I wasn't entirely sure why I wasn't feeling something more, or how I was processing it. How, then, exactly, was I supposed to reassure her?

"Had you ever seen those men before?" I asked.

She shook her head.

"Do you know why they'd want to hurt you? Or who might have hired them to do it?"

Max's head rocked farther and farther to each side, more forcefully each time, until finally she threw it all the way back and a guttural noise sounded in her throat. "God, the FBI asked me all these same questions. I told them, I don't know. I don't know!"

Even with her eyes pointed at the ceiling, I could see them well up and tears start streaming down past her ears into her hair. Before I could say anything, though, she wiped them away with her arm and looked at me plaintively. "Is there someplace I can lie down? I just . . . my brain isn't . . . I'm so tired."

"I know," I said. "But we can't stay here long. There are a few things—"

"Please? I just need to close my eyes. Please?" Max's voice cracked on the final word.

I checked the windows: the last remnants of daylight were still visible. Darkness would give us better cover. Plus, it would take me a little while to gather up what we needed.

Glancing back at Max, I saw her breathing had become ragged. With her head tilted, her shoulders slumped, she looked like she might crumble to pieces.

"Okay, c'mon." I said. "You can sleep while I pack."

Silently, she followed me back toward the kitchen and up the open staircase to the bedroom. I showed her the bathroom and offered her my one remaining clean T-shirt as a sleep shirt. After I retrieved a few things off the vanity, she closed herself in with her purse, which left me time to grab a small duffel from the closet and the three extra magazines I keep in my gun safe. One went into the pocket of my jeans, the other two into the bag.

I brought the duffel downstairs with my toiletries and returned before Max emerged from the bathroom. When she reappeared, the T-shirt hung nearly to her knees. That, plus her hair, now freed from the braid, made her look even smaller and younger than before. Her eyelids drooped, and she seemed almost to sleepwalk to the bed.

I wedged the little purse into one of the pockets of her hoodie and set it at the foot of the bed in case she got cold. Then I knelt by the side, tucking the covers around her. "I'll wake you in an hour or two, but don't worry. The alarms are all set, and I'll be on guard downstairs.

If anything bad happens, that light"—I pointed to the corner of the room, where I'd installed a red strobe—"will start to blink. If you see it, get up and get ready to move. But don't make any noise. I'll come for you. All right?"

Max nodded, her eyes already closed.

Back downstairs, I filled several water bottles and grabbed what few snacks I had in the pantry, then brought those and the duffel down to the garage. I stuffed some clean clothes from the dryer into the bag on top of the magazines and loaded everything into the Jeep. Without Max's suitcases, she didn't have anything beyond what she was already wearing, but we could pick her up something on the road. Thankfully, since I'd gassed up before flying to New York, I had nearly a full tank.

On my way back up, I hesitated at the landing where the half flight of stairs from the garage joins the half flight from the front door. Part of me said that there was little-to-no chance that the "gang"—I'd started referring to them that way in my mind for lack of a better term—could know about the house. After the break-in and the exposure of my identity to the press, I'd changed all the deeds and property paperwork so my name didn't appear anywhere. You might be able to look it up historically, but that'd take some work.

Of course, the FBI's plan to meet us at LAX should have been a much more closely guarded secret, and the gang had still managed to decipher that. I had to assume they could obtain my address, too.

The crazy woman had broken in by climbing up from the street onto the balconies, taking advantage of the fact I'd left the bedroom slider ajar. Now, in addition to always locking those doors and adding all the sensors and alarms, I'd fortified the edges of the balconies with those spike strips they use to discourage pigeons from landing. I figured the three-inch metal needles jutting out ought to make even the most deranged individual think twice about trying that route.

With the balconies as secure as they could be, though, this narrow staircase up to the main floor was the weakest link. I'd played around with some ideas for what to do if I ever needed to secure it—now seemed like the perfect time to try them out.

I plodded back down to the garage, a two-car space that I'd turned into a mini workshop where I could tinker. I've got a fully outfitted workbench down there, as well as a bunch of larger tools and equipment. At the bench, I flipped on the lamp, twisting its arm so the bulb pointed toward the staircase entrance. Then I grabbed a signal generator—a heavy, gray box the size of an old VCR—and lugged it upstairs, setting it just inside the door.

The next step required my stereo system, or at least its speakers, so I went to the living room to retrieve them.

When it comes to music, I have to admit that I've become another version of my dad, hunting down the highest-quality components that generate the biggest, richest sound profile. Most people know that speakers are absolutely critical to a good system, but they tend to focus on the wrong things when picking them out. It's really the frequency/response curve that determines whether you're hearing pure sound or not. Although lots of people pick models that accentuate bass, going too far can muddy a song, almost blurring the notes together. If a speaker overemphasizes treble, though, music sounds shrill and harsh. Ideally, you want components with a flat frequency/response curve: they apply identical amounts of energy to every sound frequency, so the proper balance between high and low is maintained.

Although Neat Acoustics isn't as well known in the States, I'd heard some of their speakers demoed at a conference in Brussels once and decided I needed a pair if I could ever afford them. When I bought the house, I settled on a pair of Ultimatum XL6s. Only three feet high, they use some neat engineering tricks to generate a much fuller frequency range than you'd expect. For example, each speaker contains an isobaric bass chamber, with two drivers lined up one behind the other inside the closed compartment. With the two woofers rigged so their cones move simultaneously, you can create the same bass sound in half the cabinet space.

Unfortunately, the trade-off for such a compact design is density, of which I was severely reminded as I lugged each of the seventy-five-pound, wood-paneled boxes from their pedestals over to the edge of the stairs.

The final piece I needed was an amp. I use a special vacuum-tube amp for my stereo, but I had a cheaper, solid-state one down in the workshop, so I went and retrieved it.

Using some books, I propped the back feet of the speakers so they pointed down the stairwell. Then I connected the speakers to the amp and plugged the signal generator into the amp's RCA jack. Setting the buttons on the generator so it would produce a simple square wave pattern, I switched that box on while leaving the amplifier off. This way, I could trigger the whole system with the amp's remote control.

Making sure I had that, the Sig, and my laptop by the couch, I circled the living area, dousing all the lights. Then I returned to the sofa and fired up my computer.

Since being removed from flight duty, my new title at the Air Marshal Service had become Tactical Law Enforcement Liaison and Principal Investigator. I decided if I was going to help get Max out of this mess, I'd better start living up to that and get to investigating. Max's world was so totally different from mine, I had a lot of catching up to do.

I downloaded as much entertainment news as I could find on the Internet. *Hollywood Reporter*, *Variety*, *Billboard*, *Rolling Stone*, plus a bunch of the tabloids. Anything I could get my hands on referring to Max, I ran through the text-to-speech software and loaded it onto my audio player.

That done, I considered waking Max up to get going, but my eyelids felt heavy. I checked the on-screen clock: nearly midnight Pacific. No wonder, I'd been going since early eastern time. If we were going to put some real distance between us and the gang, a quick catnap might help me, too.

I set an alarm on my phone for thirty minutes and settled back on the couch. It was a little short for my body, so when I tried stretching across it, my legs ended up propped on the arm. Turning to one side, I pulled my knees up and managed to fit, but the seam between the two cushions dug into my waist. I folded Shirley's blanket into a kind of cushion to fix that problem, then set my head back on the pillow.

I'd just gotten settled when the red strobe on the ceiling started blinking.

CHAPTER 4

My phone buzzed across the table, echoing the alarm. A text message said the front-door sensor had been compromised.

They were coming.

I bolted to my feet, deactivating the alarm on the phone before grabbing the Sig and the amp remote. As my adrenaline surged, I yanked the earpiece out of my ear and jammed it down into my pocket along with the phone: I wouldn't need either one for a while. Stepping behind the speakers, I pointed the gun down the stairs and waited.

Human balance is controlled by semicircular canals in your ear. Three loops, each filled with a dense fluid, oriented at right angles to each other so they cover the three planes of movement: up/down, right/left, forward/back. As your body moves, the fluid inside the canals spins, pressing against tiny hairs that feed the motion back to your brain.

The system isn't perfect. If you spin enough in one direction, the fluid gains momentum and keeps spinning after you stop. Your brain thinks the world is still turning, and you fall down, like kids in the izzy-dizzy relay races at school. The hairs inside the canals can also become overstimulated if you move repetitively for too long, giving you the sensation of still being on that boat or plane ride hours after it has ended.

But the canals have one other weakness. Because they're inside the ear, they're susceptible to sound waves. Something my team had accidentally discovered back in my former life as an engineer. We were testing audio players in the lab one day, and Tim Jennings, one of the techs, accidentally plugged his headphones into the wrong jack. Instead of the MP3 player, he connected to the signal generator, the box we used to create test signals. Rather than music, the earpieces bombarded him with a solid burst of sound waves: Tim fell right off his stool and landed squarely on his ass. Once we'd all finished laughing, he showed us what had happened.

My old mentor, Clarence, had still been in charge back then. He liked a good joke as much as anyone—his weakness, really—so we'd called him down to the lab and ambushed him with a blast from the speaker. He landed so hard, his glasses fell off his face, and no one had laughed more than he had.

I smiled at the memory of his delight over the juvenile use of our discovery. My setup on the stairs was exactly the same as the one we'd rigged up in the lab. Except ten times more powerful.

Thanks to the workbench lamp brightly backlighting the stairwell, I saw the intruders as darkened silhouettes. One, two, and then three shadows stepped into the narrow hallway, snapping me back to the moment.

They were edging forward carefully, quietly.

Signaling silently with their free hands while carrying some kind of submachine gun in their others.

With all the lights extinguished, I knew they could see nothing at the top of the stairs save the blackened rectangle of the doorway. Still, having them staring right at me was more than a bit unnerving.

As my pulse raced, I tried to keep my breathing from getting too choppy. I waited until the leader reached the halfway mark, then pressed "Power" on the remote.

Although no sound was audible, the pressure wave from the speakers jolted me.

Taking a half step back, I re-aimed as the three shadows dropped like pins struck by an invisible bowling ball. I fired two shots each at what looked like their heads, then retreated to the side of the doorway.

No return fire came.

Crouching, I spun back into the doorway and surveyed the stairs. None of the shadows moved.

Any sense of accomplishment faded immediately as my mind flashed outside. The gang wouldn't have brought just three people to try and take down two. There'd be others, and they'd have heard my shots.

Leaving the speakers on, I sprinted for the staircase up to the bedroom. My right foot had just touched the bottom step when gunfire exploded through the living room windows.

I launched myself upward, taking three steps at a time, trying not to think about the shards of glass and metal hurtling around the room. I felt two hits, one in my shoulder, one in my thigh. The shoulder felt like no big deal—just a scrape, I hoped. But the thigh strike was solid: a strong, charley-horse punch right to the muscle.

Whatever it was, I could deal with it later. Assuming we got out of this mess.

Reaching the top of the stairs, I found the bed empty. I picked up Max's hoodie and scanned the rest of the room.

No Max.

I called her name. Once. Twice.

That's when my heart really started thundering, and the bottom dropped out from my stomach. Panicked sweat flashed across my skin.

Could they have already gotten her somehow? Had she run?

Bullets continued to careen from outside up into the bedroom, but less noisily now that all the glass had fallen to the floor. She'd been nowhere near the glass. No traces of blood.

"MAX!" I screamed it with every bit of breath I had.

The closet door was cracked a fraction of an inch. My brain scrambled to recall if it had been like that earlier, but before I could even finish the thought, my legs had me over there, and I was pulling it open.

Max lay on the floor, knees drawn up to her chest like before, rocking slightly and crying.

"We've gotta go." I yanked her to her feet, ready to throw her over my shoulder if necessary, but her legs seemed stable beneath her.

The gunfire fell silent.

They'd be sending others in now. The speakers might slow them, but not for long.

There was only one way out: up.

I dragged Max to the far side of the bed and jumped as well as I could on the bad leg for a rope dangling from the ceiling. My fingers snagged it on the second try, and a folding ladder extended down behind it. I climbed up quickly, threw open the trapdoor, and led Max onto the house's flat roof. As she was taking her final steps up, another burst of shots echoed from inside the house.

So much for my $15,000 speakers.

Searching downstairs wouldn't take long—they'd be on us in a minute.

I flipped the trapdoor closed, but there was no bolt or lock on the outside, no way to secure it.

Dumb, dumb, dumb—I should have thought of that.

I pulled Max over to the sole security measure I'd installed on the roof. The extension ladder lay flat against the tar-and-gravel surface, as if forgotten by workmen. In actuality, I'd bolted its feet to hinges at the roof's edge so it would flip up and over, stretching down to my neighbor's open-air patio one story below.

The aluminum clunked loudly as I adjusted the two sections to the right length, then clattered and shook as it struck the edge of my neighbor's stucco wall. I urged Max down first, alternately watching her and the trapdoor.

The night air felt warm against my face. You could hear waves crashing in the empty distance, while swarms of lights stretched in either direction along the coast.

For a split second, all I could think was what a shame it was to be running for our lives on such a beautiful night.

As Max finished climbing, I started my turn on the ladder. Heights are far from my thing, so to avoid knee-liquefying vertigo, I kept my eyes locked on the trapdoor instead of looking down. I'd gotten maybe three steps when a hail of bullets erupted upward through it.

I paused, drawing the Sig and bracing myself across the ladder. When a dark shape appeared at the mouth of the trapdoor, I let off two quick shots.

Although the silhouette disappeared back down the hole, I wasn't crazy enough to think I'd hit anything. Hopefully I'd bought us more time.

Eight bullets used. That meant I had four left in the mag.

Descending as fast as I could, I shouted for Max to take cover behind the stone walls surrounding my neighbor's barbecue grill. My sneaker had no sooner found tile than bullets ripped the air around me. I brought the gun up along with my eyes and let off the final four shots, causing the shadows on the edge of my roof to retreat momentarily.

Holstering the Sig, I adjusted the end of the ladder so it would pass over my neighbor's wall, let it go, and watched it clatter against the side of my house, extending down to its full length. Then I turned and scrambled to join Max in her hiding place.

As shots landed dully against the stone all around us, I loaded a full clip in the Sig and checked Max to see if she was ready to move. "There's a trellis on the other side of this wall. When I say *go*, climb down it and wait for me at the bottom. Got it?"

She nodded in a way that didn't provide any reassurance, but there wasn't much else I could do. The individual shots ringing out from behind had changed to random sprays of automatic fire—I'd need to give her some cover.

"Ready . . . ," I said, pivoting up to one knee. "Go!"

I jumped to my feet and let off two pairs of shots with a small break between them. By the time I recovered behind the grill, Max had disappeared over the wall.

I'd seen at least three shadows up on my roof. The automatic fire began again, in bursts that sounded like a chain saw revving. "Who's gonna cover *you*, genius?" I muttered to myself.

Eight bullets left, but if we actually made it to the street below, I'd need some there.

Three was all I figured I could spare.

Gritting my teeth, I pivoted again, then took a deep breath, and stood. I let off two shots individually as I backed toward the wall, my free hand feeling for it.

The gunmen weren't intimidated this time, though. Instead of withdrawing, they started to bring their fire to bear on me. As sparks began shooting up from the grill, I squeezed off one final shot, then turned and rolled over the wall, grasping for the edge with my free hand.

By rolling, I stayed close to the wall, but my hand bounced off or ripped through the first few trellis bars it touched. At that point I'd picked up enough speed—air rushing by my cheeks and over my scalp—that I didn't know if I'd ever find a handhold.

As if it were falling slower than the rest of me, my heart slid up into my throat and nearly closed it.

I was just about to open my eyes to face the oncoming blackness when my fingers found a bar and stuck there. My arm felt like it was being ripped out of its socket, but I told myself that was the only way I was dropping any farther. Once I'd hung on for a moment and become convinced that first hand was set, I holstered the Sig and grabbed on with the other.

I wanted to check around for Max, but I didn't dare. My pulse was still thundering in my ears from the drop, and just the thought of looking down into the black chasm below me caused my stomach to flip.

After forcing myself to take three shallow breaths, I set my feet and started descending. The air grew darker and seemingly thicker as I lowered into the narrow gap between buildings, the thin strip of starry sky receding above me. After what felt like an endless climb, I reached a point where my feet found nothing below them. No more trellis rungs, no solid ground. They simply dangled in space, scraping the stucco wall in front of them.

In the pitch blackness, I had no idea if I was two feet off the ground or ten. My mind said the former, but my stomach wasn't so sure. Hand over hand, I worked myself a few rungs lower, then squeezed my eyes shut and let go.

The fall took just long enough to worry me it might continue forever. Then, suddenly, my feet struck solid ground. Somehow I managed to remain standing, although on impact the thigh that had gotten hit felt like it was exploding.

Electric jolts of pain were still reverberating through me when something grazed my right arm. I immediately recoiled, bracing for a fight, then saw flowing hair silhouetted by the light at the end of the breezeway. "C'mon," I whispered, extending my hand. When Max's narrow fingers found mine, I turned and, despite my leg's objections, began leading her in the opposite direction.

My neighbor's breezeway is capped at both ends by tall, ornate wooden gates. While I figured the gang probably had forces stationed on both sides of the house, all the gunfire had come from the walking street, and that was also where the foot soldiers had entered. To me, that made the alley worth trying.

I stopped just short of the gate, peeking through some of the holes carved into the wood. A dark SUV blocked the alley, but I couldn't tell if it was the same one from the airport. Lights off, it pointed uphill—away from us but toward the main streets. Perfect for a getaway.

With the gunfire stopped, the normal quiet of night had resumed, and I cocked an ear. Besides the sound of my own heavy breathing, there were muffled voices—obviously angry, hissing indistinguishable words—while sirens had begun wailing in the distance.

I ran my hands down both edges of the gate, feeling for cold metal against the warm wood. I found hinges on one side first, then the latch on the other. It was the type you lifted and slid, with a heavy handle, the thickness of rebar. I moved it incrementally, pausing each time I could feel the friction increase or hear it scrape. Finally, it slipped free and the gate gave way, but I held it closed to take another peek into the alley.

No one nearby. No movement.

Pushing the gate open just enough to slip through, I flattened myself against the wall of the next house. Max followed suit. Once she was next to me, I jerked my head toward the opposite side of the alley.

She gave me a curt nod in response.

I grabbed her hand and squeezed it. Checking the SUV, I took a deep breath and launched off the wall, leading Max in a crouched, limping dash.

The gate directly across the alley is featureless and flat, rising only to the middle of my chest. I felt around for how it was secured, but finding nothing, I knitted my fingers together to give Max a boost. She stepped into my hand and sprang over it, landing silently on the other side. After a quick glance back at the SUV, I grabbed the lip of the gate and swung myself over.

My feet cleared the top of the gate, no problem. But on their way down, they caught something. I winced even before any sound rang out, but when it did, my heart sank. This house had metal trash cans, and they struck the ground with a loud, hollow gonging sound.

I didn't bother looking back. As soon as my feet landed, I began running, grabbing Max's hand somehow on the way by. Voices behind us—still angry, but louder now—started following.

A security lamp flicked on as we continued down the breezeway, creating an island of light we quickly dashed through. Just as we reached another gate at the far end, a short burst of gunfire sounded over our shoulders. I threw Max's hand up toward the top of the gate to encourage her to climb it, then pirouetted, drawing the Sig and squaring myself on the path.

Three gunmen charged into the light, and I let off a shot, dropping the leader and causing the other two to duck and retreat.

After holstering the gun, I vaulted the gate, landing on soft grass next to Max, who'd crouched to wait for me. Unlike the alley, where there'd been no light to spare, here the old-fashioned lamps along the walking street cast dim, yellow light toward the houses, creating long, eerie shadows across the lawns. We started uphill, but after just three steps, she tripped on something in the shadows—a flagstone, a garden gnome, something—and fell onto her stomach. Since I was holding her hand, she yanked me downward as she fell, doubling me over.

Probably saved my life.

At that moment, machine-gun fire ripped through the air just above our heads. Glancing back, I spotted the arm holding the gun extended up over the top of the gate, spraying bullets wildly in our direction.

I helped Max to her feet and turned us back downhill and across the concrete walking street. The yard on the opposite side had a short, knee-high stone wall we both hurdled. Bullets thudded against the rock as we cleared it.

The wrought-iron gate to this house's breezeway must've been unlocked, as Max pushed her way past it without any problem. Following her, I slammed the door closed behind me, hoping there was some kind of latch on the door that would catch.

I heard a metallic click as it shut; then something struck the gate with a clang.

Ahead of me, Max was squirming through a tiny gap between a thick stand of banana plants and the wall of the house. I started to follow but had more difficulty: leaves smacked my face while stucco scraped the hell out of my back and the back of my head. I was only halfway through when the gate began shuddering under heavy blows. Wriggling faster, I had narrowly cleared the plants when the gate burst open with a tremendous crash.

I kept my head turned, looking behind me as I began running again, wanting to count the pursuers and gauge their progress. Because of the pain in my right thigh, I loped along unevenly, my left leg leading the way and doing more of the work. Although I could sense the breezeway widening around me, I didn't think much of it—until my left knee struck something that felt like a sledgehammer.

My body twisted in the air as I fell so that my shoulder hit first. But what it contacted was as surprising as the blow to my knee: ice-cold water that quickly enveloped my arm, my chest, my head.

Struggling to sit up, I found myself in the basin of a large fountain built into the courtyard of a U-shaped house. The water was only six inches deep, but my entire upper body was now completely soaked.

Before I could find my feet, something moved in the direction from which we'd come, and I instantly drew and fired two shots. No idea if I hit anything, but no return fire came, so I climbed out and began running again. My knee and thigh now both screamed, but I refused to listen.

I found Max at the opposite end of the courtyard—she'd avoided the fountain—and we dashed down the shortened breezeway to the alley. The picket gate here was locked with a heavy chain, so I flipped Max up and over it before following awkwardly myself. Bullets sounded against the concrete path—as soon as I reached the other side of the gate, I pulled Max away from it. Shots sliced through the wood as we raced up the street.

I wanted to gain as much distance as we could before zigzagging inward again. We made it maybe three houses before a pair of headlights turned onto the street ahead of us.

Not seeing any flashers—the sirens were growing louder, finally—I steered Max left to a house with a low metal gate. While she fumbled with the latch, the engine behind the headlights roared, and they bore down on us.

As the headlights drew closer, you could see they belonged to something big.

A quick glance at Max said she wasn't getting anywhere with the lock.

Although every instinct warned against it, I took two steps out into the alley and pulled the Sig.

Trying to visualize the front of the truck, I fired my last two bullets down and to the side of the right headlight, hoping for a tire.

A metallic crump told me one bullet had found the bumper. When no other sound registered, I assumed the other was a miss.

But then suddenly there was a loud pop followed by a metallic squeal. Yellow sparks erupted from the truck's wheel, tracing short, bright arcs that stuck in my vision. The headlights lurched right, then suddenly back to the left.

At that moment, Max got the gate open and dashed through it. I sprinted after her, but once inside, we both stopped and looked back.

Light grew brighter and brighter against the frame of the gate. Then another scraping noise pierced the air—a high-pitched, screeching sound that raised the hair on my arms. Finally, the truck's bumper slid across the face of the gate and struck its far side with a loud crunch. The bumper and tire seemed to be wedged into the frame, blocking it. Although the engine roared twice, the truck didn't budge.

With my free hand, I pounded on Max's back to urge her on.

We sprinted at least ten more blocks before stopping for breath.

Worried still more reinforcements might be coming, I kept the breather short. After a moment's break, I got us on the move again, down the hill to the Strand.

Except for a few late-night joggers and one couple making out on the benches, we had the concrete path and the night to ourselves. Just as well—we must've looked like quite a pair: Max in a nightshirt, me limping along in wet, stained clothes. My knee was gradually locking up, and now I noticed how much my thigh ached each time I moved my right leg.

As the adrenaline dwindled, my condition started back up. My mind began clicking, the thoughts coming faster, but before it got too bad, I popped the earpiece in. The background noise settled my brain down and let me focus on next steps.

I couldn't bring Max in, not now. Whatever leak had compromised our airport arrival had obviously struck again. Until Lavorgna or the FBI could sort out how the gang was getting its intel, handing Max over would be a death sentence.

The gang—if that's even what it was—seemed more like an army tonight. They still bothered me. I couldn't understand their connection to all this. Their targeting of Max struck me as so peculiar. I felt that if I could only understand that variable, then I could solve the whole equation.

But how, exactly?

Max was a mess. I was worse, and completely out of ammo. No place to go, and no transportation to get there. And I couldn't call Lavorgna or anyone else official for help.

Once I thought it through that way, it was pretty easy to know whom to call. There was really only one person left I could trust.

CHAPTER 5

Thursday, July 16

We followed the Strand all the way back to the pier. When we stopped there, Max leaned her side against the metal railing, bending over it as much as her spine would allow.

I checked the time on my phone. Just before 1:00 a.m.

Music and chatter from bars still open up on Manhattan Beach Boulevard floated down the hill to where we stood. After everything we'd just been through, it felt easy to be angry at those people: enjoying their little lives, oblivious to what was happening just a few blocks away.

I looked at Max. Was she feeling it, too?

There was no telling. Whatever fire had burned inside her earlier seemed long since extinguished now. All the rage and venom sketched across her face had been replaced by a slack-jawed stare.

I went to touch her arm, to try and break her trance, but my left shoulder—the one I'd hurt hanging from the trellis—gave me a sharp stab of pain when I tried to move it. "It's gonna be okay," I said instead, realizing afterward how big a liar the blood and injuries likely made me seem.

"They're not gonna stop, are they?" Max's voice was flat. "They'll just keep coming. Till they finally kill me." She turned to face the water, slumping over the railing again.

Using my good arm, I placed my hand on her back. "I won't let that happen. We've just gotta figure out who they are, why they're doing this."

She remained silent, staring off into the darkness.

"We'll start digging tomorrow. Tonight, we need to get you someplace safe, get both of us some rest."

Even in profile, I could see her chin starting to tremble. She turned back to me, eyes already flooded. "Safe?" A single sob erupted from her mouth, like a loud gasp. Then another. Soon she had her head against my chest, resoaking my shirt with her tears.

I wrapped my good arm around her shoulders and squeezed her tight.

I recognized the big Lexus by the shape of its headlights as it came down the hill. That, and the fact it was driving a shade too fast.

Finally, an SUV on our side.

Tires chirping, it pulled a hard turn in front of the concrete plugs blocking the entrance to the pier, then stopped suddenly. I staggered over to it as quickly as I could and opened the rear door for Max. A 12-gauge shotgun was waiting on the back seat.

Seizing it, I ushered her inside, then followed. "Ready," I said, and the car lurched forward, helping me close the door.

The driver didn't turn around. He simply asked, "What am I looking for?"

"Dark SUV, lots of damage to the right front bumper." I noticed he had one hand on the wheel, the other on the grip of a Glock 22 resting on the console between the front seats. He prefers it because it doesn't have a safety: it's always on. "Glad to see you came prepared," I said.

"You said to come hot."

Late as it was, the road was virtually empty, and he pushed the SUV well past the speed limit. Now that we had our ride, I dug out my cell and switched it completely off. "Max, I need your phone."

Without protest, she pulled it from one of the pockets in her hoodie and handed it to me. I deactivated it as well and tucked it away with mine.

"Any others?" When she didn't answer, I bent down to catch her eye. "Phones? Any other phones? They can track them off the cell towers. We need to turn them off."

She stared at me for a moment. Then, jamming her hands into her pockets, she shook her head.

"Okay, good." For the first time in several hours, I managed to crack a smile as I turned forward. "Thanks for coming to get us. Everyone should have a lawyer like you."

A pair of bright eyes popped up into the rearview mirror. "Client satisfaction, that's my motto."

"Max, meet Dan Shen. He writes the patents on my inventions."

Her face showed the most emotion I'd seen since LAX. "A—a lawyer? That's the best you could do to protect us?"

"Shen here is no ambulance chaser. After Caltech, he spent two tours as an army MP in Iraqi villages you can't even spell. Plus, as you can see, he's an ardent supporter of the Second Amendment."

"God bless the USA," Shen said.

"Shen, this is Max Magic. She's a—"

"No way." His eyes bobbed in and out of the mirror. "*The* Max Magic? Wow. It's really, I mean . . . just . . . wow."

"You know her?"

"Dude, her song? It's like, *the* dance song these days. Brian's gonna flip when we get home."

Shen sped out to the 405, then grabbed the 110 north, eventually passing the downtown skyscrapers—still lit like prime time—and heading up through Echo Park to Silver Lake.

Max started nodding off the second we hit the freeway and slept the remainder of the drive, head against the door frame.

By silent agreement, Shen and I didn't talk, instead letting her sleep, but that was fine. I had plenty of thoughts to toss around in my head.

Having listened to the entertainment articles about Max for a while now, I'd learned a lot. For starters, she was more than just the one-hit wonder Lavorgna had made her out to be. Although "Baby, I Love You" was easily her biggest hit, she'd released two albums before that. The first had just been an EP collection of four songs, covers of powerful singers like Mariah Carey and Christina Aguilera that had gotten her noticed. The next one contained a mix of covers and stuff Max had written herself. The covers—ballads or dance tunes—got most of the airplay, but critics seemed to prefer the more personal stuff. Especially after her latest album, whose songs had turned much darker, they'd described Max's writing as "mature" and "well beyond her years."

I'd also discovered that Max apparently didn't reserve her unique brand of charm exclusively for flight attendants and me. It seemed she'd managed to piss off almost everyone she'd come across in the entertainment industry at one point or another. Canceling a tour, dropping out of projects at the last minute. She'd even disappeared to the Caribbean for a month without telling anyone, although releasing her latest album shortly thereafter had earned her some forgiveness.

And then there was gossip.

Tons of it.

The tabloids contained a lot of teen, angsty, "Who is she dating?" type stuff. There were questions about everything from eating disorders to drugs. Especially recently, she'd been photographed at parties and events in ways that made her seem drunk or high, but you could never tell if those were merely awkward moments. The trade papers wondered if she was getting along with her dad, if he was the right one to steer her career, and whether she'd flame out like so many other teen stars.

Of course, absolutely none of this helped in the slightest when it came to answering the question I really cared about: Why was this crazy group of tattooed nightmares trying to kill her?

We'd seen nine gunmen now—add in some drivers and you were talking at least a dozen men. Well armed. The way they coordinated their attacks and movements, they'd been well trained, too. The more I turned it over, the less sense it seemed to make. These guys ought to be off holding up an armored car somewhere, not trying to kill the girl at the top of the pop charts. That suggested someone had hired them, but who?

I'd need to get Max's take on that tomorrow.

As we exited the freeway, I tried to push thoughts about the gang—or the militia, or whatever the hell they were—out of my head. We'd inflicted enough casualties; they'd probably spend the rest of tonight licking their wounds and regrouping. And although they'd found my house, I was pretty confident there was no way they'd find out about Shen's place.

LA is so developed, all cars and concrete, that twisting up through the tree-lined hills to Shen and Brian's house always feels slightly magical. The structure itself bends around a small patio and pool—they like to entertain out there—and compared to the rat's nest of my neighborhood, it's such a pleasant change to be outside and not hear anything or see anyone.

Shen's headlights were the only source of light for the final quarter mile of the drive, and I felt my own eyelids starting to sag. Drained completely of adrenaline now, I urged myself to hang on just a little longer. Get Max inside, get her safe. Then I could collapse.

She didn't stir, not even when we pulled into the garage and Shen silenced the car. I'd intended to carry her inside, but when I saw Shen had already scooped her into his oversize arms, I was relieved. Circling back around the passenger's side, I maneuvered ahead of him to open the door to the house.

No sooner had I entered than Shen's partner, Brian, stepped into view.

When he saw me, his hand flew to his mouth. "Oh my God, Seth. Get yourself into the powder room—I'll be in there in a second."

I hesitated a moment, but a glare from Brian sent me limping off to the small black-and-white bathroom off their entryway.

It's funny. As a couple, Shen and Brian couldn't be any more different. On first inspection, Shen's the imposing one: my height, with close-cropped military hair and enough muscle his shirts always seem too small. Brian's smaller, thinner, and moves with a kind of quickness that makes you think his bones are hollow or something. But he also has a force of will. When his mouth sets underneath that crimson beard of his, you don't question whatever he's telling you to do, no matter how many pounds or inches you've got on him.

I was surprised at what I saw in the mirror when I reached the powder room. My face looked pale and ragged, my entire sleeve now rusty brown. My pants were even worse, the ripped right leg soaked several shades darker than the left.

Brian appeared in the doorway with a small canvas pouch and winced when he saw my jeans. "Do I even want to know?"

"It looks worse than it is," I said. And in terms of pain, I wasn't lying—the shoulder injury from the trellis hurt way worse than the leg. I hadn't even bothered to check it during the drive.

"Okay, well, get them off so we can have a look."

I complied, unbuckling, then easing the pants down.

"I can't promise you'll ever get those stains out, but—" Brian winced again, and I glanced down. A jagged shard of glass, two or three inches wide, protruded from the side of my thigh, which was weeping red in small pulses.

"I—that's . . . way beyond me and this little medical kit," he said, dangling the bag slightly.

Shen appeared behind him. "Everything okay in here?"

"How's Max?" I asked.

"Asleep. Never even stirred. How're you?"

Brian turned and said over his shoulder, "We need to get him to the emergency room."

Shen raised his eyebrows. "You sure?"

I couldn't see Brian's face, but from Shen's reaction, I could imagine the look he was giving him. "Guys," I said, "no hospitals. The people who did this found us at my house—at a hospital, Max will be a sitting duck."

Brian's head turned slowly around, wearing an expression even grimmer and more determined than I'd imagined. "You've lost a ton of blood. I think you're damn lucky that glass didn't hit the artery; otherwise you wouldn't even be sitting here. But if we don't get you treated, you could still bleed to death. Bad guys or no bad guys—"

"What about Anjali?" Shen asked.

Brian didn't turn around, so I asked, "Who?"

"Orthopedist from UCLA, lives two houses over. I know it's the middle of the night, but . . ."

Brian squeezed his eyes shut for a moment. "All right, run over there. But tell her how bad it is, and if she says we've got to go in . . ."

Shen grinned and winked at me over Brian's shoulder. Then he dashed away.

Sighing, Brian turned to my other shoulder and said, "Let's see if I can do anything for this while we wait."

Like I'd thought, Brian found the shoulder wound from the gunfire superficial. Although it stung like hell, he cleaned and bandaged it, no problem. I volunteered to stay in the powder room so as not to spread blood through the house, so Brian brought me a blanket to help keep me warm as I sat on the tile floor.

Although he kept glancing nervously at my leg, my other shoulder worried me more. It looked weird in the mirror, like the deltoid had crumpled or something. Trying to move it at all sent sharp jolts of pain thundering down my arm and into my chest.

The only good thing about the pain was that it kept me awake. Shen was seemingly taking forever, but I reminded myself houses were a lot farther apart up here, and he'd probably had to wake the poor woman up. Still, when Brian started checking his watch more frequently, I knew my sense of timing was right.

Finally, Shen reappeared, trailed by a dark-haired woman in a sweat suit carrying a small gym bag.

"Sorry that took so long," he said. "We made a quick supply run. Seth Walker, meet Dr. Anjali Enjeti. She treats three of the Lakers."

"Thanks so much for coming, Doctor." The words felt like an effort, which concerned me a bit.

Enjeti slipped between the guys and squatted next to me. "Don't thank me yet," she said. Although the bags around them suggested she could use a cup or two of coffee, her eyes twinkled in a reassuring way. "Let's see what we've got."

Retracting the blanket, she said in an offhand, almost casual tone, "Oh. Well." She unzipped the bag and started rummaging through it. "Your shoulder's dislocated. I'll need to reduce that. But the bleeding's the more immediate concern."

Enjeti pulled on gloves and took out a needle and an IV bag filled with clear liquid. Then she looked me squarely in the eye. "Mr. Walker, before I do anything, I'm going to warn you, I'd be better off treating you at a hospital. I know my malpractice carrier would feel better about it."

I shook my head. "Treating me here is a law-enforcement necessity, I promise you. The federal government will make sure no one gets mad at you, even if you kill me." I cracked a small grin, hoping to get a rise out of her.

It didn't work. She calmly nodded. "That's what I thought you'd say. This is saline. It'll help get your fluids back up." After she plugged the bag into my arm and set it up above us on the vanity, Enjeti unwrapped a syringe and needle and filled it from a small vial. "This is a local anesthetic. I'm going to numb your leg a bit before—"

"Lidocaine?"

She glanced up at me. "No, but you're close. Bupivacaine. They're related. You know your drugs—are you allergic?"

"I know lidocaine from a case I worked. But no, not allergic."

"Okay, then," she said. "Here we go."

Needles have never bothered me much, obviously—I was never one of those kids scared to get his shots—but I tensed as the syringe neared my thigh. There was enough blood and muscle exposed, it looked more like raw steak than a leg, and I figured the needle was gonna kill.

It didn't, though. Enjeti must've stuck me forty times as she worked her way around the wound, but each time there was just a little prick, followed by lots of little popping tingles as she pushed the drug in.

"Not too bad," I said once she was done.

She gave me a little smile. "Unfortunately, that was the easy part. We'll give the bupivacaine a minute to work, but I've got to warn you, even that's not going to make what we have to do next pain-free."

"Taking the glass out?"

Enjeti nodded. "Can I get a flashlight?" she asked Shen and Brian, who both ran off and then returned with one. After carefully looking it over from different angles, she glanced up at me and said, "It's wedged in so far, there's not very much to hold on to. When I grab the glass, I need to be careful not to break it, otherwise we could be picking pieces out of there for a week. I need you to be still now. Are you with me?"

I forced a swallow down and nodded.

Enjeti brought out a wrapped package of long, tonglike metal forceps and tore them open. Then she glanced up at me. "Here we go."

I watched as she inserted the tips of the forceps on either side of the glass. They felt weird wriggling their way down into my leg, like being tickled, but on the inside. Enjeti's fingers flexed, and I knew the bad part was coming. I squeezed my hands into tight fists and flexed every muscle I could to brace myself.

At first she pulled and nothing happened. The glass didn't budge, but there wasn't much pain, either.

She gradually increased the force, though, and eventually the glass gave way. When it did, a pulse ripped through my leg, like she'd pulled out something that had been intentionally attached. As the glass moved outward, it seemed like I could feel every little millimeter of it sliding against the muscle on either side. It was like being stabbed, but in slow motion. I couldn't watch anymore, and turned my eyes to the ceiling. My face burned, and sweat beads were popping out all over my neck and scalp. I ordered myself not to scream, but I couldn't stop a low, guttural growl from erupting in my throat.

My lungs begged for a breath, so I grabbed a quick one. Then another.

"Halfway there," she said.

My stomach dropped at the words. I squeezed my eyes closed and could feel the tears that pressed out onto my cheeks. I started repeating "Almost there" to myself, faster and faster until the gap between the words disappeared, and they ran together.

"Got it; it's out."

With a giant heave, I pushed all the air from my lungs and pulled in a new, deep breath through my mouth. *Thank Christ.*

"We're not done," she said.

I opened my eyes, hoping she was kidding. Some kind of perverse doctor joke. But her face was deadly serious.

"The glass was in extremely deep. You can see here." She raised the bloody shard with the forceps like a piece of gruesome sushi and traced the edge with her finger. "It looks like some chunks are missing." Sure enough, you could see several small, curved gaps in what was otherwise a straight edge. "Maybe it hit the bone, maybe it was pressure from you moving around. Anyway, I can't leave those pieces in there. I'm going to have to fish them out."

I swallowed and nodded again.

She asked Brian to shine the light for her, then spread the gap in my leg open with her fingers. I was just noticing how weird the cool air felt pressing against the interior of the muscle when she moved in with the forceps.

Each time Enjeti went after a piece, the tips of the forceps would scrape bone in a way that reverberated through my whole spine. The pain wasn't just in my leg anymore, it was everywhere, and despite all my efforts to control it, I screamed. Loud, angry screams with whatever air I could draw in on short, ragged breaths.

After what seemed like several hours of that, she finally said, "That's it. The worst part's over."

"This next bit is going to feel a little weird," Enjeti said later.

She'd finished with the leg—stitches now held together both the muscle inside and skin outside—and I was taking quick, shallow breaths as she examined my shoulder.

"Weirder than you rummaging around inside my quad?"

She smiled meekly. "Hopefully not that bad. The shoulder is a ball-and-socket joint." She made a fist, then wrapped her other hand around it. Twisting her fist inside the hand, she said, "The ball turns in the socket, but we've got muscles and tendons and ligaments to keep it in place. You've got a dislocation, not all the way, just partially—that we call a subluxation." She moved the knuckles of her fist hand out to the thumb of the covering hand. "I need to manipulate the shoulder to put it back in place. It's going to feel much better once it's back in—right now it's pressing on things it shouldn't be, and that's what's giving you the pain."

Taking two deeper breaths, I closed my eyes and said, "Okay."

"I'm just going to slowly move your arm out here," she said, rotating my hand away from my stomach, "and then when we get to thirty-five degrees, I'm going to raise it . . ."

As she started to lift the arm, the pain started. Not a stabbing feeling, like with the glass, but a burning, hot fire that spread down into my lungs and up into my neck. Suddenly, I felt something shift inside with a jerk, and everything cooled. Opening my eyes, I saw Enjeti's smiling face. "That's it. Done."

I let out a huge sigh. Although my skin was drenched in sweat, I felt suddenly cold and shivered slightly. "Thank—thank you."

Enjeti patted my knee. "You won't be saying that in a couple of weeks when the rehab starts, but I appreciate it for now. I brought you a sling—keep your arm immobilized until we can get you into a hospital for some tests." She cocked her head and looked sideways at me, reminding me of Loretta. "And I *mean* immobilized, got me? Everything in there is torn up, so if you go moving it, you can do a lot more damage, and it's likely to pop out again. Understand?"

I nodded. The gang probably wouldn't mind me fighting one-handed.

"And whatever national emergency this is, you need to promise it's going to end in the next forty-eight to seventy-two hours, okay? You need to come into the hospital and let us test you, let us see exactly what's going on inside there. Promise?"

"Okay." I had absolutely no idea if I could actually pull that off, but where was the harm in trying? She'd been so nice to help, it seemed rude to disappoint her.

As I was listening to Enjeti talk, things started to dim around the edges. I tried to concentrate on what she was saying, but it was as if my body knew she'd finished everything important, and now it could shut down and rest. All my muscles started yielding—my eyelids drooped, my head sagged to my chest.

Last thing I remember, she was talking to Brian and Shen. "Have him ice it on and off for twenty-four hours to reduce swelling. Then he can take ibuprofen or naproxen for the—"

CHAPTER 6

Pain.

Everywhere.

I had no idea what time it was, or how long I'd been unconscious. When my eyes finally opened, they found the room filled with bright, natural light and decided they'd rather go back to being closed. The earpiece was chattering in my left ear, as always, and now the background noise felt particularly reassuring.

Gradually, my brain reached out to each extremity in turn, asking how it felt, gauging the damage.

I was surprised at the results.

My whole body throbbed with a dull ache. Various parts were colder than others. But overall, it could have been worse. Much worse.

The fact I'd slept straight through the night was a pleasant bonus.

I decided to force my eyes open again, and shortly after I did, the doorknob turned.

Shen ambled in and, seeing I was awake, smiled. "I was coming to change your ice."

"Time?" My voice croaked; my throat felt raw and sore.

"Almost four in the afternoon."

I went to swallow, then realized I didn't have any spit to do it with. "Max?"

"She's up and around. Been eating like a horse." Circling to the opposite side of the bed, he pulled bags off my shoulder and knee. I heard the ice crunching and shifting, but as I tried to roll and see where he put them, I realized I was wedged in place by stacks of pillows on either side of me.

"Anjali didn't want you rolling over. Said you needed to stay flat on your back to avoid messing up your shoulder."

Only now did I realize I was wearing different clothes—one of Shen's T-shirts and some baggy athletic shorts. My left arm remained bound up in the sling, draped across my chest. The skin on my shoulder started to tingle where the ice bag had been, but otherwise the whole area felt pretty numb.

"Lemme up," I said, realizing I needed his help with the pillows.

"Sure, but sit here a minute and drink something. She said you might be dizzy if you stood too fast. You still need more fluids."

Shen helped me sit on the edge of the bed, then handed me a glass of water. I held the first sip in my mouth for a moment, letting my tongue bathe in it. Then I swallowed, the cold liquid slipping down my throat, smoothing out the roughness and convincing me I needed more. I downed the rest of the glass in two large swallows and said, "Okay, I'm ready."

Pushing myself off the bed with my good arm, I noticed Shen readying himself just in case, but my legs felt reasonably strong. "I'm all right," I said. "I'm good."

He started out of the room, glancing back at me periodically, and I began to follow. But where standing had been easy, walking turned out to be harder. My left knee had turned a deep purple, with a tangerine-size knot swollen on the top of it. With the stitches, my right leg felt oddly stiff, and I didn't want to flex the muscle too much. Together, the injuries on both sides left me unable to limp, so I kind of staggered, each leg shuffling forward awkwardly, then pausing for the other to do the same.

Slowly, I made it to the hallway, and then to the kitchen, where I moved a bar stool so I could stand at the counter.

"You don't wanna sit?" Shen asked.

I tried to crack a smile. "I'll never get up again if I do."

Max was seated across the bar, talking to Brian, who was moving around the kitchen with his usual flair. Whatever he was cooking, it had a deep, warm aroma. She was munching on an apple and looked the healthiest I'd seen her since the plane ride.

"Hey," she said, noticing me, "you're alive."

Nodding, I said, "You, too."

"Thank you," she said. "For last night. I'm sorry you got so . . ."

I shrugged. "Risks of the job."

Max's lips pressed against each other, like she was going to say something else. But she paused, and then glanced to each side. "You have cool friends."

"Yeah, they're the best." In my peripheral vision, I caught both guys smiling. "I don't suppose you've thanked them for taking us in?"

Max opened her mouth, but before any words could pop out, Brian said, "She has, actually. We've been having a nice conversation."

She gave me a teasing smile. "They were telling me how you used to be some kind of giant tech nerd. Back before you learned how to shoot people."

"I think I still am. A giant nerd."

"Oh yeah." Shen nodded vigorously at Max. "Biggest smarty-smart I know. And given the people I work for, that's saying something. Gimpy over there ran an entire division of the electronics company that probably makes half the devices you own."

"Really?" She turned her gaze to me. "Why did you—"

"Long story," I said, realizing it was past time to change the subject. "How are you feeling?"

"Better," she said. "Sleep helped." You could see her thinking for a moment; then her face fell. "When are you turning me back over to the FBI?"

"I'm not."

She perked up at that, but I'd already focused on a pad and pencil sitting in the middle of the counter. Stretching desperately for them, I found they were just out of my reach. I'd just resigned myself to having to shuffle around to them when Shen came over and pushed them closer. My cheeks grew hot, and I wondered if I was still pale enough for the blush to be noticeable. "Thanks."

Shen shook his head before returning to the back of the couch he'd been leaning against.

"I'm thinking someone must've hired those guys to come after you. We need to make a list of all the people that could've done that."

Max cocked her head. "Hired them?"

"I don't think they're trying to kill you 'cause they hated your last CD. You said you'd never seen them before, never had any dealings with them, right?"

"Right."

"Okay, so they must be working for someone else. As I see it, that's one of two kinds of people: either someone criminally connected, or someone who's rich and powerful. Let's start with criminals. You know anyone with a record? Drug dealer, maybe?"

Max's eyes narrowed and burned at me. "I don't do illegal drugs."

"You drink."

"Alcohol's legal." She started scratching at her forearm with the nails of her opposite hand.

"Not for someone your age."

Sighing, she rolled her eyes so hard, it tossed her head back slightly. "Haven't we had this argument already?"

"C'mon," I said, "you're a rock star. You've never smoked pot? Never tried anything?"

"I *don't* have a drug dealer. The tabloids say all that stuff, but the only person who's ever given me any drugs is my pediatrician."

"Okay, okay." I held up my hands. "Anybody else? Anybody you can think of who might be tied in with sketchy people who do sketchy things? What about that bodyguard your dad fired?"

"Brad? He'd never try to hurt me."

"Wasn't he angry when your dad got rid of him?"

"Sure. But you heard the FBI—they checked him out."

"At this point I don't think we can necessarily trust their work. What's Brad's last name, and where's he live?"

"Brad Civins," she said. "He used to live in Austin, where we live. Now, I don't know."

I wrote down the name. "Okay. Anybody else with criminal connections? Roadies, anybody tough?"

Max shook her head definitively.

"All right. Let's try the rich-and-powerful angle. Who've you pissed off that has more money than God?"

She tilted her head back and stared at the ceiling for a moment, then started twisting the stool so her knees swung from side to side.

"And don't tell me nobody," I said. "I've listened to enough news pieces—I know there are some serious grudges out there against you."

"I'd say probably the person who was the most mad at me—like, yelling, angry, flipping out—was Nancy Irvine."

I made another note. "Who's that?"

"She's a movie producer in Hollywood."

"What happened?"

Max smiled dismissively and shook her head. "This was, like, forever ago. But I was supposed to star in this musical she was doing. Just before shooting was about to start, my dad caught her trying to screw with my contract. When she refused to fix it, he had me 'withdraw from the project.'" She made air quotes with her fingers.

Although I seriously doubted some Hollywood producer would be out hiring a tattooed militia over something like that, I scribbled some notes on the pad. "You said she flipped out?"

"Yeah, she called me on my phone and yelled at me. Called me names and all this other crap. Said blonde little brats like me were a dime a dozen, and I should be on my knees thanking her 'cause she was so important, and she'd never been so insulted, and she'd end me over it."

I glanced up. "She actually said she would 'end you'? Those were her words?"

"Uh-huh." Max nodded, then smiled with her chin raised in the air.

"Did you tell the FBI about this?"

"No."

"Why not?"

"They never asked. They never asked *me* any questions, they just talked to my dad."

I looked at Shen, then Brian. They were often better judges of character than I was, particularly with women. Both raised their eyebrows at me as if they were thinking the same thing. I turned back to Max. "Okay, we'll look at her. Anyone else?"

"Well, if you really want to know who I think is out to get me, it's Charlie."

"Charlie?"

"Charlie Garcia."

"Who's that?"

She shot me a look like I said I'd never heard of George Washington. "He's president of my label."

"Your record label? Why would he want to get rid of you? You must make him piles of money."

"Yeah, but he doesn't care about that. Not anymore. The label was pure Tejano before I got there, and he wants to dump me so he can go back to that."

"You really think so?" I asked.

"Charlie said so. Told me I'm too much of a hassle, and that he wished I never came along. After everything I've done for him." Max's voice had picked up a nasty edge.

"It doesn't sound like you and Charlie like each other very much."

Max shook her head and looked wistfully off into space. "For a while, it was good. I . . . trusted him. But then my dad figured out Charlie was screwing me on royalties. He still owes me a ton."

"Did your dad confront him about the money?"

"I think so. And that's when things changed. He'd always been cool before, but he turned . . . I don't know, controlling. Always telling me what to do. Where my career should go, what kind of songs to record. Yelling at me." Max paused, then leaned back in her chair. Her eyebrows rose, and a smile spread across her face.

"Why are you smiling?" I asked.

"'Cause Charlie's in for a big surprise."

I checked both sides again, but the guys looked as confused as I was. "What do you mean?"

"He thinks he's gonna ditch me, but I'm totally getting rid of him first. My contract is up the day I turn seventeen, and we haven't worked out an extension. So on my birthday, I'm walking, and Charlie can go back to searching those scrubby little barrio clubs for his next big thing."

"You told me your birthday's coming up, right?"

"Twenty days."

"Does Charlie know about this?"

Max shook her head. "Of course not. That's why it's going to be so great. The look on his face when he finds out is going to be awesome."

"What about your dad—does he know about you wanting to switch labels?"

Max hesitated before answering. "It was partly his idea."

It seemed like there might be even more there, but I didn't press any further. Instead, I looked down at the pad and scribbled something unintelligible to keep Max from seeing the expression on my face. I wasn't totally sure I bought the idea that this Charlie Garcia was actively trying to chase off the biggest act on his label. But if she was about to double-cross him and walk out? That was plenty of motive. And while Max didn't think he saw it coming, I guessed he might be more observant than she was giving him credit for. Garcia had just jumped to the top of my list of suspects.

"Is there anybody else we should talk about?"

Max looked up at the ceiling again. "I don't think so."

"Where does Garcia live?"

"Austin."

"And Irvine's out here?"

Max nodded. "I went to her house once. Big place, right on the beach."

An electronic timer sounded in the kitchen. After consulting the pots and pans, Brian announced dinner would be served in twenty minutes. Max snatched her little purse off the counter and said she was going to the bathroom.

I turned to Shen. "Can you and I take a little drive?"

Climbing into the passenger's seat of the Lexus with all my injuries was a painful chore, but I told myself at least it wasn't a Miata. As we were backing out of the garage, Shen asked, "Where to?"

"Someplace crowded," I said. "Lots of cell towers."

"I'll take us down into Hollywood."

Shen guided the Lexus along a series of winding streets. As we moved down the hill, the foliage gradually disappeared, and the houses grew closer together. After two silent minutes, he asked, "You think it's one of those people Max said?"

I shrugged. "Garcia sounds like the best bet. Although I was surprised the producer said she'd 'end' Max. That was weird enough to make me wonder about her. What'd you make of it all?"

He grimaced and shook his head. "Trouble."

"You think Max is lying?"

"No. I just think she's trouble."

I grinned the best I could manage. "I thought you were a big fan."

"Let's just say the idea and the reality of her are two different things." He paused a beat. "She's not your responsibility, you know."

"My job is to keep her safe. Literally."

"No, your job was to fly her ass from New York to LA. Which you did. Now you can turn her back over to the big boys who do this all the time."

"'Cause they've done such a bang-up job so far?"

"From what you said, they got caught off guard at the airport. That won't happen again." He paused until I looked him in the eye. "You ain't up to this. Not right now."

"Anjali did a good job patching me up—"

"I'm not talking about your body, fool. How much time did you have to grieve over Sarah, five minutes? Now you're back, doing this again?"

"Look, if you're worried about Brian and the house, I'll get us out ASAP."

We'd reached a red light, and Shen turned to face me. "That's not it, dude. You know—"

Nodding, I said, "I do. And I appreciate you looking out for me. But don't worry. I'm just going to chase down a couple of things—"

"That's what you said last time."

The light changed as he said it. But as the Lexus lurched forward, it felt like I left my stomach behind at the intersection.

I looked to my forearm, where the tattooed initials seemed to sizzle on my skin. Despite all the other things on my mind, even over the hum of the earpiece, all the images of Sarah I'd tried so desperately to file away came spilling back out of their hiding places.

The bright sparkle in her eyes. The way she'd seemed to fit so naturally in my arms.

The expression of fear and betrayal she'd worn that last time we'd talked. When she'd actually fallen for the frame-up and feared I was a killer.

The last time I'd seen her before . . . before she was never the same.

After the initial shock of it, my brain rushed to clean up the mess, even as my muscles tightened and my fists clenched. "Last time was different," I said, doing my best to make sure Shen knew I believed that. "Here, I just need to see if I can get the heat off Max. Or at least figure out where it's coming from. She's a kid, for chrissake."

Pursing his lips, Shen nodded silently, like I imagine he does at work when he realizes one of the patent examiners isn't going to budge on a point. Still, he didn't argue any further, and that was a relief. I needed to think through exactly what I could and couldn't say on this phone call.

Shen turned from Sunset onto Santa Monica Boulevard. With the summer days at their longest, the sun was still a couple of hours from setting, and it painted the street and sidewalks with bright, golden light that half blinded us as we pressed westward.

Once we reached East Hollywood, Shen asked, "Anyplace special?"

"No. I just didn't want them getting a fix on your house." Even before integrated GPS, you could track a cell phone by triangulating the distance between it and the surrounding cell towers it was using to communicate. Now, the second your phone made contact with the tower, the carrier likely had your exact location.

As Shen pulled into a spot at LA City College, I turned on the phone and dialed. The number rang three times before Lavorgna answered.

"Vince, can you talk?"

"Seth, thank Christ! We heard about your house—local police roped us in once they figured out who owned it. I sent Linda out to stand guard."

Linda Vasquez pretends to be Questar's daytime receptionist. She sits at the front desk, answers the phone if it ever rings, and signs for packages when the FedEx guy arrives each day. A five-foot-two-inch mother of three, Vasquez wears conservative clothes, glasses, and a "mom" haircut. She also keeps an H&K MP5 submachine gun hidden underneath her desk and is a black belt in three different martial arts. My house would be in good hands.

"Thanks."

"I have Special Agent Franklin and Max's father here in my office—they flew out after what happened at the airport yesterday. I'm going to put you on speaker."

The background noise on the other end changed, deepening, until Franklin's subtle drawl appeared. "Mr. Walker, how are you? I assume Mr. Drew's daughter is with you?"

"Yeah, I've got Max. We're both safe."

"Mr. Walker, this is Gregory Drew. I cannot thank you enough for saving my little girl."

"You're welcome, sir."

"The Bureau owes you a great debt, too," Franklin said. "Five of the seven agents from the LAX detail survived yesterday's assault. From the reports I've heard, that's mostly thanks to your quick thinking. Leading the shooters away probably saved their lives, so again, thank you."

Although that hadn't been my concern at the time, I was glad for the result. "I'm sorry about Moore. He never had a chance."

Franklin remained silent, leaving my mind to replay the feeling of Moore's blood splattering against my cheek.

Lavorgna's Philadelphia accent cut in. "Where are you now, Seth?"

Clever, asking the question before Franklin could get to it. Keeping control of the conversation. "We're mobile," I said. "Figured a moving target would be harder to hit."

"We'd obviously like to work out a time and place for you to come in," Franklin said.

"I'd love to. But I think we may be better holding off until you track down the guys who hit us. What's the status on that?" Now we'd see how forthcoming Franklin was going to be.

"Honestly, we're not totally sure who they are. The ones at the airport took two of the three bodies with them—the only one they left was wedged into the luggage chute. Same thing last night. We found lots of casings, bullets, and blood trails around your house, but no bodies."

"I know I nailed at least a couple. So they're a gang that takes their casualties home with them? I would think that's weird enough to be an identifier all by itself."

"We're looking," Franklin said. "We just don't have any answers yet."

"You said you got one body. What about those facial tattoos . . ."

"Again," he said, "we're processing them. But they're not like anything we've seen before."

"Did you get anything helpful? Age, prints, anything?" I asked.

"Coroner put the guy in his early twenties. No hit on his prints. We're working on all those angles. But I think everyone here would feel better if Mr. Drew's daughter was under the full protection of the Bureau."

"I can appreciate that," I said, not really meaning it. "But like I said, I just don't know that I'll feel comfortable bringing her in until we really know what we're up against."

"All due respect, Mr. Walker, these guys already found your house. Don't you think she'd be better—"

"Exactly. They found my house. And before that, they found us at the airport. Both secrets people were entrusted to keep. You told me at JFK that we were likely facing a lone psycho, yet in both places you had large details outfitted for an attack, and one of those still got slashed to pieces. So, no, I don't think Max is better off with you, at least not yet." My pulse was pounding harder than I'd expected.

"So you're not going to hand her over?"

"Nope."

"Not going to give us your location?"

"Nope."

"Mr. Walker, this is Greg Drew again. I realize I'm just the father here." His tone suggested he thought he was a lot more than that. "But I think it stands to reason that Max can be much better protected in an environment like an FBI office than wherever you are, on the road, as you said. No offense—you've done a wonderful job. But, she is—quite literally—a multimillion-dollar asset. I mean," Drew chuckled slightly, "if you're holding on to a priceless statue, you don't just throw it on the front seat of the car and go rumbling around the dirt track. You very carefully set it down on a pedestal at the museum and let the guards patrol around it."

I'd lost a lot of blood and had been unconscious, but I had to check myself to see if Max's father had really just compared her to a piece of artwork.

Franklin's drawl cut in. "Vince, maybe you could help Agent Walker understand—"

"Oh, I think my air marshal understands the situation better than all of us, considering he was the one dodging all those bullets last night. I think what he's saying is that the gang appears to have some source of intelligence on this end, and we need to plug the leak. Once we do that, I'm sure he'll feel perfectly comfortable returning Max to your purview. Do I have that right, Seth?"

"Exactly what I meant, sir." I remembered the way an FBI friend of mine had once squirmed in Lavorgna's presence—he was pretty much Bureau royalty—and I wondered what Franklin was thinking right about now.

Drew's voice appeared on the line again. "I just have to say, I don't find this acceptable, not acceptable at all. Leading her out of the airport was one thing. But now you're proposing trusting my daughter's safety to a single man—not even an experienced bodyguard, but some kind of . . . of . . . airline rent-a-cop—to—"

"Be very, very careful right now, Mr. Drew," Lavorgna said. "My job is overseeing those 'rent-a-cops,' as you just called them, and I can tell you they're far more than that."

"I don't mean any offense. I'm sure your men are very good at what they do. Blending in, protecting the airlines—when I saw Mr. Walker at JFK, I never would have guessed someone who looked like him was in law enforcement. But you're talking about an impressionable sixteen-year-old girl here. You're trusting some . . . some lone wolf to escort her through who-knows-what-kind of environments . . ."

"I'm sure Agent Walker will—"

"See, it's wonderful that *you're* sure. But as her father, I'm not. I don't know Agent Walker from a hole in the wall so—again, no offense—I have absolutely no idea if he's the kind of man who can be trusted with a girl my daughter's age. Maybe you haven't seen pictures of her, Mr. Lavorgna, but—"

"Enough." Lavorgna didn't yell the word, but he said it with enough force that the call went silent. I could imagine the grim line his mouth had formed beneath his beard. "While I appreciate your concerns," he said, more calmly than I expected, "I can tell you with absolute confidence that Agent Walker is the best we have. I would trust him to protect my own family. So—no offense—I would appreciate it if you avoided impugning him, or any of the rest of my air marshals, any further than you already have. Franklin, Walker's not coming in until you've got the leak plugged on your end. Clear?"

Before Franklin or Drew could say another word, I hung up.

"That got heated," Shen said.

"Yeah," I said. "Max's dad went a little overboard."

He shrugged. "Hard to blame the guy."

I nodded silently, but my wheels had started turning. After a minute, I said, "Let's get out of here. I don't want to see how fast the FBI can fix a cell position."

"Plus, Brian's gonna be pissed. We're late for dinner."

CHAPTER 7

Shen's prediction proved correct: we found Brian standing in the kitchen, flipping the pages of a magazine so hard, I thought he'd rip them out. A large pan sat on the stove next to him, and although it was covered, the whole space was filled with the subtle aroma of saffron.

"Sorry," Shen said.

"Oh, it's no problem. I cooked half the afternoon, but no one's going to eat the damn thing until it's cold."

"It's my fault," I said. "I forced Shen to drive me down to where I could call the office. I didn't want to be too close, in case someone tried to trace the call."

Brian's face softened at that, and he nodded.

I glanced around. "Where's Max?"

"Still in the bathroom, I think. She's been in there since you guys left."

As fast as I could go on my gimpy legs, I tracked back to the powder room where I'd spent so much time the night before and knocked softly. "You okay in there?"

The toilet flushed and the sink ran for a few moments. Then the door popped open, and Max came out with her head down. She beelined for the kitchen, but I grabbed her elbow, spinning her back around.

"Hey, I asked if you were okay."

Her eyes stayed locked on the floor. "I'm fine."

"What took you so long?"

"Jeez." Max lifted her head, but instead of rage, her voice sounded flat, almost defeated. "Can't I even go to the bathroom in peace?"

The way she squinted made me uncomfortable, as if I'd intruded on her in a way that wasn't appropriate. "I—I'm sorry."

Her chin rose slightly. "I'm . . ." She paused. "I'm a little . . . plugged up." Her voice trailed off at the end, her eyes sliding to the side. But then they came back to glare at me, and her voice rose again. "Happy? Now you know all my intimate details."

"I just . . . I was . . . worried about you."

She blinked at me as if she expected me to say something more. Then she spun on her heel and stalked off toward the kitchen. As she disappeared around the corner, I kicked myself a little bit.

The saffron smell turned out to belong to a giant pan of vegetable risotto, which Brian left on the stove as he served us at the counter. I hadn't realized how hungry I was until the first bite hit my mouth, but then I quickly gobbled an entire plate of creamy rice, mushrooms, and other vegetables. Solid and warm in my stomach, it made me feel stronger than I had since waking in the guest room.

Glancing around the quiet table, Shen was shoveling food into his mouth like it might be his last meal, but Max had her head down and was just sort of toying with hers.

"So, Max," I said, "what's the best part of being a superstar?"

"Huh?" She glanced up from her plate. "What do you mean?"

"I've never met anyone as famous as you, that's all."

"I met Norman Schwarzkopf once," Shen said between bites.

"Who's that?" Max asked.

"A famous general," I said. "Before your time, probably. But c'mon, what's the best part? What do you like the most?"

"I don't know," Max said, sweeping her hair behind her ear. "I mean, I love singing, but I've always loved that. Maybe photo shoots? Those are kind of cool. You get to dress up, and sometimes they let you keep the clothes."

"I would be so self-conscious," Brian said. "I can't even take a regular photo without closing my eyes."

Max giggled; then her face straightened. "I was kind of nervous the first couple times. It's weird, you know, them giving you directions and stuff. But eventually you figure it out and just get into it."

"The night before we met at JFK," I said, "I saw a couple of your photo shoots online. There wasn't much clothing to take home." At the time, the cheesecake photos hadn't seemed like a big deal. But now that I knew Max, thinking back over them felt . . . awkward.

"Did you see the *FGO* one? *For Guys Only*, in the white bikini?"

"I don't know . . . maybe?" I absolutely remembered it: draped across a boat in that one, Max had on a strapless top, and wore bottoms with metal rings at the hips to show more skin. In full makeup, she'd looked twenty-five.

"God, I hated that one."

I relaxed slightly. "Really? Because I—"

"That bikini was totally wrong for me. The color washed me out, and it made my ass look too big and my boobs look too small."

"Wait, what?"

"Didn't you think it made my ass look too big?" She was staring directly at me, expecting an immediate answer, as if she'd asked what time it was.

"No . . . I . . ."

She smirked. "So you like a girl with a big ass?"

My cheeks flushed. "I didn't say that, either . . ." I looked to either side, but Brian and Shen weren't offering any help.

"Did you see the spread in *Men's Quarterly*?"

"Was that the one on the rug?"

Max leaned back in her chair, crossed her arms, and nodded. "What did you think of that one?"

"I don't know," I said, hoping my glances around the room might be sufficient cover. When she continued to press me, I said, "I was kind of surprised . . ."

A proud smile bloomed across her face. "I *loved* that spread." Speaking to Shen and Brian in turn, she said, "They shot me from the side, on my hands and knees. They got awesome sideboob." A little sigh. "I wish I looked more like Kate Upton. Her boobs are so fantastic . . ."

"Wait a second," I said. "Doesn't it bother you when—"

Max's smile disappeared. "When what?"

"When they . . . make you pose that way? So . . ."

"So . . . what?" Max's eyebrows rose, and her nostrils flared like she knew exactly what was coming.

"So . . . sexually."

"Didn't you think I looked good?"

"Looking good isn't the issue . . ."

She nodded. "So I *did* look good. You just don't want to admit you liked it."

My face burned even hotter now, and realizing Max would probably notice only made it worse. "It's more that you're only sixteen. No sixteen-year-old should—"

"Should what? Should be proud of her body? I should be ashamed? Is that what you're saying?"

"No, I didn't say that. I just don't know that everyone should see . . . everything."

Max's eyebrows furrowed, her mouth drawing to a point. "Oh. So I shouldn't be allowed to embrace my own sexuality? We're going back to the 1700s now, or something, and women should just go off to the back room?"

"'Embracing your sexuality'? Is that really what you were doing rolling around topless on a rug?" My voice rose. "Because it looked more like you were just trying to get a bunch of guys lathered up."

"And what's wrong with that?" she asked. "Why should you or anybody be allowed to keep me from doing what I want with *my* body? If I want to show it off, that's my choice."

"You don't think it sends the wrong message?"

"I think the message I'm sending is to buy my records. And I think a lot more guys'll buy them if I let them see the side of my boobs. Do you know how much publicity I got from those shoots? It was probably the difference between gold and platinum. All for just being in a bathing suit I'd wear to the beach, anyway."

I leaned in over my plate. "Doesn't it make you feel like a piece of meat?"

Max didn't retreat. The opposite—she leaned in as well, planting her palms on the table, her voice continuing to rise. "What makes me feel like a piece of meat is people like you controlling me. Telling me what I should and shouldn't do. *I've* got the talent. *I'm* the one people pay to listen to. So why does everybody else think they get to tell me what's best for me?"

"You mean like Charlie Garcia?"

"Charlie. The FBI. You." Max paused for a moment, but the muscles in her neck flexed, and she looked up to the ceiling. "*Everyone.* I just need to get away. Away from everyone so I can decide what happens in my life and my career." Her eyes dropped back down on me. "So *I* can be in charge for once."

Although she was glaring, when our eyes locked on each other, I thought I saw a spasm of sadness flash across Max's face. Just a quick twitch of it before she pressed it back down. But even that brief glimpse was enough to force me back in my chair.

Trying not to show it, I took a deep, cleansing breath.

While the moment was still hanging there, Brian piped up. "Have you gotten to go anyplace exotic for your shoots? I love to travel."

She blinked at me a few more times, then turned to Brian, her face softening. "Um, no. No place that exciting."

"I read you went to the Caribbean for a while," I said, my voice deliberately gentler now. "Did you do any shoots down there?"

Max's eyes darted at me, like I'd said something poisonous. "No," she said, clipping the word.

"I've been trying to get him"—Brian nodded at Shen—"to take me, but it's never the right time. Which islands did you see?"

She glanced all around, as if maps were printed across the walls and ceiling. "Um . . . a few different places. The Bahamas." She paused. "Saint Lucia." She looked down at her plate and fell silent for a moment. Then she turned to Brian. "I'm sorry—you cooked a wonderful meal, but I'm . . . I'm not feeling quite right. Do you mind if I—"

"No, no, of course, sweetie," he said, rising and smiling. He touched her shoulder as she turned to go. "If you need anything in the middle of the night, you just let us know."

She gave him a weak smile, then dropped her eyes and headed off toward the bedrooms.

Once she was gone, Brian shook his head. "Poor thing."

I glanced over at Shen, only to find he was already staring at me, attempting to remind me of his warnings about Max during our earlier conversation.

Wincing slightly, I apologized for the scene. Then I told them what she'd said outside the bathroom, whispering in case she was listening. "I shouldn't have pressed her."

"She'll be okay," Brian said.

"Think so?"

"She's traumatized. Who could blame her?"

Shen nodded. "Question is, what's next for you two?"

I took another deep breath. "You heard Max: Nancy Irvine lives right up the road. So tomorrow, I think we'll go pay her a visit."

CHAPTER 8

Friday, July 17

I slept in again the next morning, although not as late as Max.

When I woke, I found my knee felt much improved. The knot had shrunk by half overnight, and although still sensitive to the touch, it had stopped affecting my movement. The other thigh still felt oddly stiff, but part of that could have just been my own fear of ripping out the stitches. The new combination left me with a pronounced limp that was infinitely preferable to my stiff-legged shuffle of the day before. My scraped shoulder itched, but otherwise my upper body felt positively normal compared to my legs. The arm in the sling didn't hurt at all.

After a quick shower, I began poking around the house for signs of life. The kitchen stood empty, and clocks on the appliances agreed it was somewhere between 11:05 and 11:07. Max was still sprawled facedown across her mattress in the second guest room.

I found Shen in his office, back to the door, typing away while wearing the noise-reducing headphones I'd given him for Christmas a couple of years back. I started toward him, figuring I'd need to tap his shoulder to get his attention. But before I'd even made it halfway, he spun around on his chair. Slipping off the headphones, he shook his head. "Can't sneak up on me, dude."

I raised my one free hand as if to show I was unarmed. "What's up?"

"Not much. I gotta meet a client this afternoon, so Brian went to his studio early. He should be back in a few."

"And here I thought I was your only client."

Shen's eyebrows rose. "I'm having to diversify. You've been a little less prolific lately."

"Ouch." I covered my heart with my hand and took a mock stagger-step backward with the good leg.

Shen continued staring at me, and I realized he wasn't going to let me off the hook.

"I've just been in kind of a rut," I said. "Nothing on my mind, you know? At least, nothing electronic."

He shrugged. "That's natural. You need some time—it hasn't even been a week."

I nodded slightly.

Shen cocked his head. "I miss her, too, you know."

"Yeah," was all I could manage.

"You need to let yourself feel it."

Feeling my eyes starting to well up, I squeezed them shut.

"What happened to her wasn't your fault. You've got to remember that."

I nodded again, not because I actually believed him, but out of some hope it might cover the way my chin was trembling. As my throat clenched, I swallowed hard against it and prayed he'd move on to some other topic.

"Good news is, we've got plenty in the pipeline . . ." Thankfully, he turned back to his computer and started ticking off the status and next steps on a handful of my patents. That bought me time to wipe my eyes and get it together.

All told, Shen had filed about two dozen applications on circuits and gadgets I'd designed in my spare time. He'd also helped me approach companies about licensing them. The first couple had gone well enough—they'd paid the down payment on the house and let me bank some money on the side. I wasn't exactly rolling in it—I sent a chunk of money to Shirley in Texas every month to help with my god-kids, plus now I had Sarah's five weeks of ICU bills to cover—but none of that seemed particularly important right now.

As he turned back to me, Shen smiled. "You don't care about any of this, do you?"

"Not really."

"What are you thinking?"

"I just keep tossing all this stuff about Max around in my head. None of it makes sense—what on earth would make someone want to kill a kid?"

Shen's mouth tightened into a grim line. "Only three reasons anybody ever kills anybody: fear, anger, or money."

I searched for some reason to disagree but couldn't find any. He was so damn good at that.

"You gonna wake her?" Shen asked.

"Is it okay if I don't? I'm thinking it'll be easier getting in to see Nancy Irvine flying solo. And safer for Max—the less she shows her face around town, the better."

"Sure. One of us will be here. We can go shopping for you, too—it's not like you have a ton to wear."

He had a point. Max had borrowed a T-shirt and shorts from Brian, who was closer to her size, while I was still trudging around in the athletic stuff they'd dressed me in after Enjeti had patched me up.

"Thanks," I said. "I'll pay you back, obviously."

He grinned. "I'll just add it to your tab. You need anything else besides some new duds?"

After listing off a few quick things, I added, "Can I borrow a car? And your phone?"

Although I offered several times to take what the guys call the "paint truck"—an old pickup Brian uses when moving canvases to and from his studio—Shen didn't think the rusted-out shell with multicolored splotches would play well in Malibu. He insisted I take the Lexus.

Cruising along the 10, I realized I could've been in one of Irvine's movies: a helicopter shot might have pulled up and away from the sunroof, panning forward to show no traffic ahead, only bright sunshine and blue water. The Southern California people elsewhere dream about, where every day is eighty-five degrees, sunny, and you never glance back to see haze smearing the views of downtown and the mountains.

I hit Santa Monica in less than thirty minutes and turned onto PCH, where I switched off the AC and lowered the windows to let the breeze roll through.

I'd only driven out to Malibu twice before, both times to surf. This time, I found myself paying more attention to the buildings than the beach. In most of LA's coastal neighborhoods, the majority of houses are little bungalows, shacks built back in the 1920s that people pass off as "historic" to justify their price tag, as if a few arched doorways and outdated plumbing make eight hundred square feet worth $1.5 million. There are some huge mansions right along the beach, but usually, they're the exception.

Not on this drive.

After turning north, cliffs sprout up on your right, eventually rising hundreds of feet overhead, their sandy soil covered in just enough brown scrub to fool you into forgetting it could all tumble down on you at any minute. The only man-made structures along this stretch sit on the ocean side of the road, blocking much of the view. It's as if the rich are sending everyone else a middle-fingered message: you can't touch this.

By the time you hit Malibu proper, though, the money's too much even to be bothered with messages. Cliffside houses pick up again, large and opulent, while the beachside places recede back behind tall hedgerows or security walls so all you can see are a few unassuming roofs. Hunkered down behind those barricades, built right on the dunes, are huge, multimillion-dollar mansions. Irvine's address put her with the most elite of these: the so-called Billionaire's Beach, a stretch of houses owned by software CEOs and rock stars.

And, apparently, the occasional movie producer.

As the house numbers gradually approached Irvine's, I started searching for a parking spot. No easy task in Malibu. Decades ago, California decided almost all its beaches should be public property, with access every one thousand feet. Given the prices they paid, many of Malibu's residents take great offense to that. Particularly along Irvine's stretch, homeowners pull all kinds of tricks to keep people out, everything from posting privacy signs on public easements to blocking potential parking with orange construction cones.

Funny thing, though: grassroots groups have banded together and fought back. The coolest thing they've come up with is a phone app showing all the public parking and access ways. I used the app to find a street spot for the Lexus, which left me a quarter mile walk back to Irvine's house. With the limp, it took me longer than usual, but after being cooped up, the hot sun on my scalp felt more invigorating than withering.

Irvine's number was posted on a whitewashed stucco wall that stretched at least a foot over my head. Midway along it stood two gates, both constructed from dark-stained wood. The larger one guarded the driveway: small, gray cobblestones peeked out beneath its bottom lip. The smaller one, shaped like a door with an arched top and glass insets, was obviously for pedestrians, but it bore a large lock and was monitored by a small security camera. An electronic call box was mounted into the stucco next to it.

I pushed the "Talk" button on the box to see what would happen. A deep voice squawked through the speaker. "Can I help you?"

"I'm a federal investigator. I need to speak with Ms. Irvine."

"You have an appointment?"

"No," I said. "This concerns something fairly urgent."

"Ms. Irvine is unavailable at the moment. You can make an appointment through her office. That number is—"

"There's no time for that. I need to speak with her now." I took out my badge and held it up to the camera lens, although I realized I wasn't exactly dressed to look the part.

"Ms. Irvine is unavailable at the moment."

"That's all you're gonna give me?"

"She's unavailable."

"And if I come back here with a patrol car and a warrant? We can block traffic on PCH, make the evening news."

"She's unavailable."

Damn. It was a total bluff, but I'd hoped it might crack him. "Fine, I'll call her office." Although I turned back the way I'd come, as soon as I was out of the camera's view, I had my phone out, checking the beach-access app again.

Following its map, I walked three houses down, where a narrow asphalt path cut between two tall fences. Dark, steep, and shadowy, the path looked like a drainage swale, its entrance blocked by a wooden sawhorse and some large plastic trash bins. As I double-checked the map, though, a strong breeze blew up through the channel and smacked my cheek.

The air smelled rich with salt.

The narrow passageway was particularly slow-going with my limp, but I emerged at the bottom onto a broad strip of white sand. A flock of gulls huddled to my right, but otherwise I counted only five visitors on the entire beach, all sunbathers spread across their towels. Although the wind whipped in off the water, the surf was placid, just tiny wavelets collapsing at the tideline.

I could see why you'd want to keep this place to yourself.

Starting back toward Irvine's property, I took just a few steps before removing my sandals. Hot from the bright sun overhead, the deep sand scalded the bottoms of my feet, encouraging me along faster.

While no part of Irvine's house had been visible from the street, from the beach you could see the entire thing: a sprawling, three-story mission-style mansion, built directly into the hill so its series of rear terraces all faced the ocean. The house's whitewashed walls gleamed so brightly in the sun they put even the powdery sand to shame. The tiled roof was a deep, bloody crimson that, juxtaposed against the walls, gave the building just the slightest feeling of a lighthouse. A small path snaked its way down from the bottommost terrace to the sand through dense patches of ice plant, whose normally dull, fleshy, blue-green shoots were adorned with bright purple flowers.

No security was visible along the winding path, but I hurried as best I could just in case. Remarkably, I found the door to the lowest terrace unlocked, so I quickly entered and peered into the windows of the house's bottom floor: a small gym and a bedroom, both darkened and unoccupied.

Stucco steps led up to the next terrace, but unsure what awaited above, I climbed them cautiously. At the top, I found myself looking across a swimming pool toward a series of umbrella-covered tables on the opposite side. A white-haired woman sat alone at one, reading in the shade, glasses perched on the tip of her nose.

I began rounding the pool, but activity on the next terrace up caught my eye. Two burly, suited men, running.

I drew my badge and gun. Holding each in an outstretched hand, I called across the water. "Ms. Irvine?"

The guards had reached the steps now, descending two at a time. While I kept them in my peripheral vision, I locked my eyes on the woman. Her calling off the dogs was the only way this would end nicely. She glanced up at me with a look of genuine surprise.

"Ma'am, my name is Seth Walker. I'm a federal investigator, and I need to ask you some questions."

When the guards reached the bottom of the steps, they split up, one moving to protect Irvine, the other continuing toward me. Each was reaching inside his jacket.

"I'm sorry to disturb you, but I'm afraid this can't wait, ma'am. It's a matter of life and death."

The runner had covered half the distance between us, clutching a pistol in the low ready position, but Irvine still hadn't said anything. Next to her, the bodyguard was drawing a bead on me.

Stepping sideways, I let the runner eclipse my view of Irvine, which also meant he blocked his partner's shot. Then I dropped to a knee and brought the Sig around. "Stop right there, buddy. Keep the gun down."

The guard pulled up awkwardly, and for the first time, I got a good look at his face. Big, bulbous nose over a goatee. Dark eyes, flitting up and down between my face and the barrel of the Sig.

I waved the badge as best I could in my free hand, despite the sling. "I really don't want to hurt you. Or your boss. I'm just doing my job here, but I've gotta ask her some questions, okay?"

He hesitated. I could see his muscles flexing, yearning to do something. But his brain wasn't quite sure what.

"Julian." It was a female voice, stern and strong, and the guard turned in time to see the white-haired woman step to his side and seize his arm. She needed both hands to circle his bicep, and had to reach up to her own eye level to do it. "Julian, it's fine. We don't need any shoot-outs before lunch. Blood will be hell to clean out of the pool." She shook her head dismissively. "Let the man ask me his questions. I won't melt."

Gradually, the guard relaxed, until finally he tucked his gun back inside the jacket.

The woman turned and waved me up off my knee. "Come on, Mr. Walker, it's hot out here. Join me for a glass of iced tea."

CHAPTER 9

Once we were seated across from each other at one of the shady tables, Nancy Irvine shooed Julian and the other guard away.

"If it'd make you more comfortable, they can stay," I said. I'd considered leaving the Sig on the table in front of me but decided it would be more polite to holster it.

She shook her head. "They're nice boys, but they only need to do two things: protect me from being kidnapped, and keep every waiter and waitress from the Valley from showing up on my lawn with their screenplay. Given that both my senators are still Democrats"—her lips pulled back to reveal teeth bright enough to match the walls of the house—"I doubt the government sent you to haul me to Guantanamo, and I don't see a roll of pages under your arm, so we should be good. Although I have to admit, you're not dressed like any federal agent I've ever seen."

I shrugged. "Undercover," was the best thing I could find to say.

She nodded at the sling. "You get that in the line of duty?"

"Yes, ma'am. Part of the reason I'm here."

Although her brows rose at that, Irvine kept her pale-blue eyes trained on me in a way that was slightly unnerving. Her hair—stark white, with just a hint of a curl where it ended at her shoulders—agreed with what little I'd read, putting her into her sixties. But her face was devoid of lines, the skin still supple and smooth. If she'd had work done, it had been masterful: she lacked the tight, catlike expression you found after a bad face-lift or the stiffness of someone who'd been Botoxed. Instead, she looked like a thirty-year-old woman who'd gone prematurely gray.

I glanced around. "You have a beautiful home."

"Thank you. I've always loved the beach, and it's great for entertaining."

"You might want to secure that beach gate a little better, though."

"I'll have the boys look into it." Her eyes bored into me harder. "You said something about life and death. I think the architectural features will keep."

"I've been assigned to protect a star who's been receiving death threats—"

Irvine rolled her eyes. "Welcome to being a star."

I cocked my head.

"Seriously. I don't know anyone on the talent side of this business who doesn't get threatened now and again. It's part of the price of being in the public eye."

"Well, these particular threats were followed by machine-gun fire from a small army. I was lucky to get away with just this," I said, jabbing my chin down toward the sling.

Irvine pursed her lips, but otherwise didn't react. "Who's the star?"

"Someone I think you know. Her name is Max Magic."

Now Irvine's cheeks pulled back into a full smile, and she glanced off to the horizon. "That poor little bitch."

"Excuse me?"

"Max and I worked on a project together. Or started to. But I'm guessing you knew that. Extremely talented kid, but she's got some issues."

"Yeah, Max mentioned you two had history. That's why I'm here."

Irvine leaned back in her seat.

"Well?" I asked.

"Well, what?"

"Do you have anything to say about what happened between the two of you?"

"You mean"—Irvine looked at me as if I were hard of hearing—"you're actually thinking I might be involved somehow?"

"It's sort of my job to figure that out."

Irvine burst out laughing and clapped her hands together. "Don't get me wrong, Mr. Walker, I'm actually kind of flattered. The idea that anyone would think of me as some mobster, ordering hits on people. As you've seen, I don't exactly have an army at my disposal, and no, I haven't dispatched Julian and Reynaldo to take out Max Magic."

Now I got to return the favor, pressing her with my eyes. "Weren't you angry at her for holding up your movie?"

"Angry? Sure, I was angry. For the day or so it took us to round up a handful of nearly as talented, more-committed replacements. I mean, my Lord, Mr. Walker, do you have any idea how hard it is to get a fucking movie made? If I let a star dropping out send me off the deep end, they'd have carted me off to the loony bin a long, long time ago. Do you know what we ended up turning on that picture?"

"Turning?"

"We originally had a twelve-million-dollar budget. Dealing with Max and then replacing her pushed us three million dollars over. But with Ayannah Morris, Max's replacement, the film grossed thirty-eight million dollars domestic, plus another twenty-nine international. A four hundred percent margin is nothing to sneeze at, Mr. Walker. Even in this business. So yes, while I was quite angry, I managed to get over it." Irvine took a long sip from her iced tea.

"You said some fairly threatening things to Max."

"I did?"

"You don't remember telling her you'd 'end' her?"

"I might have."

"So you can see how someone might view that as a threat."

"To end her movie career, sure. To kill her? Hardly."

I continued to stare at Irvine, and her eyes dropped back to the table again. Her long nails clickety-clacked against its glass top as she drummed her fingers. "I should have known better," she said.

"About what?"

She looked up at me again—despite their color, her eyes seemed on fire. "Do you have *any* idea how hard it is dealing with child stars? The lengths we have to fucking go for them?"

I gave her a one-shoulder shrug. "Enlighten me."

"Normal actors have an agent. You negotiate the contract with them; then the actor shows up and does his or her thing. They might have some special requests, but it's all about leverage. The bigger the star, the more they can get because they're bringing more to the table. But kids . . ." Irvine let out a chuff and shook her head.

"What's the problem with kids?"

"Where do you start? I mean, just to be able to hire them, the studio has to have a special permit from the state. Then, before any arrive on set, we have to get a special permit from the Department of Labor for every single one of them. Just to get that permit is a giant pile of paperwork, including educational records and so on. And at any point, the state can send someone to come inspect us and shut down production if we're doing it wrong.

"Once we actually get the kids on set, then the fun really starts. For someone Max's age, guess how many hours a day we get to shoot?"

I shrugged. "Eight?"

"Five if it's during the school year, seven if it's not. We have to have a studio teacher available to them, one specially certified teacher for every ten kids. Plus, a parent or guardian has to be present for every second of work. Not just filming, but hair, wardrobe, makeup, PR, everything. And a SAG rep sits on every set, just waiting to blow the whistle if we do something wrong.

"Did I mention travel to and from locations counts as work time? Did I mention the twelve hours that have to elapse between the end of one workday and the start of the next? Or the files I have to keep on all of this crap for three years after the project is completed, just in case I get audited by the state?"

Irvine's voice had risen to a crescendo, and now she looked off toward the horizon again, as if searching in the distance for some sort of refuge from it all.

"So you did all that for Max?"

"Absolutely. We had to, just to get the project started. Then the little diva herself showed up."

"How was she?"

"Difficult."

"Difficult how?"

"Well, she was only with us for about five minutes. But in that short time, she was surly. Wanted what she wanted and thought it was everyone else's job to get it for her. Penny-ante bullshit, but it's still a pain in the ass. Then you throw Daddy in on top of it all . . ."

"What was wrong with him?"

"Oh, he comes out here dressed like some slick Silicon Valley CEO and thinks he's going to run circles around my thousand-dollars-an-hour lawyers. Honestly, he was much worse to deal with than Max. Talent's almost always difficult, but no one likes an asshole lawyer."

I cracked a smile. "Aren't they all assholes?"

"Absolutely. But there are two kinds, you know. Some are doing right by their client. They drive a hard bargain, but that's their job. You may not like them, but you can respect them. Then there's the ones like him. I mean, talk about not knowing the business—what kind of showbiz father doesn't have a Coogan account set up by the time their kid gets on set?"

"A what account?"

Irvine took a sip of iced tea and swallowed it slowly. "A Coogan account. Named after Jackie Coogan."

I shook my head.

"Coogan was a child star back in the twenties. He was the little kid in that Charlie Chaplin picture. Anyway, Coogan woke up on his twenty-first birthday to find that his parents had spent every nickel he'd made."

"What happened?"

"He did what anyone in Hollywood would do—he sued. Sued his parents. Didn't get much out of that, but they passed a law with his name on it to protect kids' earnings, and it's been in place ever since."

"So what's a Coogan account?"

"Back when he was working, wages belonged to the parent. The Coogan law changed that, made the parents fiduciaries, with an obligation to look out for their kid. Plus, it forces them to create a special account, a blocked trust the parents can't access for themselves. Fifteen percent of the kid's wages have to get deposited into that account, and California law says we can't issue a paycheck until it's established by the bank."

"But Drew didn't have one for Max?"

"Fuck no. He didn't have that, which is one of the most basic things anyone who knows anything about entertainment would know. But then he takes our employment contract and starts trying to rewrite it. I mean, he wanted to work over every section. My lawyers were pulling their hair out—he was calling them every five minutes."

"Max and her father gave you that much grief, and yet you still didn't feel the urge to do anything about it?"

Irvine's voice picked up a bit of a snarl. "Oh, I did something about it. Make no mistake. I fired her ass before she ever made a dime. I turned around and replaced her. And after that, I made damn sure to throw a large, extravagant party for all my producer friends, whom I told all about my dealings with Max Magic and her lawyer father."

"What was their reaction?"

Irvine's face relaxed again into an easy smile. "Sympathy. For a moment. But their general response was to toss back a big slug of whatever they were drinking and think to themselves, 'There but for the grace of God go I.' Because every last one of them has horror stories like that. We take risks on talent because talent is what makes the magic happen. And, if you're talented enough, you get several shots. I hear Max is about to start work on another project very soon."

I stared at her, not blinking.

"What, you think I'm trying to kill her out of jealousy? Because she's making this other movie instead of mine?"

"It crossed my mind."

"What I think you're missing, and where I think you're giving Max's imagination about my power and influence too much credit, is that I really have no need to do anything that drastic."

"How do you mean?"

Irvine raised her eyebrows. "Whatever I do, or don't do, whether Max makes this new movie or not, do you really think that kid's still going to have a career in two years?" Irvine shook her head. "She's a flash in the pan. Sure, she's got talent, but if you've spent time with her, you must have seen, she's not committed to anything but herself. The great ones—the ones who emerge from childhood with something still to do—they're humble, they're committed to it. They love it. They want to learn to get better. Not just strike it rich and drink all the Cristal they can find. But those are few, we're talking one or two in a generation. And none of them have parents like that father of hers, I can promise you."

"So?"

"So you think I hired some . . . some army to kill Max Magic? No one hires an army to kill a moth, Mr. Walker. And that's what these stage kids are: moths. They've got a twenty-four-hour life span if they're lucky, and if you just leave well enough alone, they'll fly themselves right into a flame. If I wanted Max Magic to never be seen or heard from again, I wouldn't have to *do* anything. I'd just sit back and watch."

Irvine crossed her arms and leaned back in her chair again. A psychologist friend of mine once said that was a sign people were trying to create emotional distance between themselves and the situation before them. I didn't get that sense from Irvine, though. This was about confidence. Power. She radiated it now, the same way she had when ordering Julian to holster his gun.

"Okay. If you haven't tried to hurt Max, do you have any idea who might?"

Irvine raised her eyebrows again, eyes growing wide as if she was scanning something in front of her. "I mean, let's be honest, a huge part of her popularity is the Lolita angle, so I'm sure there are millions of men who fantasize about having their way with her. One or two or five of them are probably completely psychotic, with little shrines to Max in their basement, and if one of them went off the deep end the right way, he might want to hurt her. But that's not gonna get you an army.

"On the other hand, knowing how she behaves, I'm sure there's a line around the block of people Max has pissed off. But then I think you have to ask, who'd stand to gain enough from doing it that they'd actually go through with it? What's the *motive*?"

"Revenge isn't enough of a motive for you?" I asked.

She shrugged and smiled like she'd just taken a bite of something unpleasant and was trying not to let it show. "I'm a businesswoman. And, let's be honest, my business is all about money: who's got it, who can get it. In my experience, there's very few hurt feelings money can't salve over. Now, if you told the people I work with they could have a billion-dollar hit on their hands and all it would take was one little murder, yeah, they might take a crack at it then. But not because they got pissed off."

I might not have agreed with Nancy Irvine on human psychology, but I was fairly certain my first instinct was right: she hadn't tried to kill Max. "Thank you for your time, Ms. Irvine. And for keeping your guards from shooting at me. I've had enough of that this week."

"My pleasure," she said, her face breaking into a relaxed, easy smile. "But if that's all the questions you have about Max Magic, can I ask you something?"

"Yes, ma'am."

"Have you ever done a screen test? Auditioned for anything?"

"Me?" I chuckled and shook my head. "No, ma'am."

"Oh, you should." She leaned forward, nodding, and for the first time the robe she'd kept tightly wrapped around her gaped open just a little, revealing the swimsuit underneath. "You're good-looking, ambiguous ethnicity . . ."

"I already have a job, ma'am."

Irvine cocked her head. "There's precedent for it, you know, people leaving law enforcement for the movies. What are you, twenty-seven, twenty-eight?"

"Thirty-one."

"See," she said, resting her chin in her hand and blinking slowly at me. "That's still plenty of time to get you started. Men age gracefully— they get good parts into their forties. I know I could find a place for you."

I checked up and around, but found I was still sitting in the shade. The heat I was feeling wasn't coming from the sun.

"If you did it, you'd need to lose all the 'ma'ams,' though. With the tattoos and the muscles and the shaved head, you'd need to be a bad boy." Irvine's eyes glistened. "Give it some thought. Let me know."

"I certainly will. Ma'am."

CHAPTER 10

My drive back down PCH stalled as the Lexus became mired in midafternoon traffic. The line of cars stretching to the horizon left me time to gaze wistfully out at the water and consider where the meeting with Irvine had left me.

If Nancy Irvine hadn't organized the attacks on Max, that left former bodyguard Brad Civins and Charlie Garcia, the head of Max's label, as my remaining suspects. The FBI had supposedly cleared Civins. While I wasn't inclined to give that too much weight, Garcia had always seemed the most likely to me. If Max died in some shocking, tragic fashion, didn't that increase his chances of selling a whole bunch more records before she faded from memory? There'd be tribute albums, previously unreleased recordings. Who knew, if Papa Drew had mucked up the contracts, Garcia might even own her rights going forward. Taking Max out might give him complete control over the whole operation.

Although I didn't know yet where Civins lived, investigating Garcia meant traveling to Austin. Normally, I wouldn't have batted an eye at that: a quick call to Loretta and I'd be on my way, maybe even tonight.

But now I had complications.

The first was what to do with Max.

I could leave her with the guys, like I had this morning. That would have been easiest, at least for me. And, the truth was, part of me was convinced she'd be perfectly safe with them; any trail the gang had been following had gone cold now. As long as we kept a low profile, the chances they'd catch on were awfully slim.

But I couldn't guarantee it. Not 100 percent.

They clearly had my name, and Shen and I did plenty of business. If the gang was desperate enough, or resourceful enough, they might piece that together.

A quick glance at my forearm reminded me of the price for guessing wrong.

I couldn't expose the guys that way. They'd already risked themselves enough taking us in. While Shen was more than capable of defending himself, the thought of something—anything—happening to him and Brian . . .

I wouldn't go there.

I just couldn't.

That left the possibility of moving Max, depositing her someplace else. But where? She was only sixteen; I couldn't leave her alone. I couldn't trust the FBI. Everyone at work was likely being watched.

There was really only one option left. It wasn't ideal—hell, being honest, it was colossally stupid—but Max would have to come with me.

That left the question of how we should travel.

We needed to get there—and fast. That meant flying. But there was no way we could go commercial. Paying for tickets would mean using a credit card, and I had to assume the FBI was watching those. Maybe the gang, too. Even if Loretta managed to book the tickets for us, our names would be on the passenger manifest. We'd have to show IDs to check in and clear security. With no idea how pervasive the gang's contacts were, we couldn't risk that many people knowing who we were and where we were going—it'd be LAX all over again.

Of course, I didn't exactly have any forgers on my contacts list to make us fake IDs, either.

But as I considered it, there was another option. A way to fly that wouldn't generate much attention. Something most people wouldn't think of.

The more I turned the idea over in my mind, the more perfect it seemed. It would take some phone calls to arrange, but looking at the traffic, I had plenty of time.

As I dug Shen's cell out of my pocket, I realized I probably needed to check in with Lavorgna before we headed out of town. Calling the office would be too risky—Franklin could be monitoring those lines—but I had a work-around in mind for that, too.

I set the rendezvous at a Santa Monica supermarket, the kind where the store is built over an underground parking garage.

Although there were plenty of empty spaces, I parked the Lexus down on the bottom floor, off by itself. Then I rode the elevator up, grabbed a basket, and started strolling the aisles, trying to pick ingredients that looked like they went together. I was in "Baking Supplies," between the flour and the muffin tins, when I heard a voice behind me. "What are you making, a cake?"

Spinning around, I found Lavorgna. He was also holding a basket, his bearded face twisted up in a grin. I stuck out my hand to shake, but with his free arm, he wrapped me in a hug, patting me on the back hard enough that it hurt my shoulder.

He glanced to either side and said softly, "Been a while since I've had a clandestine meeting like this." With a flex of his arms and fingers, he added, "Feels good." He started walking slowly toward the rear of the store, and I fell in beside him. "First things first," he said. "I see the limp, the sling. How are you?"

"Better than some of the guys on the other side. Thanks for meeting me, sir. I'm sorry for bothering Judith at home. I just didn't want to risk—"

His face straightened. "You did good. And calling her was smart—Franklin and the girl's father have nearly taken up residence in the office. Drew's no sweat, he's on his phone the whole time. But Franklin's listening to everything. Now, I don't want too many details from you so I don't have to lie, but are you getting anywhere?"

I shrugged my good shoulder. "Trying. There just aren't that many suspects. I interviewed one today, but I think we can rule her out."

"Speaking of which." Lavorgna dug in his pocket and handed me some folded sheets of paper. "The name you asked us to run. I haven't looked at that, but I'm told it gives you their latest address . . . and particulars."

"Great." I tucked the packet away without opening it. Now I'd know where to find Civins.

As we reached the end of the aisle and began rounding the corner to the next, I glanced at Lavorgna's basket. It was loaded with cans of tomatoes and boxes of pasta.

He caught me looking. "When Judith told me where you wanted to meet, she gave me a list. But I also stopped and got you a couple of other presents on the way. They're down in the trunk of my car." With his free hand, he produced a key, which he dangled in front of me. "I'm on B1. You know the one, right?"

I nodded.

"Good. I've got a spare, so just lock this inside on the driver's seat when you're done." Lavorgna pressed the key into my hand. "Wherever you're going, don't use plastic unless you absolutely have to. Franklin hasn't said, but I can guarantee you they're monitoring your cards."

Lavorgna slowed to a stop. "Listen, I know this has turned out to be a lot more than either of us expected—I'm sorry for that. The Bureau's playing catch-up, but it's going to take them a while to get anywhere. You're the best hope the girl has." He gave me a curt nod. "Be careful, Seth."

Then he started off again, heading toward frozen foods.

I wove back to the front of the store, then downstairs. Grabbing the Lexus, I swung it up and around the concrete ramps of the garage until I spotted Lavorgna's Honda. Fortunately, there was an open spot next to it.

People at the office didn't tease Lavorgna much, but the Odyssey was one of the few topics that earned him some ribbing. He insisted the minivan was an SUV, but he wasn't fooling anyone. Plus, there was the color. Lavorgna called it "cherry red," but I didn't know anyone who liked their cherries that shade of maroon.

In a paper bag in the trunk, I found three extra magazines for my Sig, three boxes of ammunition, and an envelope with $1,000 inside. Apparently Lavorgna was a better gift giver than I'd given him credit for.

After leaving Lavorgna's key the way he'd requested, I headed back to the guys' house in Silver Lake.

By the time I arrived, it was nearly six. Brian was busy in the kitchen, wok'ing a vegetable stir-fry that crackled sharply and filled the room with the smell of soy and ginger.

"There you are," he said. "We were starting to get worried."

"Thanks. Everything's fine. I just had to make some arrangements for the next few days. How are things here?"

"We're doing all right. Max didn't get out of bed until after I got home at lunchtime. It took her a while to get moving, but once I told her Dan would be hitting the stores on the way home, she perked up.

She seemed particularly interested in the idea that she got to pick out clothes for you."

All of a sudden, I felt slightly afraid.

"After that, she asked to borrow Dan's office so she'd have a quiet place to work. She's been in there ever since, writing music. She popped out a couple of times for a snack, but that's about it."

"So she seems . . . better?"

Brian nodded. "I think so. Heck, there were moments today she was downright polite." He raised his eyebrows and smiled. "I won't swear to it, but I think there might actually be a sweet little girl lurking in there, somewhere. Buried underneath all the money and hormones."

Within thirty minutes, Brian had the food finished and arranged along the bar. As if drawn by the aroma, Max appeared, Shen walked in from the garage, and the four of us sat down to eat.

Before popping a first bite into his mouth, Shen asked, "How'd today go?"

"I talked to Irvine. I'm pretty sure she's clean—"

"She admit what a bitch she was to me?" Max hissed the words, earning a sharp look from Brian that drove her eyes down to the table.

"—but that means we need to go check out Civins and Garcia."

Max straightened in her chair. "We're going home?"

"Yes."

"What time's our flight?"

"Early," I said, "so no sleeping in for you tomorrow."

"Won't they be watching the airlines?" Brian asked.

I nodded. "We're flying private."

"Ooooh," Max said, eyes gleaming.

"Don't get too excited," I said. "It's not *that* kind of private plane."

Max looked confused, but before she could ask another question, Shen slid a plastic bag across the table to me. "Wherever you're going, this should help. That's got the burner you wanted, plus seven hundred and fifty dollars cash."

"Thanks, I'll hit you back."

He grinned. "Already on your tab."

"Speaking of phones," Max said, "can I have mine back? I need to—"

I leaned over and stared at her hard. "No. You can't talk to anybody."

"Do you even know how the music business works? My fans follow me on social media. They haven't heard from me in days. If I don't—"

"You've got to stay quiet," I said, raising my voice slightly. "If you log in from anywhere, they can trace it. No one can know where we are, and no one can know we're going. Not my boss, not the FBI, nobody. It's all got to be a secret."

Max half rolled her eyes.

"Seriously, this is to keep us safe." I tapped the plastic bag Shen had passed me. "We can't trust my phone, either—that's why I had Dan get me this burner. I worked it out with the FBI and your dad. Everyone understands it's safer if we're off the grid. So you've got to promise me: no communicating. Okay?"

"When I don't have any fans left, it's going to be all your fault."

"You'll be alive," I said. "They'll come back to you."

"Fine. Whatever. I promise."

"Which way are you going?" Brian asked, his eyes flickering. Although Shen had been in the military, he was much more the homebody of the two. Brian had left the Midwest seeking adventure, and he was still always up for a trip. Or to hear about someone else's.

"Our first leg is LAX to Phoenix," I said. "Then we'll catch a smaller plane to Las Cruces. Spend the night there, then hop a flight to San

Antonio. I haven't worked out the last little bit yet, whether we'll fly or drive."

Max looked at me sidelong. "So we'll be there Sunday. You're sure?"

"You got someplace else to be?"

"Just answer my question," she said. "Sunday night, at home?"

"Yep," I said, "unless something unexpected happens."

CHAPTER 11

Saturday, July 18

Knowing the drive to LAX would take us at least thirty minutes, I rose at five to finish getting ready.

Truth was, though, I'd packed almost everything the night before. The clothes Shen had bought us went into an oversize duffel, along with the ammo and magazines from Lavorgna. Shen had also insisted I borrow at least one extra gun from his collection. I'd considered the Glock, but not wanting to deprive him of his favorite, I'd settled on the shotgun from the other night. It'd be slightly tricky to handle with my arm in the sling, but I thought I could manage. And while it wouldn't be any match for the volume of shots the gang could get off with their machine guns, every shot I did take would pack quite a punch and give me some margin for error when aiming. That I'd slid into the duffel, too, along with a box of shells.

The other thing I'd stocked up on for the trip were articles about Charlie Garcia and his company, Otra Records. In addition to all my usual tech blogs and audiobooks, I now had a full collection of everything that had been written about the man.

After a quick shower, I pulled on my new clothes: black jeans, a white button-down with narrow purple stripes, and black leather shoes that had a slight heel to them. Way more stylish than I normally wore, but I left the shirt untucked and rolled the sleeves to my elbows. Although the jeans fit snugly, I still managed to wedge the Sig's holster into the waistband.

My next task was waking Max. I shook her shoulder multiple times until one blue eye finally cracked open. "C'mon," I said, "it's time." When the eye shut and didn't reopen, I yanked the covers off her and pulled her up into a sitting position.

"Hey . . ."

"I mean it. Gotta go."

I went to the kitchen to give her some space, and found both Brian and Shen sitting at the bar, sipping mugs of coffee.

"Sorry for waking you guys," I said. "I was trying to be quiet."

"How did you think you were getting to the airport?" Shen asked.

"Calling a cab."

"Not a chance," he said.

Brian nodded toward a bag sitting in the middle of the counter. "I packed you both some food."

The guys had nearly finished their pot of coffee by the time Max finally emerged. Hair in a loose ponytail, the Sweet Tart shirt was thankfully gone, replaced by a pink tee that covered both shoulders. It bared her stomach, though, revealing her belly button and a silver charm dangling from it. She wore a different pair of cutoffs that were quite possibly shorter than the previous ones.

"That's your idea of subtle?" I asked.

Her eyes, still half-closed, stared at me for a moment. "What? The places you said we're going are all in the desert. It's gonna be crazy hot."

"All you had them buy for me were jeans and long-sleeve shirts."

"Yeah. But now you look better."

I took a deep breath. "Let's get moving."

We all piled into the Lexus, the guys up front, Max and me in the back. Given the hour, the ride went quickly as Shen took the 10 to the 405. The sun, just peeking over the horizon, cast long shadows that stretched across all four lanes of the freeway.

As we neared LAX, I directed Shen onto Century Boulevard, the main artery in and out of the airport. While tourists and travelers usually focus on the tall, glass hotels and fast-food joints lining the north side of Century, almost all the airlines have offices along their south side. Their buildings—just a few stories tall, with nondescript, opaque windows—don't attract much attention. What folks don't necessarily realize is that they back up onto the runways.

At my instruction, Shen turned onto a narrow access road, then into a small fenced parking lot surrounding an off-white concrete building.

"What is this place?" Max asked, peeking over her sunglasses as the Lexus slowed to a halt. The single-story structure looked more like a warehouse than anything else, its sides lined with rolling cargo doors, several of which were occupied by tractor trailers.

"Azimuth Airlines," I said.

Before she could complain, I hopped out of the car and circled around back to grab the duffel. By the time I'd shut the rear hatch, Shen and Brian stood together on the driver's side. Max was starting their way, but dragging her feet. I passed her, gave Shen and Brian each a quick one-armed hug, then started toward the entrance to the building.

I glanced back in time to see Max throw her arms around Brian's neck. She whispered something in his ear; then he whispered back and gave her a squeeze with his eyes shut and a wide smile on his face.

Shen, too, embraced her. Even after he lowered his arms, she clung to him for several moments more, whispering in his ear before stepping quickly—almost running—past me to the door.

I felt a pang in my chest watching Max saying goodbye. I beamed at the guys one last time before they climbed back into the SUV.

As I turned for the entrance, I hoped I'd make it back here to see them again.

Just inside the building, a receptionist's desk sat empty. As I searched for a bell or some other way to announce ourselves, a man in a pilot's uniform appeared from around a corner. Everything about him was tall and thin, from his tie to the dark pants that seemed to be hiked up well past his waist. He had one of those narrow builds where the bottom of his rib cage seemed to jut out wider than the bony points of his shoulders. Although we'd never met, I recognized him immediately. "Tom Musselman."

His lean face split into a broad smile. "You must be Seth Walker. Finally come to see how the other half flies?"

I smiled back. "Well, your brother's been telling me for so long how he's the better pilot—I figured I'd better come gauge for myself."

Musselman shook his head. "After this trip, you may never want to go commercial again. C'mon back, I'll get you settled."

He spun on his heel, leading us through the office and out a back door onto the tarmac. The sun had risen higher now, and you could feel and smell the heat starting to rise off the concrete, while a warm breeze buffeted us from the side. A steady hum of mechanical noise filled the air.

Fifty yards away, a white 737 sat waiting. A rolling set of stairs had been wheeled up to its side door, while just aft of that, a large hatch had been built into the side of the plane. A forklift was loading a large silver container through the gaping opening.

From behind me, Max called, "We're flying on that?"

"I told you it wasn't *that* kind of private jet."

When we reached the stairs, Musselman took them two at a time, almost by necessity with his long legs. I followed him up, duffel slung over my good shoulder.

Inside, the plane looked like some kind of retrofit. Overhead compartments lined the ceiling all the way aft like on a normal plane, but other than two rows of seats at the very front, the cabin floor had been cleared. Workers were sliding the most recently loaded container rearward, where several other containers were already secured to the deck.

Musselman turned to face us, and extended his hand toward the seats. "That's it for our extensive boarding process. Sit wherever you like. We always ferry a couple of deadheads with us to Phoenix, but there'll be plenty of room if you want to spread out. That"—he nodded at my bag—"can go in one of the overheads."

"Thanks," I said. "It's four-star dining back here, right?"

He chuckled. "Absolutely. If you brought a hot plate, you're welcome to boil up some of the cargo—I don't think anybody will miss one or two of the smaller guys." Musselman's face straightened. "I've got to go run preflight, but I'll check in with you before we take off." With that, he turned and disappeared into the cockpit.

As I stowed the duffel, Max asked, "What were you two talking about?"

"Just joking around. There's no flight attendants on here, no drinks or food. That's why it's good Brian packed that for us." I nodded at the bag of provisions he'd handed her.

"What'd he mean, 'boil up the cargo'?"

"Lobsters," I said. "Fancy restaurants need fresh seafood, but Phoenix isn't anywhere near the ocean, so every day or two it gets flown in. That's one of the things this company hauls—they help out the commercial carriers with loads they're too full to carry."

"How do you know him?"

"I don't," I said. "Not really. His twin brother's a pilot for Delta. I helped the brother out a while back, and we've kept in touch. This flight is him repaying the favor."

Max shimmied in against the window while I took the aisle, leaving an empty seat between us. Although she gazed outside for a few moments, soon she leaned her forehead against the bulkhead and closed her eyes. I checked the time on the burner phone—still not even 8:00 a.m.

Maybe ten minutes later, a few men stepped into the cabin. All wore uniforms like Musselman's, although some had only three stripes on their epaulets rather than four. I eyed them as they scattered themselves among the remaining seats, but none seemed to pay us any attention.

Finally, Musselman returned. His pilot's cap was gone, revealing dark, slicked-back hair. "We're just about ready. You two all set?"

"Yep. Thanks a bunch for letting us stow away."

"No problem. You off on some hush-hush air marshal business?"

I shook my head. "Nothing like that. My niece over here"—I jerked my head at Max—"came out to the coast for a couple of weeks, but now she's got to get home. I figured I'd tag along, but everything was sold out."

Musselman nodded. "Tim said you're good people, so happy to help. It's not a long hop—only about forty-five minutes once we get in the air."

After Musselman returned to the cockpit, I switched my audio player over to the Charlie Garcia articles. As we rumbled through takeoff, I closed my eyes and focused on the words coming through my earpiece.

According to industry profiles, Garcia had grown up in one of San Antonio's nastier neighborhoods, the youngest of seven children and the only one to finish high school. The stories all mentioned how he'd avoided joining a gang, thanks to older brothers who'd been members themselves but had shielded him from it.

In my mind, though, that raised questions: Had Garcia really avoided the gangs? Or had he merely become their legitimate face? The men at my house hadn't been speaking Spanish, but I certainly didn't know all the different gangs operating in Texas.

Garcia had worked the graveyard shift at a local Tejano radio station to pay his way through junior college. When the money hadn't added up quickly enough, he'd dropped out of school but expanded his role at the station. Soon, he was emceeing local concerts, hosting music festivals, getting to know the scene in a way no one else could. After two years, he left the station to start Otra.

I wondered how difficult it would be to start a music label from scratch like that. You needed recording space, a lot of equipment. If Garcia had lacked the cash, could he maybe have sought a loan from his brothers' friends, instead of a bank? Possible, and one way he could be connected to whatever group was after Max.

Otra's first successful signing was a small family group named El Fenix. Using his contacts to get their single on the radio, Garcia was eventually able to crank out an El Fenix LP. That, in turn, allowed Otra to expand, attracting bigger and better acts like Cesar Casarez, Aggie Zaragoza, Los Coyotes, and Chicos de los Rios. Several won Tejano Music Awards. Los Coyotes were even nominated for a Grammy before they got rid of the Tejano category in 2011. But none was a major commercial success. None had crossover appeal.

Until Max.

One article compared her signing with Otra to Elvis's arrival at Sun Records in 1954: a game changer. As her albums started going gold, Garcia received much of the credit. Suddenly, Otra was competing with the big boys in terms of sales numbers, and Garcia was signing acts in new genres: rap, hip-hop, R & B. While Max had taken off and gone platinum, though, none of the others managed to replicate her success. The more time passed, the more Max looked like a bolt of lightning rather than a product of Garcia's genius.

All the more reason to keep her, I thought.

Or prevent her from going someplace else.

I'd finished listening to about half of the articles on Garcia when I noticed we'd begun banking our way through the approach to Phoenix.

As the plane turned, Max started to stir. Physically at first, shoulders and arms twitching while her eyes remained closed. After a few moments, though, she bolted upright, her head jerking to each side. Realizing where she was, she yawned and smacked her lips. "We there?"

"Almost," I said. "Just need to land."

After a soft touchdown, we taxied back across the airport to the cargo area. With no seat-belt light to obey, I watched the deadheads. As soon as we stopped moving, they all unbuckled, so I did the same and retrieved the duffel from the overhead.

Musselman emerged from the cockpit wearing his cap again. As he opened the side door, an intense blast of heat and noise entered the cabin.

I motioned for Max to follow me, and we got in line behind the other crew exiting the plane. When we reached the door, I thanked Musselman again and set the duffel down to shake his hand.

"Try and keep cool out there," he said. "You know where you're going?"

"We've got to meet someone over at general aviation."

"There's a shuttle bus you can call. Just ask inside."

Max and I dashed from the plane to the Azimuth office and then out to the shuttle at top speed. Each time we exited the air-conditioning, it felt like stepping into an oven.

The shuttle bus wound us along a narrow access road that circled one end of the runways before heading for a series of stand-alone buildings lining the opposite side. Many resembled Azimuth—single-story warehouses receiving cargo from tractor trailers. Ultimately, though, the bus pulled into a parking lot belonging to a newer two-story building constructed of steel and tinted glass.

Once again, we dashed across the few yards of asphalt to sliding doors that yawned open as we approached. A loud gust of AC blew over us as we entered. The lobby of the building was constructed as a two-story atrium, with a reception desk on one side and banks of sofas and comfortable chairs on the other. I steered Max toward the seating.

"What is this place?" she asked.

"An FBO."

"An FB-what?"

"Fixed base operator. They're like rest stops on the highway. Almost every airport has one so private planes have a place to fuel up or tie down." I wedged the duffel beneath a chair that backed up against the glass wall and faced the front door, then sat with my feet splayed on either side of it. Max plopped into the seat next to me.

"So we're taking a private jet on this next leg?"

"Something like that," I said. Although we were alone in the seating area, I scanned the rest of the space, looking for anything suspicious. "We're meeting our next contact here, but it's going to be a little while."

"What are we supposed to do? Just sit here?"

I nodded at an interior wall perpendicular to us, where a large TV was running cable news on mute. Spinner racks of newspapers and magazines stood on either side. "Read," I said, "or watch TV. It'll just be a couple of hours."

"Hours?" She made the word sound three syllables long.

Over the next thirty minutes, people filtered in and out of the FBO. With a copy of *Sports Illustrated* open in my lap, I eyeballed each new arrival. Virtually all were men, mostly middle-aged or older. No tattoos or guns; they seemed more interested in the urns of free coffee than Max and me as they stationed themselves in various chairs around the seating area.

A few minutes later, Max announced, "I'm going to the bathroom."

"I'll—"

She glared at me. "It's right over there." She pointed toward the reception desk. I had an open line of sight to the door.

"Okay. Don't talk to anybody." But Max was already off her chair and several steps away.

As I scanned back across the seating area, I could see several men's eyes following her.

A couple then turned to look at me.

I met their gaze for a moment before glancing elsewhere.

Max and her damn clothes.

Was she really so desperate to have her ego stroked that she'd risk us being spotted over it?

Apparently, yes, she was.

When Max reappeared, she angled toward the TV wall. Pausing at the corner of it, she fished in her pocket and pulled out some money. I heard a hollow clunk, she bent down, and then she was sauntering back to our chairs, sucking on a Popsicle.

Again, heads followed her.

The smile she wore, while slight, was unmistakable.

I didn't say anything as she slipped back into her chair. I just glanced back down at the magazine. Several moments later, she gave the Popsicle tip a particularly loud suck, then whispered, "Why are you all angry?"

"I'm not angry."

"Yes, you are."

"No, I'm not."

"The little veins on the side of your head look like they're about to pop."

I sighed again. "I didn't like the way those guys were looking at you."

"Aw," she said. "You jealous?"

I snorted. "I think you're asking for trouble."

"How?"

"Dressing like that."

"Like what?" Her voice had grown singsongy. She was enjoying this. It took effort to keep my voice quiet. "You know exactly what I mean."

"If guys want to look," Max said, folding a leg underneath her, "I think it's flattering. Besides, maybe they recognize me. Maybe they're fans." After drawing out the last syllable, she stuck the Popsicle back in her mouth.

"They're a little old for you. And they weren't looking at your face."

She withdrew the Popsicle again, releasing a little giggle with it.

I decided to drop the issue there, although my stomach continued to churn. Ten minutes later, Max reached into the bag Brian had packed. "You want something to drink?"

"No. Thanks."

She flopped back around into her seat, holding a bottle of water. Cracking it open, she sucked down a third of it. She drank so fast, in fact, the rippled sides of the plastic crackled and snapped as they compressed.

"Really?" I asked.

"What's wrong now? I'm drinking too loud?"

"It's not that."

"Then what?"

I sighed. There was no winning at this.

In my peripheral vision, it looked like Max was smiling again, but when I turned to check, she'd donned her sunglasses and begun staring out the window.

We both remained quiet for a long time after that. Whether it was the silence, the air-conditioning, or something else, I didn't know, but gradually the heat seeped out of my face. Although my earpiece had shifted back to playing the tech podcasts I usually listened to, they weren't holding my attention. Fortunately, the seating area had cleared out—only one guy was left, reading a newspaper over at the far end of the space.

"What's going to happen to your movie now?" I asked. "The one you were coming out here to make?"

"What do you mean?"

"Are you worried they'll replace you if you don't show?" Irvine's comments about child actors echoed in my head. So far, although the LAX shoot-out had become national news, no one had connected it to Max, so the people producing this new film would have no idea why she was AWOL.

"I hadn't really thought about it," she said, "till now. Thanks. I'm sure my father will be as thrilled about it as you are."

"I'm not trying to gloat or anything," I said. "Really. I was just asking. What does your dad have against you being in movies, anyway?"

Max's head slid back against her shoulders, her eyes pointing up at the ceiling. "He just hates the idea of me having any freedom at all. Of me doing anything I want."

"Oh, come on. He can't be that bad. I'm sure—"

"He is, okay?" Max's voice spiked, and she glared at me. "Can we please not talk about my father? Like, ever?"

"Sure," I said. "Let's talk about going home. When we get to Austin, it's going to be a little weird for a while. You're not going to be able to see your friends or anything until we make sure we have all this under control."

"You don't have to worry," she said. "I don't have any friends in Austin."

"What do you mean?" Last night she'd seemed awfully eager to get home. If it wasn't to see friends, I wondered exactly what it was.

"I just don't. We lived in Missouri most of the time I was growing up, until we moved to Texas to try and get Charlie to sign me. Since then, I've been too busy for stuff like that."

"What about the kids you go to school with, or play sports with?"

"I don't really go to school anymore. I have tutors, sometimes. But that's about it."

"How can that be legal? You've gotta—"

"My dad's a lawyer. Don't you think he knows exactly what's legal and what isn't?"

My eyes flashed to the guy with the newspaper. He looked up at the sound of Max's voice. I turned back to her and said very quietly, "I'm sorry, I—"

Max ripped the sunglasses off. Her eyes had narrowed to slits, but tears were swelling on either side of them. "Bullshit. You're not sorry—not at all. You've been all over me, criticizing me about everything since we met. God! My clothes, my career—now school? Where do you get off judging me? I've made more money at sixteen than you'll probably ever make. So fuck you!"

With that, Max slumped down in the seat and turned her back to me. Her shoulders shook slightly, and I guessed she might be crying.

I glanced back at the guy who'd looked our way. He shot me a dirty look, but then returned to his newspaper.

I started to say something once or twice, but didn't get past opening my mouth. Max was wrong on the money thing—she didn't know about my patents, obviously—but otherwise, she had a point. When I was her age, all I worried about was school and whether I could maybe get a girl to kiss me someday. My idea of a job was summer landscaping work for six bucks an hour. Nothing like the pressure of supporting a family.

Or an entire record label.

◆ ◆ ◆

Over the next thirty minutes or so, the FBO began to fill again. Apparently this was the postlunch crowd, as they went for sodas and chips from the vending machines instead of the coffee.

Finally, an older guy entered through the sliding doors. Bushy white curls poked out from beneath his red Wisconsin baseball cap. The hat seemed to match what the sun had done to his ruddy complexion: it was like all his freckles had connected beneath the white hair on his arms.

He ambled over to the edge of the seating area, then yanked the aviator shades off his face. Jabbing the tip of one earpiece between his lips, he glanced around until his eyes settled on us. That's when he pulled the glasses from his mouth and made a beeline for our chairs.

"You Seth Walker?" he asked in a nasal voice.

I stood up. "Yes, sir."

"Jerry Norgard. Glad to meetcha." An impish smile spread across his face as he extended a hand to shake.

"Thanks for making room for us."

"Oh, no problem. I gotta make the trip, anyway. And any friend of my Christa is welcome to grab a ride. You got all your stuff?"

I glanced at Max and the bags. She still wasn't looking at me. "Yep."

"Okay, great. Let me hit the little boys' room, and we'll get out of here."

Norgard shuffled back toward reception, following the same track Max had traveled earlier. When he returned, the sunglasses were perched on the brim of his hat, and the collar of his white golf shirt had been turned up. "Let's get a move on, kids."

I slung the duffel over my good shoulder and shepherded Max to follow him out the sliding doors and around the building. *Intense* was the only word to describe the heat—the way it attacked your skin felt deliberate and threatening. Unlike back home, there was no breeze here; the air sat perfectly still other than a slight updraft off the concrete. Despite some scattered clouds, the sky above us was unrelentingly bright. The sun blazing overhead seemed to have bleached everything—the tarmac, the terminal buildings—to the same drab tan.

Even from behind, I could see Max's head checking each of the sleek jets we passed to see if it might be the one. But Norgard led us past all of them to an area filled with smaller prop planes. Max's gait slowed and gradually he pulled ahead, eventually ducking under the wing of a white Cessna adorned with Wisconsin-red stripes.

Max stopped short of the plane, and her head whipped around to face me. "That? You think I'm going to ride in *that*?"

My lips drew into a narrow line, and I nodded.

"Oh no." She started shaking her head. "That thing is way too small—"

"It's perfectly safe," I said. "I hate heights, but I'm not afraid of planes like these. As long as you're enclosed, it feels like riding in a car."

I could see her throat muscles clench as she swallowed hard.

I moved past her and stepped under the wing. Although the shade dropped the temperature at least five degrees, the air still felt like it would boil water. "You don't sound like you're from around here, Jerry," I said, loud enough for Max to hear.

"Nope. Grew up in Wisconsin. Been down here fifteen years now, though. Better for my arthritis. And my cholesterol," he added with a chuckle.

"How long have you been flying?"

"Uncle Sam taught me a couple of decades before you both were born," he said.

I glanced over at Max and tried a soft smile. It didn't seem to help. When she still hadn't moved after I buckled the duffel into one of the rear seats, I crossed back over to her. "What's going on?"

She shook her head. "I need . . . I need to go to the bathroom."

I rolled my eyes, then called to Norgard that we'd be right back. Although Max stayed silent as we retraced our steps, she walked quickly, and I noticed she kept her arms locked straight, her fists clenched.

Once we got back inside, Max went directly into the ladies' room. I took up a position next to the door to wait for her.

After a minute, I checked the time on the burner phone. Then I kept checking, until five and finally ten minutes had gone by.

I knocked on the door. "Max? You okay in there?"

When no response came, I wondered whether I might need to repeat the gesture, or do something even more drastic.

But then she reappeared. Although her hair was damp with sweat, her arms now hung limply by her sides.

I placed my hand on her shoulder and leaned down so our faces were just inches apart. "Are you okay? What's going on?"

She kept her eyes down, her chin almost touching her chest. "I'm just . . . I was . . . nervous."

"Did you get sick?"

She nodded weakly.

"I'm sorry. We don't have a choice—"

"I know," she said. "I'm ready now. Let's go."

"Are you sure? We can wait a few—"

"No," she said. "Let's go."

She led the way outside, and when we reached the plane, Max headed straight for the empty rear seat.

Norgard watched her buckle herself in, then turned to me. "Everything okay?"

I shrugged. "Hope so."

"Then let's mosey."

Max remained quiet through taxi and takeoff. When I finally glanced back from my seat in the front, I found her leaned against the duffel, eyes closed and mouth open.

"She all right back there?" Although he was directly to my left, Norgard's voice sounded distant over the intercom.

"Yeah. She's tired, and I don't think she's ever flown in a little plane like this. But she's asleep now. You make this run often?"

"Couple of times a month. Since I retired, I been flying almost every week. Last year, a guy I know at the airport asked if I'd pick something up for him—Las Cruces ain't a major hub, but folks still need parts and stuff. He paid me a hundred bucks plus fuel, so now I do this on and off, and it helps cover some of my costs."

Norgard remained chatty, telling me about his daughter, Christa, one of the first flight attendants I'd met upon becoming an air marshal, and his dream to island-hop through the Caribbean on a seaplane. Before I knew it, the altimeter on the panel in front of me said we'd begun descending, and Norgard began talking with the tower about our approach.

Although dull-brown mountains ringed the horizon, the terrain beneath us seemed to be nothing but a wide expanse of desert sand freckled by dark scrub. A single ribbon of highway stretched from right to left as far as you could see—I-10, I guessed from my earlier looks at the map—while the city itself loomed off to our right as strings of white dots surrounding collections of weird, flat shapes traced on the ground.

The airport below had three runways—two longer ones arranged perpendicularly in an X and a third connecting their southern ends. We banked a couple of times until the third, shorter runway stood as a straight, pale line directly ahead of us. Through the seat, I could feel Norgard bleeding off speed and altitude. As we descended even farther, the ground revealed an added third dimension: suddenly you could discern the variations between hills and ditches. Finally, the runway widened before us, Norgard angled up the nose, and the airplane bounced softly onto the ground.

We continued down the runway until all the plane's excess speed had dissipated. Finally, near the end, Norgard slowly turned the Cessna toward a series of buildings and hangars that lined the tarmac.

But as he did so, a loud, chattering sound filled the cabin.

The noise eclipsed the sound of our engine, and while I heard Norgard asking the tower about it in my headphones, a quick check out my window revealed a white helicopter overhead, following the direction of the runway.

The chopper couldn't have been more than fifty feet in the air— low enough that I could make out the seams between the panels on its underside. It continued along its course for another hundred yards or so before banking sharply and turning back toward us.

Norgard managed to let out a "What the hell?" before the helicopter landed directly in front of our nose, blocking the path to the hangars.

My heart started racing when I got a glimpse of the pilot and copilot through its glass canopy.

Both had tattooed faces.

"Jerry," I shouted, "we need to get out of here. Now!"

Norgard continued turning the plane until we faced the direction from which we'd come. And that's when I realized why the rotor noise was so loud.

A second helicopter had landed directly behind us, blocking the runway.

CHAPTER 12

The second helicopter was painted navy blue, but its crew was similarly inked.

"Jerry, these are bad, bad guys," I said. "We need to move!"

"Hold on," was his only response.

Men started to emerge from the rear doors of the blue chopper. Each carried a machine gun.

But suddenly they, the blue helicopter, and all the scenery behind them began sliding to the right. Norgard was turning the plane again.

Without warning, he gunned the throttle, and the Cessna jolted forward.

"What's going on?" Max said from the back.

"Our friends found us again," I said, trying my best to sound calm. Shifting in my seat to face her, I saw the same bug-eyed expression she'd worn inside baggage claim at LAX. "Don't worry. We'll be okay."

I glanced back out the windows, wondering if I truly believed my own words. Both helicopters had left their rotors spinning, and now the blue one's tail angled up into the air as it started to lift off. "They're gonna follow us, Jerry."

"They might try," Norgard said.

We rolled onto the longer runway that joined ours at an angle. As we lined up, Norgard opened the throttle. The engine's buzz rose an octave, and the plane pitched forward, pressing me back into my seat.

Out my side window, I saw the blue chopper racing to catch us. Nose down, it was gaining quickly. Over my other shoulder, I could see the white helicopter on the opposite side of the plane, doing the same. Both were also squeezing closer to us, trying to pinch us between them.

Shots rang out, and I spotted muzzle flashes coming from the rear door of the blue helicopter.

"Faster, Jerry," I said. It felt like we should have been airborne already, and I wondered what Norgard was waiting for.

"This is max power," he said. "Just hang on."

Without warning, our wheels popped off the ground. Norgard yanked hard on the yoke, and we moved into a steep climb.

When they realized we were taking off, both helicopters swerved in toward us. But as Norgard's maneuver lifted us up and out of their way, they ended up nearly colliding, veering away from each other at the last moment before their rotor blades touched.

In the pilot's seat, Norgard seemed oblivious to the action below. His face and body were perfectly calm, as if this were all routine. But he left the throttle open and continued to pull back, the angle of the nose steepening until it felt more like a roller-coaster climb than anything else. I could sense the raw mechanical power through my seat.

"You okay, Jerry?" I asked.

"I don't like people shooting at my aircraft."

"I can explain—"

"Save it," he said. "We got speed and power over those helos. So we're gonna climb up into the sun where they can't see us and get the fuck out of here. Once we're someplace safe, you can do all your explaining."

"Run away?"

"From bad guys with guns? Absolutely."

"Where?"

"El Paso's closest. Less than fifteen minutes."

"But even if we pull away from those choppers," I said, "they can just radio for reinforcements. They'll have someone waiting in El Paso before we get there."

Norgard paused for a moment. "So what's your idea, genius?"

"Return fire. Take them on here."

He chuffed. "With what, exactly? I left my Sidewinder missiles at home."

I pulled out the Sig.

He glanced over quickly. "You kidding? You can't hit anything with that up here."

"You get me close enough, I'll hit something."

Norgard's eyes remained forward. We continued climbing.

"They're going to follow us," I said. "Trust me, Jerry—if you can dodge them, I can shoot them."

His face turned. Even behind the aviators, I could feel the old man's eyes measuring me. Finally, he shrugged one shoulder slightly. "I've always wanted to see what this girl could do if I really turned her loose."

With the adrenaline pumping now, I pulled the earpiece out from where I'd snaked it beneath my headset. I also called to Max behind us. "Can you dig out the extra magazines from the duffel?"

When no answer came, I looked back at her. "Max?"

Still wide-eyed, she didn't respond.

"Max!"

Finally, her eyes ticked over at me.

"Magazines. In the bag. Get them. I need ammo, now!"

Her head started to bob. Slightly at first, then more of a nod. As she reached for the duffel, I turned to Norgard. "Let's go."

He eased the yoke forward, and backed off power slightly. As we started leveling off, he said, "The engine and the rotor assembly on those things aren't as fragile as you think. Aim for the tail rotors. Or the pilot."

"Got it."

Max passed me the three magazines, and I wedged them between my thighs. Then I unlatched the side window. Hinged at the top, it swung outward at the bottom—only a few degrees, but enough that wind began shrieking through the cabin. I braced my right arm on the sill with the Sig barrel pointed forward. That helped steady my grip.

"Ready," I called.

"Then here we go," Norgard said.

He eased the yoke forward and cut power. The nose of the plane dipped toward the ground, and we started descending. Slowly at first, but working with gravity now instead of against it, the plane seemed to gather speed exponentially.

"There," Norgard said.

Although I looked all around, I didn't see anything at first. But as he maneuvered us slightly, something glinted in the sun. A tiny speck against the sandy-brown backdrop.

The sparkling speck began to move, sliding left to right across the windshield, flashing as it went. We continued toward it, as if following some kind of blinking lodestar.

Gradually, ground details came into sharper relief as the earth grew closer. The speck grew large enough for me to see it was the blue helicopter.

I couldn't tell whether it was actively running from us or if Norgard had simply circled us behind it. But over the course of several seconds, it changed from a pinprick dot to a small teardrop. I kept my eyes locked on the shape, while in my back and legs I could sense Norgard applying power, leveling off to maintain our angle of approach.

"Thirty seconds," he said. In the windshield, the helicopter had grown to a quarter inch.

Steadying my arm on the sill, I eyed down the sights. Between the gusts of wind still pressing their way into the cabin and invisible bumps in the air, my platform was anything but stable. Still, I did my best to focus on the tail of the teardrop shape, to picture the rotor spinning at the end of it.

"Ten seconds."

The dark-blue helicopter was bigger now, maybe a half inch in my vision. But I was still way out of range.

"Five . . . four . . ."

Although Norgard went silent, I continued counting in my head. We were close enough now that I could see the chopper clearly, and I locked in on the tail. At two, I guessed we were in range for the Sig and let off four shots.

The helicopter flinched as if it were alive and startled by something. But if I scored a hit, it wasn't enough: the chopper not only kept flying, it banked back in the direction from which we'd come.

Almost immediately, Norgard tilted us into a steep left turn. As he did, I heard automatic gunfire, and the white helicopter flashed by.

"Told you this was a shitty idea," he said.

As we cleared the turn, Norgard opened the throttle again, and we soared upward. This time, though, instead of a smooth climb, he rocked the wings every few seconds.

Gunfire rang out again. Two hollow thumps sounded, then the side window next to me broke, causing me to pull my arm back inside the cabin.

"Hang on," I heard.

Suddenly, the climb became a dip. We bounced several times as if clearing invisible hills before dropping into a sharp right turn. Almost as soon as we'd entered it, though, we were pulling out into an even steeper climb than before.

After several seconds soaring upward, Norgard said, "Okay, we're clear. You're sure you don't want to rabbit while we can."

"One more chance," I said.

Without another word, the plane pitched to the left, and we started another dive. Like the climb, this one was steeper than before, and

I frantically searched the drab tan expanse below for any sign of the helicopters.

"One thirty," Norgard said. "White one."

Sure enough, just right of the nose, I saw an impossibly small white dot. With no idea how Norgard's vision could be that good, I reassumed my firing position at the windowsill.

Locked in on the white chopper, though, I wasn't expecting the plane to juke hard to the right. As it did, I tumbled to my left, my seat belt the only thing keeping me from spilling into Norgard's lap.

Gunfire crackled, and I saw why Norgard had made the sudden move: the blue helicopter had swooped in from the side. Executing a turn across our path, I saw flashes from its windows and heard two more dull thuds hit our fuselage.

Norgard had no choice but to pull up hard.

As he did, though, a buzzer began to squeal: the stall warning.

The airplane lost momentum, then twisted around. The nose now pointed directly at the ground, which started to spin slowly.

Over the electronic squealing, I heard Max scream.

"It's okay," Norgard said calmly over the radio. He idled the throttle and jabbed his feet until we stopped turning. As the airplane smoothed out, he pulled back gently on the yoke until we were level. The squealing stopped, and now Norgard applied power again to push us upward once more.

The blue helicopter hadn't gone far—it continued circling above us like a shark.

As we climbed toward it, the chopper disappeared behind us, then reappeared on my side of the plane. "Get ready," Norgard called.

The helicopter kept turning in front of us, remaining at the same altitude. Norgard applied more power, pulling us up well past the chopper's level, before abruptly banking us over to the left. Exchanging altitude for speed, we swooped down through a turn, ending up directly behind the blue chopper.

"There's your shot."

I scrambled to line up the tail rotor in the Sig's sights. Although the copter tried to waggle back and forth, to alternate speeds, Norgard matched its every move. After a cleansing breath, I let off a steady stream of eight shots in a line.

Two, then three, flashes erupted from the tail. Suddenly, the helicopter's entire back end started swerving wildly. It began shedding altitude, but before my eyes could follow it downward, Norgard pulled us back up into another climb.

"That's one," he said.

As I reloaded, Norgard made periodic left turns, giving himself a chance to search below us. He continued to steal glances toward the ground until finally, he said, "Gotcha," and pitched the nose over. "Two o'clock moving to three."

This time the spotting was easier—the white chopper stood out against a dark-brown mountain framed behind it. I got into position in the window and waited as the dive pushed my stomach farther up into my chest than I'd prefer.

The helicopter was still only the size of a fruit fly when it abruptly changed direction. Norgard moved to match its course, and we continued descending on it, creeping ever closer. As we settled in just behind and above it, the white helicopter began flying erratically, weaving this way and that.

When it veered hard left, I anticipated it coming back right and laid down a line of six shots where I thought the tail would end up.

I was too early—the chopper did come back, but the bullets were long gone.

The helicopter continued dancing up and down, left and right. I guessed again when it would cross our nose and emptied the rest of the magazine.

The shots were too high this time, as the helicopter dipped before swerving.

As I reloaded again, Norgard's voice sounded in my ears. "I can't stay on him forever."

Once I had my eyes back in the sights, I let the chopper swing back and forth a couple of times to get a sense of its rhythm. Then I let off a diagonal line of shots.

At least one of the six was a hit. Sparks erupted from the helicopter's tail. The rotor seized, and almost immediately the body of the chopper began to spin.

Looking up from the Sig, my focus widened, and I suddenly realized how close we were to the mountain: the nearest peak was no longer a vague brown blob, but a sharply defined, craggy chunk of rock. The chopper must have been leading us in a dive through the entire pursuit.

As the helicopter careened forward and down, Norgard pulled us into the sharpest turn yet. My head jerked to the side while the force of the turn squeezed me back against the seat.

Although I didn't see the helicopter strike the ground, the impact and explosion jolted the Cessna. Norgard once again seemed oblivious, focusing only on banking us away. With the nose down, though, as the airplane's turn steepened, we didn't level out of it as I expected.

Instead, the Cessna banked even farther.

Suddenly, the nose was pointed at the ground again, and we were spiraling downward.

"Hang on," Norgard said over the radio. Although calm, his voice betrayed obvious effort.

This time seemed different from the last, the aircraft more helpless. My insides, already jumbled and uneasy from all the maneuvering, started to feel queasy.

We went through several rotations—I had no idea what our altitude was, but it sure didn't seem like we had much to spare. Each turn revealed more detail below us: what had been brown lines across the desert sand blossomed into visible dots of scrub.

There was no stall warning this time. No noise except the engine humming as Norgard wrestled with the controls.

As the fall pressed me deeper and deeper into my seat, my heart seemed to pound against the inside of my rib cage.

Soon, I could see cracks and fissures in the ground instead of a matte floor.

A check of the instruments showed everything spinning. Already dizzy, I looked away to avoid becoming totally disoriented.

Seconds stretched into what seemed like minutes as the turns kept accelerating and the ground approached. It grew harder and harder to breathe.

"C'mon, baby," Norgard said through gritted teeth.

Finally, somehow, he flattened us out and brought the nose back up to the horizon.

Once we were back cruising, Norgard glanced over, wearing a broad smile. "Everybody awake?" he asked. "Let's go land somewhere."

CHAPTER 13

Although we could have gone in any direction after the attack, because we didn't know the exact fate of the blue helicopter, I convinced Norgard to head north to Albuquerque. It was farther than El Paso, but the airport was larger and would give us more cover and more options.

Not wanting to provide too many details, I told Norgard I was delivering Max to the FBI in Texas after the gang had attacked her in LA. Thankfully, he didn't ask any questions. And while we all remained on alert through the rest of the flight, it was uneventful. Our landing—to the southwest, as the sun swelled and painted a bright-orange band against the horizon—was beautifully boring.

As Norgard tied the Cessna down, I helped Max out of the plane and retrieved the duffel. It was obvious all the adrenaline had faded for us both. I had my earpiece back in, but my muscles felt totally wrung out. Her eyes drooped like she wanted to go back to sleep.

Finally, Norgard circled back to our side of the plane and stuck out a hand. "That was an adventure," he said.

"How'd you learn to fly like that?" I asked.

"North Vietnamese triple A is a pretty good tutor. But I'll tell you, I shot down two MiGs, and neither was a fight like that."

"I'm so sorry about your plane," I said. "I'll pay to—"

He scrunched up his face and waved his hand. "Don't worry about it, kid. You get to be my age, a little excitement like that is worth hammering out a few dings."

We shook hands, then went our separate ways.

A quick search on the burner phone's GPS showed the airport was adjacent to the freeway, surrounded by a cluster of motels. Figuring we'd need food and supplies, I opted for one whose parking lot connected to a Waffle House and a 7-11. Twenty minutes later, we were locked in our room, Max poking at a salad, me wolfing down large bites from a bacon cheeseburger.

"You've barely eaten today," I said.

She stabbed a chunk of tomato with her plastic fork and stared at me over it. "I'm just not very hungry."

"Okay. But tomorrow's gonna be another long one."

"What time will we get home?"

I shook my head. "No way we're getting to Austin tomorrow. Not with this little detour."

Max's face flushed, and she burst out of her chair. "We have to— you promised!"

I shrugged. "What do you want me to do? We just had to come two hundred miles north. Right now, I'm thinking we fly to Dallas. I've got some police friends there from my last case—we can check with them, see if they know anything about the gang. Then we'll head to Austin on Monday."

"That's a whole extra day!" Her eyes were wide, the hair on her arms standing at attention.

"I know. But as long as we get there safely, what's the difference?"

"It's just—" Max looked down, her eyes darting to different places on the floor. Then she let out a noise, something between a grunt and a growl, and stormed off to the bathroom.

After the door slammed, I heard the lock click.

Not in the mood to chase down another of her tantrums, I stayed where I was and slowly ate the rest of my food. Although I tended to avoid red meat, after the events of the day, I was hungry enough that the burger tasted absolutely gourmet. By the final bite, I felt warm and sleepy.

After cleaning up my own trash, I wrapped up the remnants of Max's salad. I was on one knee, tucking them into the minifridge, when she reappeared. Visibly calmer, her arms were draped at her sides, her eyes tracking the ground in front of her feet.

Resisting the urge to ask if she was all right—it felt like that was every other sentence out of my mouth—I tilted the plastic container toward her. "Still hungry?"

"No. Thanks," she said slowly. "I'm sorry for freaking out."

I shrugged and smiled. "Been a helluva week."

As I put the food away, she asked, "What happened to your shirt?"

I turned, and Max pointed at my right side. I still didn't see anything.

She stepped over and pulled the shirt around. There was a small tear in the fabric, surrounded by a brown stain. "Must've gotten hit somehow." I hadn't noticed. Unbuttoning the shirt and twisting it around the sling to remove it, I stepped to the bathroom mirror, glancing back over my shoulder. A straight line was drawn from my right side toward my spine, a couple of inches above my belt. Thankfully, just a scratch, but it was red and weepy.

We'd bought clean bandages for my shoulder—at this point, what was one more? "I'm gonna need your help," I said. "With my bum arm, I can't reach either one."

Although I worried whether Max could handle the blood, she wetted a washcloth and stepped around behind me.

The cloth stung sharply against the skin, partly from the cold, partly the exposed flesh. Gradually she dabbed at the scratch until it stopped hurting. I handed her some folded-up gauze—she pressed it against the wound and taped it down. It felt good, comfortable.

"Need to get this one next," she said softly, putting her hands on my shoulder. The tape didn't want to lift up at first, and even after that was all removed, the gauze had stuck to the wound. As Max peeled it off, I grunted: it felt like the bandage was taking some awfully big chunks with it.

"Let it breathe for a second," I said with my eyes closed. I wanted to help it heal, but the cool air also sucked away some of the burning sensation.

Max ran a fingernail across the skin of my opposite shoulder, near the sling strap. Lightly, almost tickling. "What's this tattoo? Is this . . . math?"

"Yeah. It's an equation."

"Why do you have math tattooed on your back?" She dragged the nail back and forth in a way that made me squirm slightly.

"It's called a DCT."

"A DC-what?"

I opened my eyes and smiled at her in the mirror. "DCT. Discrete cosine transform. It's used to compress audio and video. It's the reason your songs fit onto a CD."

She gave me a look like I'd dodged the question. "So, why's it on your back?"

"I told you, I was an engineer."

"That's not a reason."

I took a deep breath to give myself time to choose my words carefully. "When I . . . stopped doing that job, getting the tattoo seemed like . . . the right way to remember things."

"Did you like being an engineer?"

"Oh yeah," I said. "It was my dream from when I was way younger than you."

"So, why did you switch?"

"I told you, it's a long story."

She rolled her eyes. "It's not like I'm going anywhere."

After a long, slow breath, I said, "Not tonight." Then I handed her another piece of gauze. "Finish up back there, there's something else I need to talk to you about."

"What am I in trouble for now?"

I motioned toward the bed. "Sit down for a second."

Max sat on the edge, and I moved in beside her. "I need you to tell me who you gave our travel plan to."

She bolted to her feet. "*What?* You think I—"

I nodded. "I know you did. Only three people knew where we were going and what we were traveling in."

"They could have found out some other way!"

"No. I kept an eye out the whole day. To line up those choppers, they had to know exactly what to look for and exactly where we'd be, well in advance."

Max's hands balled into fists. "So, you don't trust me now? You think I'm trying to have myself killed?"

"I don't think that at all. But the gang has to be getting their information from somewhere. I didn't tell anybody. I don't think Jerry Norgard called them. Which just leaves you."

Max's lower lip and chin started trembling.

"Was it your dad? Did you call him to say you were okay?"

"Fuck no."

"So who was it?"

Her eyes dropped to the bed, and her shoulders slumped. "Marta."

"Who's Marta?"

"She's my nanny."

All I could picture was Mary Poppins, but that didn't seem to square with Max's life.

"Since we moved to Texas, my dad's always busy. With my mom gone, it's just kinda been me and Marta." Then she paused. "But Marta loves me. She'd never—"

I raised my hands. "This doesn't mean she wanted to help them—just that she did. But now that we know they have access to her, you can't talk to her again, okay?"

Max nodded slightly. "Do you think she's in trouble?"

"I don't know. How did you call her—what did you use?" I'd intentionally avoided returning Max's phone after she'd turned it over to me in Shen's Lexus, and before we'd left LA, I'd hidden both our handsets inside a drawer at Shen and Brian's, turned completely off so they couldn't be tracked. As smart as that seemed at the time, not searching her for other devices now seemed equally stupid.

"I called this morning, when I got freaked out about the plane. I just needed to talk to someone. I have a flip phone Marta gave me for emergencies."

I stuck out my hand. "Let me have it."

Max produced a small silver phone from her purse and dropped it into my open palm. "Other than that one call, I kept it turned off, just like you said. I usually leave it off, anyway; no one has the number, and that way I don't have to charge it much."

I checked, and sure enough, the phone was completely powered down. "You sure the only time it was on was this morning? If you used it at the guys' house, I need to know. They could be in danger."

"I swear." She stared at me unblinking, no signs of wavering.

"Well, that's something," I managed to say. I tucked the phone into my pocket. "This stays with me. No other communications from now on. No calls, no texts, no tweets. Nothing, understand? You saw what happened today when anyone knows where we are."

Max's chin dropped to her chest, and she nodded.

"Is Marta the reason you're so desperate to get home?"

She nodded again.

"How'd she sound when you talked to her?"

Max shrugged. "Normal, I guess."

"Did she say anything unusual? Did you get the sense she wasn't alone?"

"No. She sounded relieved, sort of, that I was coming." Max remained quiet for several moments, as if she were replaying the conversation in her head. Then she glanced up at me. "Do you think they'll—"

"Hurt her? I have no idea," I said, trying to wear the most honest face I could. "But since we foiled their little ambush today, the gang should want to keep all their sources of information open. That means Marta's still valuable to them. Let's get some sleep now. Tomorrow, we'll make for Dallas and try to get the jump on them for a change. Then we'll hit Austin and hope Charlie Garcia is our man."

I gave Max the best smile I could, but the worry and confusion in her eyes said she wasn't buying it.

◆ ◆ ◆

Fifteen minutes later, the lights off, Max was in her bed, and I was in mine. Over the earpiece, I listened, trying to hear if she'd fallen asleep.

The pitch-black room was silent, and I hoped that had done its trick. I closed my eyes and started to let myself drift.

And that's when I heard it. The slightest, softest noise, like what I imagined a mouse's whimper might sound like.

Was Max crying?

What a fucking day for her: almost die several different ways, then find out your surrogate mom either sold you out or might be in danger.

I'd always thought Max and I came from different worlds, but this? This put her out in some other universe. Scared, tired, afraid—it didn't seem like anything I could say would make a difference. But, staring upward in the dark, I started with, "I have to tell you, the original 'Baby, I Love You' is probably my favorite song of all time."

Max shifted on her bed, sniffling loudly. "Great. Let me guess, I fucked that up, too."

"No. Not at all." I glanced over but couldn't see her face. "I thought you had your own take on it, you know, which was really good. You didn't just re-sing it. It meant something different than the original, but it still meant something. You—you put a lot of emotion into it."

There was a long silence before Max spoke again.

"Thanks," was all she said.

CHAPTER 14

Sunday, July 19

A nightmare caused me to bolt upright in bed the next morning. A grotesque hand—wrapped in bandages like a mummy's, the skin purple, black, and blue from bruising—had been reaching out of the darkness toward me.

Sarah's hand.

My eyes popped open at the last moment.

Although the room still stood dark, enough daylight pushed its way around the curtains to expose the edges of everything. Glancing over at Max's bed, I found the sheets and covers flat and empty.

I rolled to my feet and drew the Sig off the nightstand in one motion. As I did, a click sounded, and the bathroom door opened. Max inched out, her profile illuminated by a shaft of yellow light streaming into the room.

"You okay?" I asked.

"Yeah," she said softly. "Sorry I woke you."

"You didn't." My pulse gradually returning back to normal, I placed the Sig back on the table. "I wake you?"

She nodded. "You were talking in your sleep. Thrashing around, kind of."

"Sorry."

"Was it . . . this?"

I shook my head. "Something else." After a glance at the clock, I said, "It's late enough—we should get rolling."

A quick shuttle-bus ride delivered us back to the Albuquerque FBO. Although not as large or luxurious as the one in Phoenix, it featured a little Southwestern-themed seating area with wooden beams across the ceiling and a rounded, adobe-looking fireplace in the middle. The couches were serviceable, and I set Max up in one before I approached the reception desk.

Overnight, Norgard had texted me a list of names and numbers of pilots he knew who made runs between Albuquerque and Texas. The receptionist confirmed one was in town and another would be passing through later today, so I texted them to see if we could stow away to Dallas.

Next, I considered where we might stay once we got there. Although Shirley and my godkids live in Fort Worth, just a short drive away, I didn't want to risk exposing them to Max's pursuers. They'd been through enough misery. I had some other ideas of low-profile places, though, so I called and left a few voice mails for people.

Finally, I dialed a 214 number from memory. After four rings, I was just about to give up when a man's thick Texas drawl answered, "Jim Grayson."

"You got nothing better to do on a Sunday morning than answer your phone?" I asked.

"What can I tell you," he said. "Mindy's off tapin' a story on life in the border towns, so I'm all by my lonesome."

"Then you ought to be out taking target practice at least."

Grayson chuckled. "You know, if I could just get shooting lessons from you, Seth Walker, I wouldn't do anything else but play with my gun. How the hell are you, amigo?"

"Never a dull moment. But I should be asking you that. How's the leg?" Before shooting at me, the crazy woman had poured four shots into

Grayson. Thankfully, even the worst one had only hit his leg, although for a runner like him, being out of commission must have been torture.

"Doin' all right. Rehab's coming along. What can I do for you?"

"I'm on this new case—"

"Uh-oh."

"Nothing like before."

"Good thing. I still got six weeks' leave comin' from what Berkeley did to me—I don't think I could take another one like that."

"You know somebody I could ask questions about a gang I'm running up against?" I explained briefly about the men I'd seen, and how little the FBI seemed to know.

"*No hay problema.* There's a guy over in our gang unit, Sal the Pal. If he can't answer your questions, nobody can."

"Great. I'm hoping to pull into Dallas sometime tonight."

"Let me see what I can do—it may be the mornin' before we can get ahold of him. If you need a place to crash . . ."

"I would, but I've got someone with me."

"Oh, ho, ho! That's gettin' back up on the horse, my friend."

"No," I said, "it's not like that."

"What's his name then?"

"She's a girl."

"What'd I tell ya?"

I rolled my eyes and growled a little bit, which I knew would only encourage him.

"If you need the name of a place with Jacuzzis in the rooms—"

"This is bodyguard duty, Grayson. She's sixteen."

Grayson chuckled. "Don't worry, amigo, your secret's safe with me."

"I'll call you when I get in."

"Sounds good. I should know somethin' by then."

When I returned to the couches, I found Max sprawled over one arm sideways, looking sick. Sweaty and droopy-eyed, her skin had paled to the point it looked almost gray.

I asked what was wrong, and she complained about a headache and cramps. While I wondered again if she'd been lying to me this whole time about drugs, she was so visibly miserable, I held back from posing too many questions. Truth was, whether she'd gotten food poisoning from last night's salad or was just jonesing for a fix, at this point it didn't make much of a practical difference: I was still going to need to drag her to Austin.

Mumbling that she might need to throw up, Max slouched off to the bathroom adjacent to the reception desk. I kept an eye on the door while buying her a bottle of Gatorade from the vending machine. If nothing else, I could keep her hydrated.

Over the next two hours, a visibly embarrassed Max continued making runs to the bathroom while I kept working the phone and thinking about the new variable she'd identified last night: Marta.

I'd obviously never met the woman, so I had nothing to judge beyond the facts themselves. She'd been with Max a long time—far longer, it seemed, than the gang might have been targeting her. That seemed to weigh against her being some kind of plant. But it left wide open the question of why she'd be helping them. Max worried Marta was in danger, and based on the gang's handiwork so far, I imagined they had plenty of experience making people do things. Torture, extortion—I wouldn't have put anything past them. If that was the case with Marta, we'd need to determine how to rescue her.

But what if she wasn't in danger?

Max loved Marta—I could see that in the way her eyes softened when she talked about her. Was that feeling mutual? Given what little I knew of Max's dad, I wondered whether he'd done something to turn Marta against the family. Maybe Garcia had gotten to her?

Or maybe it wasn't even that complicated. Maybe the gang had just offered her money, or something else she needed.

Ultimately, there was no way to figure it out on this end. All answers lay in Austin.

◆ ◆ ◆

A few minutes after 1:00 p.m., a woman strode into the seating area. Max and I were the only ones present, so she approached us directly, her boots clacking slightly against the dark composite flooring.

"Seth Walker?"

I rose and nodded. With a slight boost from the heels on the boots, we stood eye to eye.

"I'm Zonnie Begay," she said. "You still need a ride to Dallas?"

One of the names Norgard had given me, although for some reason I'd assumed it belonged to a man. "We sure do, if you've got room."

"Just to warn you, I'm going to Love, not DFW."

"Love is great," I said, realizing she meant Love Field, Dallas's smaller, lesser-known airport.

Her full cheeks pulled up into a smile. "Then it's your lucky day."

I introduced Max as my niece.

Begay's high, arching eyebrows furrowed. "She doesn't look too good."

"I think she might have eaten a bad salad for dinner last night."

Squatting down next to Max, Begay asked, "You okay to fly, honey? We're looking at about two hours in the air."

Max nodded weakly.

"Okay, then." Begay rose back to her full height and faced me. "We're fueled up—let's get going, assuming you're ready."

I grabbed the duffel and swung it over my shoulder.

"Need help?" As she extended a hand, I had no doubt Begay could manage the oversize bag: although her fingers were tipped with precisely manicured crimson nails, her matching sleeveless blouse revealed taut, muscular arms.

"S'okay," I said. "I'm good."

Begay led us out onto the tarmac, where a beautiful Beechcraft Baron G58 stood waiting. A dual-engine plane, it had a prop mounted on each wing, which met the fuselage at the bottom instead of across the top like the Cessna. White with royal-blue stripes, the paint job on this one gleamed as if it had been finished yesterday.

Inside, the Baron's cabin consisted of two pairs of seats facing each other. I strapped the duffel across the rear pair, then helped Max settle onto the ones that backed up against the cockpit. "You got a sore throat?" I asked.

She shook her head. "Just achy. And hot."

Her hair was damp and stringy from sweat. Pressing the back of my hand against her forehead, the skin was clammy and damp, but she didn't feel feverish. "Keep resting," I said. "Couple of hours, we'll be there, and you can try to sleep this thing off."

Whatever it was.

By the time I joined Begay up front, she'd tied her blue-black hair into a ponytail, donned a pair of mirrored Oakleys, and gone through half her preflight checklist.

I let her get through takeoff before I spoke again. "Beautiful plane," I said.

"Thanks," she said, beaming. "She's my baby. Someday I'm going to have a whole fleet of these."

"You from Dallas?"

"Nope, right here. I came in to visit the family."

"You known Norgard long?"

Begay shook her head. "Met him maybe six months ago. He was trying to get out of Dallas before a big storm, but he needed to fix his hose, and all the mechanics were too busy. I had an extra fitting, so I slapped it on for him and helped him get out. He's a nice old coot. Stares at my ass a little too much, but otherwise he's harmless."

My cheeks flushed. "You do your own maintenance?"

"Got to, for now. FAA regs say I can't qualify as a carrier without a bunch of employees, but I owe enough on this girl that I can't afford that yet. Anyway, I grew up fixing planes—my dad was an air force crew chief at Kirtland before moving over to ABQ."

As Begay pushed us up to our cruising altitude, you could feel the difference in power and control between this and the Cessna. Below, the terrain gradually shifted from desert to prairie. Although the sky remained big and blue, it became dotted by white clouds so dense and puffy, they looked like some kind of confection. The mountains disappeared, the earth flattened, and sandy soil was replaced by broad expanses of waving grasses.

Although less chatty than Norgard, Begay still shared enough details about herself that I felt slightly guilty for not reciprocating. Evidently her parents had wanted her to be a pediatrician or a school-teacher, something to give back to the Navajo Nation, but Begay had balked at that. Bitten by the flying bug early, she'd gotten her license on her seventeenth birthday and never looked back. Seven years of toiling through three jobs simultaneously had gotten her the down payment for the Baron.

Foliage picked up below, followed by signs of civilization. Doing some quick calculations, I gathered we'd reached the outskirts of Fort Worth. While my initial thought was to try to spot the roof of my godkids' house, I put that aside and started thinking about what to do after we landed.

I'd only ever flown through Love twice, compared to hundreds of connections at DFW. Despite being within sight of the Dallas skyline, the little airport had just one, T-shaped terminal. To promote DFW back in the sixties, Congress had restricted how far you could fly from Love, setting the limit at the four states bordering Texas. When Southwest had come on as a discount carrier, it had basically taken over the place. Now, even though old restrictions had been lifted and other airlines had moved in, Love was still doomed to play second fiddle.

Checking the burner, I found several texts responding to my calls seeking lodging for the night. One provided an address, and a quick check of the GPS showed it lay right next to the airfield. That was good news. Nothing from Grayson, but he'd warned me that might happen. I'd just need to contact him again once we set up at the crash pad.

Begay lined us up with the downtown skyscrapers and brought us in, taxiing directly to a hangar on the west side of the field. Once she pulled the plane inside, I moved around back to help Max. Having slept almost the entire flight, she was groggy as I forced her up onto her feet. I found Begay waiting for us just outside the cabin.

"Thanks again for the ride," I said, "especially on such short notice. I'm happy to pay you for—"

Begay shook her head. "On the house. I was headed back, anyway. But you could do me a favor."

"What's that?"

"Well," she waved an open hand around the hangar, "like I said, it's just me right now, but someday when I get my little Diné Airlines here to be a real thing, I'm going to need all the publicity I can get. Compliments from an air marshal and a pop star might—"

"Wait, what? How do you know—"

"Jerry called me before he gave you my number. He's a gentleman like that." Begay's face broke into a mischievous little grin. "He explained how he knew you, and promised you were okay."

"Did he tell you why—"

"Nope. And I'm guessing he has absolutely no idea who Max is. But just because Jerry Norgard hasn't listened to pop radio in thirty years doesn't mean I haven't." She leaned down to Max. "It was very nice meeting you. I like your songs."

"Listen," I said, "we're—"

Begay straightened and put her index finger over my mouth. "Don't worry, Marshal. Your secret's safe with me."

Her dark eyes locked on mine for a long moment.

"Okay, thanks." With the bag over my shoulder, I started to lead Max out. Then I turned back and asked, "Din-ay Airlines? What does that mean?"

"*Diné* is Navajo for 'people.'"

I nodded. "Good luck. Let us know when you're up and running."

"Oh, I will," she said. "And don't be a stranger."

As the map had predicted, the cab ride from Love's baggage claim didn't take long. Just outside the airport grounds, we turned onto a narrow street lined with single-story brick houses. Each was fronted by a small patch of sun-bleached grass.

The cab dropped us on the sidewalk outside one of the nearly indistinguishable dwellings, then sped away.

Still looking like she might fall over any moment, Max asked, "What is this place?"

"A crash pad," I said, moving to a planter beneath one of the house's front windows.

"What's a crash pad?"

I found the spare key where the text had said it would be and returned to the door. "A lot of commercial pilots and crews don't live near their home airport, so they have to commute. Airlines won't pay for that—they only cover stays in the middle of trips. Hotel rooms are expensive, so the pilots and crews get together and share a house or an apartment."

From what I knew, crash pads could vary widely in terms of quality and cost—some were essentially minihostels, full of bunk beds open to anyone passing through, while others were rigorously run, with tenants who worked out schedules in advance. This one was definitely one of the latter.

I'd met the owner, Steve Jensen, a couple of years ago at a party at Shen and Brian's house. A childhood friend of Brian's, Jensen had been a flight attendant for thirteen years; for the first ten, he'd been based out of St. Louis. But then his airline had gotten gobbled up in a merger. Suddenly, Jensen's hub shifted to Dallas. Not wanting to lose seniority or uproot himself and his family, Jensen had bought this place.

Just a one bedroom, the house gave him somewhere reliable to stay on either side of his turns; plus, he rented it to other crews on the nights he didn't need it. While it didn't generate much cash, it covered the mortgage and maintenance.

After unlocking the door, I ushered Max inside, then followed behind her. The interior was as impeccably neat as I'd expected—not a wisp of dust on the wooden floors, all the windows clean and clear.

I dropped the duffel by the door, then drew all the curtains and poked around the place. Fortunately, it seemed to be stocked with everything we might need for the night: bottled water and canned food in the pantry, medical supplies and a first-aid kit in the master bathroom.

"You should go rest some more," I told Max. "Take the bed, I'll take the couch."

She didn't argue. After she closed the bedroom door, I dialed Grayson again. He said his guy Sal Peña could meet us before their morning shift; once I explained where I was, we settled on a motel a couple of blocks away as the rendezvous.

"There's one other thing I could use your help with," I said.

"What's that, amigo?"

"We're going to need a car. But I can't rent anything without giving them my license or credit card. Any ideas?"

"You just need to take it to Austin?"

"Yeah. I don't know exactly how long we'll be there, but not more than a few days."

"Let me work on it overnight," he said. "I bet I can find you something."

After we hung up, I noticed my stomach grumbling. Realizing I hadn't eaten all day, I went to the kitchen and microwaved some soup. When it was done, I returned to the couch, only to hear noise coming from the bedroom.

I knocked lightly on the door, then pushed my way in. Stripped down to a long T-shirt, Max was sprawled across the bedspread, her head propped on three pillows to watch the TV across the room.

"Can't sleep?" I asked.

"I'm feeling better."

"Sick as you've been, you can use as much rest as you can get."

Max rolled her eyes—maybe she *was* feeling better. Then she sniffed the air. "You cook something?"

"Just some soup."

"What kind?"

I glanced down into the mug—I hadn't taken a sip yet, and hadn't bothered checking the label. "Looks like vegetable something. You want it?"

She didn't answer, but I handed her the mug. She took a dainty sip. "Good?"

She shrugged, then slurped down several more mouthfuls. Finally, she announced, "I'm gonna grab a shower. I feel all sticky."

"When you get out, I'll need your help changing my bandages."

She nodded vaguely on her way into the bathroom before shutting the door.

I returned to the kitchen, heated some soup of my own, then brought it back into the bedroom and set it on the vanity. The shower beating against the opposite side of the wall sounded like a fire hose that might rip through the plaster at any second.

As I began working to get my shirt off through the sling, I checked my reflection. The bright, white makeup lights surrounding the mirror were unforgiving, but I decided I could have looked worse. An equal amount of stubble covered my scalp and face. Dark rings surrounded my eyes, and, of course, my left arm hung limply in the blue canvas sling.

The shoulder ached. My penance for doing absolutely nothing Anjali had suggested to care for it. In the medicine kit, I found foil packs of Motrin. I managed to rip one open with my teeth, then washed down two pills with scalding broth.

Leaning against the vanity for support, I tested my right leg, pulling the heel all the way up to my hamstring, then pressing it back down. Even squeezing it hard, the quad muscle felt solid. At least the stitches were doing their job.

Although I craned my neck to try and look at my shoulder, I couldn't see anything. The makeup lights made everything behind me seem cast in shadow.

That's when the bathroom door opened, and Max stepped out wearing a towel. Her skin tone was better than before: more pink than gray. With her hair slicked straight back, several shades darker from the water, she looked like a different person.

"You ready for your bandages now?"

"Yeah, but you can get dressed first." The end of the towel was tucked directly into her cleavage, a fact I did my best to ignore.

"S'okay," she said, stepping behind me. "You might spray me with blood when I peel these things off." Before I could object, she started picking at the tape surrounding the upper wound. "Let's start with the bad one."

Once the tape was up, I gritted my teeth and braced myself. The gauze gave a squishy sound again as it peeled away with what felt like chunks of my shoulder, but not as many as the previous night.

"Better?"

I grunted.

"It looks better," she said softly. "The right side's mostly closed up."

155

Max's hands trailed down my back to the newer wound, where they scratched away at the tape until it was free. "Ready?"

Pursing my lips, I nodded. This one stuck, too, but not as badly.

Max remained silent, and, with me facing the mirror, she was completely eclipsed behind me. I passed a wad of gauze back. After she draped it delicately over the shoulder wound, I reached for the roll of tape, but she was faster, her arm shooting under mine to grab it off the vanity.

In doing so, Max's body brushed my back in a way that I wasn't completely sure was accidental.

"Stay still," she said. "I've got it." She reached around me again, for the gauze this time, but we didn't touch. I took a long, relieved breath.

All in your head, I told myself.

Max covered and taped the second wound so gently, I barely noticed when she was done. Her hands moved back up onto my dislocated shoulder. "What's this thing called again? Your tattoo?"

"A DCT."

"And what's it do?"

"It's a formula. It helps you take data, like the sounds of the notes you're singing, and shrink it down into something smaller."

"You didn't tell me why you got it."

"I know."

"But why? Seriously. Of all the cool things you could have gotten . . ."

"I used to use that equation a lot. Back when I was an engineer."

"So?"

"So what?"

"So why get it inked? And on your back—you can't even see it." Her voice light and teasing, Max left her hand on my neck while dragging a nail from the other hand back and forth beneath the spot where the numbers were.

I snorted an angry-sounding breath through my nose, buying a second to think about exactly how little I could get away with saying while still putting an end to all this. "It was something I used every day. It was important to me. But when I . . ." I paused for a second, trying to pick just the right words. "When I left that life, I got the tattoo."

I stared at my reflection. Hard. Before I could stop it, my mind flashed to Shirley and my godkids. The last time we were together . . . the kids splashing in the pool, us sipping iced tea on the porch.

"So, it's like a souvenir?" Max asked.

"Sort of."

"Sort of?"

In my head, the picture changed, from a movie of my godkids to a still image of their father. A handsome one of Clarence smiling, oblivious to the heartache that was coming.

The portrait they'd propped on top of his casket at the funeral because they couldn't leave the lid open.

While my eyes bored into their duplicates on the glass, I only vaguely noticed the muscles in my temples flexing as my teeth ground together. "It's . . . a reminder."

"Of what?"

Of Clarence. My friend. The man who'd shot himself.

"Of . . ." My throat constricted just a little, and I knew I was on dangerous ground. My right hand squeezed the edge of the vanity. "Stuff that's behind me."

"But it's always there," she said.

The words, soft and breathy, were like a swift knee to my gut. The whisper of a ghost.

I tried not to show it. Averting my eyes from the mirror, I glanced downward. Only to find the *SA* tattoo on my forearm.

Sarah.

"Why'd you leave?" Max's voice had dropped even farther now, but there was more urgency to it, like she sensed she was onto something.

My mind registered the words, but heard the voice as someone else's.

Sarah's voice. The angry tone she'd taken the last time we'd seen each other.

Why'd you leave?

"Did something bad happen?" Max asked.

Something horrible.

All because I left.

If only I'd stayed. If only I hadn't gone chasing that madwoman. You'd still be . . .

I looked up, hoping to find some sort of relief, some sort of forgiveness in my own reflection.

There wasn't any.

"Something painful?" Max asked.

Painful.

My brain began cycling between the images in my head, each one dissolving into the next.

My godkids' smiles, all teeth and dimples.

Clarence's face, naively innocent, half-hidden behind thick glasses.

Sarah's eyes, pale blue and white, accentuated by her bronze skin.

Different people, different places. Exact same result.

So much pain. So much death.

All my fault.

My chin sank to my chest. Although I tried to stop it, to hold it back, my shoulders shook with a single, heavy sob.

With my one good hand, I gripped the vanity even tighter. Pulling upward with all my might, I tried to tear the counter from the wall. To break it, to smash it.

Anything to dispel the energy massing inside me.

But it was too late. All the moisture had vanished from my mouth, while tears began gushing from my eyes. My shoulders heaved. And

I gasped for breath in between the guttural howls that rattled in my throat.

So consumed was I with the pictures in my head and trying to regain control, I didn't notice Max's hand moving. Or the sound of the towel crumpling on the floor. I only heard her voice as she cooed, "Did it hurt you?"

"Yes." With my throat clenched, the word croaked out.

"I can make it feel better."

Suddenly, all the images in my head, all the pain and the anguish— everything—evaporated. I was instantly aware of Max's skin, pressed against my back. Her lips grazing my shoulder blade. And her hand, starting to sneak down the front of my jeans.

"Whoa!" I said, grabbing her wrist and yanking it away. When I spun around to face her, I didn't let go. Although my brain registered her nakedness, I did my best not to look, to stay focused on her face. "What are you doing?"

Max looked up at me, eyes wide and inviting. "Just trying to help. Trying to say thank you."

"What . . . what are you talking about? Get dressed."

A sly smile crept across her face. "You're a man, I'm a woman—"

"No," I said, shaking my head. "No, you're not. You're a sixteen-year-old girl."

"A girl who knows what men like." Her eyes sparkled with excitement now, and she took a step toward me, raising her other hand.

I retreated, but that pressed my back against the wall, and Max kept coming. With my left arm bound in the sling, I couldn't stop her as she pressed her right hand flat against my chest. I squeezed her other wrist. "No."

She struggled against my grip a moment; then her eyes flashed again, and her smile turned wild. She ducked and spun around until she was facing away from me, my arm stretched across her belly. "This better?" She bent over, pulling me with her, and started grinding herself against my crotch. "You like it this way? Wanna take me from behind?"

Letting go of Max's wrist, I kept my arm tucked into her stomach. Then I straightened up, lifting her off the ground. Although she struggled and squirmed, I had her locked as I started toward the bed.

"This. Is. Not. Happening." I tossed her onto the mattress, then stepped back to the bathroom, where I scooped up the towel in my free hand and flung it over her.

Max curled into a ball on the bed and looked up at me as if I'd struck her across the face. Her eyes welled up, and she began bawling. "Why—why do you *hate* me?"

The words were a shock. I dropped to one knee at the foot of the bed. "I don't . . . I don't hate you—"

"Then why don't you *want* me? Want to be with me?"

She started shimmying toward me on her stomach, reaching for me with her arms, but I grabbed her shoulder and stopped her at arm's length.

"Because it isn't right."

Max looked at me through cascades of tears spilling down onto her cheeks. Her eyes were wide and round—confused and scared.

I took a breath to clear the anger and stress from my voice. "But . . . I am not going to let anything hurt you. And I am not going to leave you until you're safe. I promise you that."

Her face melted into a sobbing mess, and she lowered it to the sheets. Her whole body shook as she cried—deep, violent breaths causing her back and sides to shudder.

As the tears subsided, though, she started to tremble, to shiver. The color blanched from her skin, and she rolled onto her side, curling into the fetal position. I rose to get her some clothes, but before I could, she began coughing. A loud, choking cough that racked her whole body in spasms. After several seconds of that, a rush of vomit spewed from her mouth.

Having not eaten anything solid for hours, the puke was entirely liquid, and the greenish puddle soaked immediately into the comforter.

I ran to the kitchen and grabbed the entire roll of paper towels.

Back at the bedside, I peeled one corner of the spread up and over her body. Then I tried using the paper towels to soak up the bile, but it was too late. I settled instead for wiping Max's face and moving her away from the spot.

"Is there more in there?" I asked.

Back to shivering, Max seemed to nod her head.

"Let's get you to the bathroom." Grabbing one arm with my free hand, I stretched it across my shoulders and lifted her to her feet. She could barely stand, so I bore her weight and helped her hobble toward the toilet. We'd just gotten to the bathroom doorway when she puked again.

We spent nearly two hours on the tile floor, every muscle in Max's body spasming to eliminate what little was left inside her. At first, giant rushes of liquid came up, but those quickly shrank to a trickle, then switched to dry heaves that left Max coughing uncontrollably.

And it didn't only come out of that end.

Weak and weary, dripping with sweat, Max asked me to help her up onto the toilet. With just one arm, it took me a second to stand myself, and we didn't quite get her there before she lost control.

Doubled over, still trembling, she'd started sobbing her way through apologies I told her were unnecessary. Two rounds after it seemed like there couldn't possibly be anything left inside her, she announced she was done.

I got her up, helped her wash off, then tucked her into the clean side of the bed after stripping off the comforter. While Max shivered beneath the sheets, I started the comforter in the washing machine and then returned to the bathroom to wipe it down the best I could. In the end, it looked fine, but you could tell the smell might take a while to fade.

By the time I returned, Max had fallen into a fitful, twitchy sleep. I spotted her small purse on the bedside table and rifled through it. Not much inside: couple of tampons, a few wadded-up bills, some gum. Nothing that gave any indication of what was causing all this.

Still, any meager hope I'd been clinging to that she was suffering from food poisoning or the flu had disappeared. She was clearly in the throes of withdrawal, but from what?

And who'd given it to her?

Max had insisted several times she didn't have a drug dealer. Of course, she'd insisted she wasn't on drugs, either. Was her urgency to get home more about scoring than saving Marta?

Marta.

Now there was an interesting variable. If Marta were working for the gang, could she have provided Max with the drugs?

It wasn't immediately clear to me why the gang would want Max strung out. Maybe Marta had nothing to do with it. I'd need to press Max for answers in the morning.

I continued checking her temperature through the night. Despite all the sweats, she'd never had a fever, but I'd need to keep an eye on that. Not knowing what she'd taken, I had no idea what the rest of this withdrawal would look like, or what to research to find out. Dropping her off at some facility or a hospital still wasn't a viable option, though. I figured the best I could do was keep pumping fluids into her and get us to Austin before the trail went cold.

I had to hope she could hang on that long.

CHAPTER 15

Monday, July 20

Max's fitful sleeping continued into the early morning.

Before any light began creeping in, I slid out of bed and padded into the front room. I stayed there, consulting maps on the burner, until it was time to meet Grayson. Max hadn't shown any signs of waking; still, I left her a note explaining where I'd be.

Although the sun had barely cleared the horizon, the walk was hot and sticky. Living in California, I've lost my tolerance for humidity, and the three blocks left sweat pouring down my brow.

The neon-colored motel was one of those new-style, reduced-service chains that catered mostly to business folks. In lieu of a restaurant, the hotel lobby had devoted the area across from registration to a series of tables and booths, flanked by a wall that looked like it had been lifted from a 7-11: refrigerated cases held drinks, snacks, and prefab sandwiches, while a credenza supported bins filled with fruit, small boxes of cereal, and various breads, along with carafes of coffee and juice.

After buying a box of Rice Krispies, a banana, and a cup of decaf tea, I chose a banquette table at the edge of the seating area that provided a modicum of privacy in the otherwise sparsely populated room.

As I ate the banana, I scoped out everyone else eating breakfast. Mostly singles, noses in their laptops, except for one group of three guys, who, by the way they were fidgeting with their briefcases, looked like they were heading to a meeting any minute.

I'd finished half my tea and had just poured the cereal when Grayson strode in, followed closely by another man I guessed was his contact. I half stood so they'd see me.

Grayson's hound-dog face, tan and weathered by the sun, lit up when our eyes met. Although it was weird to see him with the cane, it gave his gait a sort of roll that accelerated as he headed my way.

"Hey, amigo." Leaning on his good leg, he wrapped me in a hug, then touched my elbow in the sling. "You get that doin' this?"

"Yeah. But from the looks of it, I'm still better than you. How much longer are you stuck with that thing?"

"Doc said two more months." His face flashed a grin. "We'll see if I can't beat that. This here's DFW's finest, Sal the Pal."

The other man stepped up. "Salvador Peña, but most people call me Chava. Everyone except him." He tilted his head at Grayson, then thrust out his hand.

"Seth Walker," I said, shaking it. Peña had one of those grips that threatened to break your fingers, and you could see why: the muscles of his chest and arms were so thick, they forced him to move in a stiff, wooden way. His nose and jaw were both cut at sharp angles. He had piercing blue eyes and dark hair cut almost into a Mohawk.

They headed for the food while I sat back down. Eventually they slid in across from me, Grayson palming an orange and a can of Diet Dr Pepper, while Peña had filled a bowl with oatmeal, yogurt, and berries.

"Thanks for meeting me out here," I said, keeping my voice down. Nodding at their food choices, I added, "Sorry the menu's not more glamorous."

"I suggested Ricky's," Grayson said to Peña, then turned to me. "Little diner off 35E. Best place in Dallas to get huevos rancheros and biscuits and gravy under the same roof."

Peña grunted as he mixed the contents of the bowl with a plastic spoon that looked tiny in his hand. "My arteries thank you," he said to me. His voice lacked Grayson's Texas twang but sounded like he'd smoked for years. "Ricky's gravy is like liquid butter."

"First things first," Grayson said. "I solved your automobile problem." He produced a car key and slid it across the table. "My ex is off visitin' her folks for a week, so I asked if I could borrow it."

Peña's face burst into a large grin. "Man, I heard your divorce was friendly, but that's some pretty messed-up shit right there."

Grayson ignored him. "It's just a little Hyundai. It ain't gonna set any speed records or anything, but it'll get you to Austin and back. Just bring it home in one piece."

We exchanged a little more small talk until Grayson finally said, "Sal here is Dallas's expert on street gangs. This group you say you're up against, what are they like?"

"Nasty." I recounted the attacks at LAX, my house, and Las Cruces. I described their weapons, the tattoos. I shared Franklin's observation that they carried away their casualties. "The FBI doesn't know who they are."

"You hear 'em talk?" Peña asked between bites.

"Yeah. They used some kind of foreign language."

He cracked another smile. "Like French?"

I shook my head. "No. It didn't sound like anything I'd ever heard before."

"Were there any glottalized consonants?"

I blinked several times, having absolutely no idea what he meant.

Peña made a couple of noises that sounded like *pa* and *key*, with each preceded by a sort of popping noise from the back of his throat, almost like he was working to clear it.

"Yeah, that sounds right."

He nodded slightly, before looking down and taking a scoop from his oatmeal. "Then you, my friend, have a big problem."

"What's that?" I asked. "Who am I up against?"

"*El Segundo Ejército Guerrillero de los Pobres.* The Second Guerrilla Army of the Poor."

"Should I have heard of them?"

"Probably not. Think of them as *Gangland* 3.0. How much you know about gang activity?"

"Little to nothing," I said.

"How much you know about Mexico and Central America?"

"About the same." My cheeks warmed at the confession; although I'd been to Asia and Europe plenty of times for business, I'd never made it south of the border.

Peña turned to Grayson. "Jeez, I thought you said this guy was smart." Then he leaned back in his seat, his face growing serious. "When you're talking about gangs in the United States, I mean, we could go all the way back to the 1700s, 1800s. The Irish in New York. Later the Italians. But practically speaking, things really kicked off in the fifties and sixties. Social unrest, housing projects, white flight from the cities. All that led to the formation of black gangs like the Crips and the Bloods."

"I've heard of *them*," I said, smiling meekly.

Peña nodded back. "In addition, you've always had some Mexican gangs, and some that were mixed race, like 18th Street. Back in the day, all the gangs, they robbed people, got into fights, slung some drugs. But when we get to the 1980s, boom." He tapped a fist on the table, making everything vibrate. "Cocaine. Crack. Demand skyrockets, and suddenly all these guys have major reasons to fight over territory. Things start to get ugly. So what do we do?" Peña shrugged. "We throw gas on the fire. As if it wasn't bad enough, there's this superpopular, hyperaddictive drug out on the streets, and we go and impose minimum sentencing for drug offenses. That sends all the juvie bangers away to big-boy prison for piddly shit. You ever been inside one?"

I shook my head.

"In there, it's like banger boot camp. Guys got nothing to do all day but lift weights and figure out how to be better criminals. So locking them up just made things worse. Gangs got more organized, more serious. And they made new friends inside: the cartels have people locked up, too. Suddenly, manufacturing is talking to retail, and we see a spike in the influx of drugs like we've never seen before."

"Okay, I get all that," I said. "But how does that get us to the Guerrillas of the Poor, or whatever they're called?"

Peña raised a hand. "Hang on. We're almost there. So, we've got all these bad guys banging around, and someone in Washington gets a genius idea: 'Hey, some of these fuckers are foreign nationals. Let's ship 'em back where they came from.' So we started deporting them. But where were we sending them? To countries with shitty infrastructure and lots of poor, disenfranchised youth. It was like saying, 'Let's get rid of the mosquitos' and dumping them in a swamp. You got gangs like MS-13—that's *Mara Salvatrucha*—going back to El Salvador and essentially taking over down there."

Peña pushed his oatmeal bowl away.

"That's the general framework. Your boys, they're Guatemalan. And that's its own kettle of fish. CIA decided back in the fifties that Guatemala might go Communist, so we installed a guy we thought would be friendly to us. Shockingly, he wasn't a very nice guy to his own people, and that left an opening for the army—who we'd trained, of course—to take over. When the Guatemalans got tired of death squads and forced disappearances, they fought back. Small groups, like the Guerrilla Army of the Poor, started a civil war that didn't fully end until '96. Since then, the politics have been relatively stable, but the country's still a mess. Average age is, like, twenty. Average income's about five grand a year. So you've got tons of young people, desperate for economic opportunity. Guess who steps in?"

"The gangs and cartels," I said.

Peña's mouth twisted into a rueful smile. "Now you're getting it. The Zetas Cartel owns the southern tip of Mexico, along the border with Guatemala. They see that Guatemalan cities are overrun by local gangs, *maras*, who keep the general populace indoors and afraid. So the Zetas put the *maras* on the payroll, and, boom, they control most of the country."

"So the Guerrillas have gone from fighting the government to working for the Zetas Cartel?"

"Nope. We're not talking about the Guerrilla Army of the Poor from the civil war. After the war ended, those original Guerrillas folded up shop and became a political party. You're dealing with the *Second Guerrilla Army of the Poor*." Peña pointed to his cheekbones. "Those facial tattoos you saw—traditional Mayan tattoos. Those weird sounds you heard"—he made the popping noises again—"Mayan dialects."

I shook my head, not understanding.

"See," Peña said, "the Mayas are the group down there that's gotten shafted the worst by everybody. They're, like, forty percent of the population, but they tend to be rural and poor. They're scattered in all these different tribes. So they've been easy pickings. Everyone who's come into power in Guatemala has picked on the Maya. Killed them, taken their land. But in the last year or two, it seems like they've finally had enough. They adopted the old Guerrilla name to try and gain popular support, and now they're standing up to the Zetas, and the Zetas-controlled *maras*."

"But if these are Mayan freedom fighters or whatever, why are they here, shooting at me and Max? That makes no sense."

Peña chuckled, as if he were truly enjoying this. "Life's complicated. You want to fight the Zetas, you need firepower. Firepower costs money. You need money . . ." He cocked his head at me.

"You commit crimes?"

"Not just any crimes. We figure they're backed by one of the other cartels."

"Which one?"

"Who knows?" Peña shrugged. "Zetas own the eastern half of Mexico. The Sinaloa Cartel owns most of the center and west, but you've also got the Juárez group, Tijuana, La Familia. All of 'em would love to take a bite out of the Zetas, or at least keep the Zetas busy. So we figure one or more of them are funneling money and weapons to the Second Guerrillas. It's the only way they could have come on so hard, so fast."

"You've been up against them?" I asked.

Nodding, Peña said, "Yep. I think every city in Texas has had at least one big incident. Three months ago, we raided a house we thought was full of them. Had a half-an-hour shooting match that cut two cruisers to ribbons and sent five officers to the hospital. Turned out it was just three guys in there. We hauled one of them in, tried to interrogate him. Normally, bangers resist, but it's all a bunch of macho bullshit. Eventually, you break through it. Not this guy. He was, like, military-level silent—name, rank, serial number."

"So, what's the best tactic to deal with them?"

All humor drained from Peña's face, and his eyes locked on mine. "Get the fuck out of their way. You say you've had a couple of run-ins already? Consider yourself lucky and steer clear, man. Let them do what they're gonna do, 'cause they've got plenty of men, they're well equipped, and they got years and years of pent-up anger and frustration, all just dying to spill out."

I glanced down at my half-eaten bowl of cereal, but my appetite had disappeared.

"Whatcha thinkin', amigo?" asked Grayson.

I looked up at my friend, and his eyes said he was nervous, even if I wasn't. I shrugged. "Max is just a kid. I've been at this almost a week, and I still have no clue why they're trying to kill her. The FBI's been zero help—"

Grayson turned to Peña. "If these Mayan guys are such a force, how come the Feebs are sayin' they never heard of 'em?"

Peña raised his eyebrows. "Dunno why they're saying that. But I *know* they know about the Second Guerrilla Army. I've sat in task-force meetings with our friends out on Justice Way where we talked about nothing *but* these guys. In fact, the running theory is that their leader, a dude named Petén, has moved north and is calling the shots from up here."

"Payton?" I asked.

"Pronounced 'peh-TEN.' It's the name of a Maya-heavy region in northern Guatemala. We figure that's where he's from. Nobody knows much about him. Some say he's a *Braveheart*-type man of the people who just got fed up and started leading. Others figure he's former military or something, the way he's gotten them organized. The folks we've dragged in who do business with Petén—not the soldiers, they love him; I'm talking about the dealers, the street runners—they're all scared shitless of him. Guy can be brutal."

Grayson turned and gave me a wary look.

I shrugged again.

"Running and hiding's really not an option here?" he asked.

"I'd love to, but where could I take the girl that'll be safe? They already shot up my house, ambushed us twice." I looked to Peña for support. "You make it sound like they won't stop coming."

He closed his eyes and shook his head.

"All right, then," I said. "Guess it's off to Austin."

After some small talk and a cup of coffee, Peña checked his watch and announced he needed to head for his shift.

When I thanked him, he nearly broke my hand again.

"You need a ride?" Peña asked Grayson.

Grayson nodded. "Meet you outside."

Peña excused himself and headed back out the sliding doors at the front of the lobby.

Once he was gone, I turned to find Grayson staring at me.

"What?" I asked.

"You know what."

"No, I don't."

"I know how you are when you get a bee in your bonnet," he said. "You got the same stupid, stubborn look in your eye right now that you did when you were trying to convince me that Berkeley woman was a killer."

I smiled. "And I was right."

"This ain't funny." The tone in Grayson's voice wiped the feigned confidence from my face. He lifted the handle of his cane above the surface of the table and nodded at it. "You saw what one badass woman could do. Now you wanna take on an army? C'mon, Walker. Use that big ol' brain of yours."

"Jim, I've got a sick sixteen-year-old girl on my hands that they're trying to kill. What am I supposed to do, hand her over to them?"

"No." Grayson rapped his cane on the floor. "That's not the only other choice here. Look"—he leaned in toward me, speaking more softly—"the FBI knows something's up. They've got something cooking behind the scenes. Gotta be. Why else would they play all coy with you? So find some nice bunker to hide in, and don't stick your head out till after the shooting stops."

"I'd love to sit this one out, believe me. But you weren't there. You didn't see these guys, the way they butchered the FBI at the airport . . ."

Grayson took a deep breath, then released it through his nose slowly before leaning back in his seat. "What's your next move?"

"Austin's her hometown. I'm thinking the head of her record label could be in with the Second Guerrillas. Plus, her nanny tipped the gang off to our route. That means she's involved, or they're using her."

Grayson directed his gaze down to the tabletop and nodded. "When're you leavin'?"

"Soon as you and I are done, I'll head back and scrape her out of bed."

We sat at the table silently for several moments.

Finally, he said, "Guess I better go. Mindy'll kill me if I miss rehab while she's gone." He started pressing himself up over the top of the cane.

I rose as well. We both stood there a moment, staring at each other. "Thanks for the help," I said. "And the car. I'll talk to you soon?"

Grayson nodded. He gave me another hug, less enthusiastic this time, then slowly cane-rolled his way out the door.

CHAPTER 16

After returning to the crash pad, getting on the road proved more difficult than I'd expected.

I straightened up the house as best I could, then went to wake Max. Even after I had her up, though, Max's skin remained ashen and clammy, her eyes half-closed. She didn't answer any of my questions—in fact, she seemed delirious. Her muscles trembled as I worked to pull clothes onto her, and then I supported nearly her entire weight as we walked to the car.

Getting her buckled into the little sedan was even harder. Just when I thought I had her settled into the tilted-back passenger seat, she squirmed and fought against my free arm, spilling out onto the sidewalk in a heap. As she struggled, she kept slurring "Gotta get away," so it sounded like one word.

"Sh," I whispered in her ear. "We're going home today. To Austin. But you've got to get in the car."

Max made a noise in her throat that sounded like an angry cat and shook her shoulders, but in her weakened condition, it was only half-hearted. I finally lifted her in, belted her, and locked the passenger door before closing it.

By that point, I was drenched in sweat.

Thankfully, the drive to Austin was far less eventful. After some construction delays around Dallas, the freeway cleared up outside the city, and I switched on cruise control. That left me freer to monitor vehicles around us. I paid particular attention to trucks; mostly we encountered tractor trailers, crawling along in the slow lane. While passing one of those, though, a black SUV zipped up behind us, causing my hands to tense up on the wheel. But as soon as I cleared the truck and merged back right, the SUV gunned its engine and passed us in the fast lane.

Although I'd heard Austin referred to as being part of Texas's "hill country," the scenery remained fairly constant as we progressed southward: broad, flat, grassy plains alternated with thick stands of trees. The sky was a darker shade of blue than it had been in the desert; the clouds, still white, were thicker and more purposeful. Above it all, the sun loomed brilliant and blazing, seemingly unwilling to leave its perch at the top of the sky.

As signs indicated Austin was approaching, I considered where exactly to go first. If Max had her way, we'd head straight for her house to try to find Marta, although now I had to wonder whether that was motivated by love, withdrawal, or something else. Regardless, though, it struck me as dangerous. We had no idea what Marta's situation was, and if the Second Guerrillas were watching anyplace for Max, it'd be her home. Plus, if Garcia heard we'd reached town, he might get spooked and run.

The safer move, it seemed to me—the move they'd suspect least— was to check Garcia out first thing.

While finding the website for Garcia's record company on the burner was easy, it didn't include a street address. Internet searches got me nowhere. As much as I hated to bother her, and as unsure as I was whether she could actually help, I called Max's name.

After several tries, she finally stirred.

"Max, I need you. Can you stay awake for a little bit? Can you answer a question?"

She nodded loosely, her head swaying from side to side.

"Charlie Garcia. Where do we find him? Where's Otra Records?"

"South . . . east," she said, in almost a whisper. She mumbled out what sounded like a street name. I took a chance and plugged it into the burner, and a dot appeared near the airport. Expanding the map, State Highway 130 branched off just north of Georgetown and then tracked along Austin's eastern side. That seemed just about perfect.

And, merging onto it several minutes later, it was. Newly paved construction, and nearly empty, even with rush hour approaching.

I glanced over and saw that Max's complexion had turned greenish, and I worried about a repeat of last night. "We're getting there, Max. You recognize all this? You're almost home."

Although I wasn't sure what she could see from her reclining position, Max seemed to try to smile, but all her muscles could manage was to turn up the corners of her mouth. Even that seemed forced.

While she remained conscious, I needed to keep her talking, get her mind working. "You glad to be coming home?"

She grunted softly.

"Think your dad will be here?"

Her eyes snapped toward me, the most purposeful movement I'd seen her make in hours. "No," she said. "Not him."

"I'm sure he's worried about you—"

"No!" Max pulled her legs up so her face was nearly buried in her knees. She was shivering.

"You know, you've told me about Charlie, and all the things Nancy Irvine did. But you've never told me why you hate your father so much."

Doubled up as she was, her answer came out as a mumble. "Everything."

"Seems like he's helped you with your career."

"Stop. Stop!" Her head shook violently.

"Okay, okay. I'm sorry." Like the problem of her possible addiction, Max's relationship with her father was something I needed to nail down, but I could tell now wasn't the time. Heck, in her state, she hardly knew what she was saying.

◆ ◆ ◆

I didn't have much time to worry about Max's feelings. Signs quickly began announcing the airport exit, and I took it.

As we traversed the ramp, the terminal loomed to our left. Seeing planes moving around the tarmac left me feeling slightly hollow, but I didn't dwell on it: the road forked almost immediately, and soon I turned right to head to east Austin.

We crossed the Colorado River—looking much more like a small creek—on a high concrete bridge. After clearing a series of freeway overpasses and underpasses, we found ourselves on a broad but plain-looking street. Unlike all the new concrete and stone that had adorned Highway 130, here the asphalt bore long, jagged scars where cracks had been sealed over with tar. The buildings were low-slung and industrial, the billboards and signs in Spanish as often as English.

Following the map, I made a few turns and, tucked back behind a series of small clapboard houses, found Otra Records. A sign with the name written in narrow cursive letters stood at the foot of a gravel driveway cut through a grassy field. The building it led to looked like a warehouse from this distance, with a corrugated roof above ribbed metal walls painted a dull yellow.

The parking lot was empty other than two large pickup trucks, one shiny white, one faded blue. As we started slowly crunching across the gravel toward them, I said Max's name. "Hey, look up for a second, I need you."

With a groan, she sat up in the seat.

"Is one of those trucks Garcia's?"

She peered over the dash before flopping back down. "White one."

Once she said it, it made perfect sense. The truck looked brand new—a big crew-cab model, with a wide bed, tinted windows, and shiny chrome accents. The plate read OTRA.

"So he should be inside. Did you recognize that other truck next to it?"

She nodded weakly. "Bruce. Sound tech."

Although both trucks were parked at the entrance, I circled the building counterclockwise, stopping along its left-hand side, pulling forward just enough that I could monitor the front door. "You think Bruce will leave at five?" If so, it'd be worth the ten-minute wait.

Max shook her head. "Could be . . . all night." Although she mumbled, her voice cracked as if her throat were rough and dry.

I glanced around and checked the mirrors. The sun still hung midway in the sky, a long way from setting. There was no foot traffic, and the row of houses blocked the view of most cars on the street.

After a moment considering it, I unclipped my seat belt. "We've got to go in before Garcia realizes we're here. But I can't cover two guys and carry you. Are you gonna be able to stand and walk?"

Max nodded the same way a drunk tells you he can drive.

I opened the door to the sedan, slid out onto my feet, and switched off the earpiece. The adrenaline was pumping now, and I could feel my senses sharpening. The only steady noise here was the high-pitched hum of traffic up on 35. Although the heat still squeezed my skin as it had in Dallas, it didn't dominate the air the same way here; the scent of cut grass filled my nose.

Shutting the sedan door as quietly as I could, I stalked around the back to the passenger's side, trying not to crunch the gravel too much as I walked. Max had gotten her door open, but hadn't made it out yet. I helped her, then watched to see how steady she'd be. After a slight wobble, her legs seemed okay, and I turned to lead us inside. "Stay close, stay behind me," I said.

A security camera protruded from the corner of the building, pointing back toward the entrance. A quick glance confirmed a matching one on the opposite corner. I kept us tight against the front wall, hoping that might help a little, but, truth was, if Garcia were watching, he'd have already spotted us.

I just had to hope he was busy.

A small awning stretched over the ramp and glass doors. I paused at the side of it, stretching to peek inside.

All I could see was an empty reception desk.

Stepping to the door, I opened it, and one of those electronic chimes sounded—ding-dong.

With a wince, I darted in and drew the Sig, letting Max slip behind me. The only other doorway led to the left, and I covered it in case the chime had attracted attention.

When no one appeared after a few moments and my breathing remained the only sound, I started in.

The door led almost immediately to a darkened switchback, sending us along what I guessed was the wall behind reception. The silence continued, while the hair on my arms detected a steady breeze of air-conditioning blowing past us. As we crept ahead, a reddish glow emanated from the entrance to a hallway, farther down on the left.

Drawing up against that wall, I peered around the corner.

Both sides of the hallway were lined with evenly spaced doors. Each was closed, with a light bulb mounted above its frame. Only one bulb was lit: the next-to-the-last one on the right.

With the Sig at high ready, I crossed the hallway and pressed myself against the opposite wall, sidestepping down to the illuminated door. There were no windows into the room, no telling exactly who or how many were inside.

I gave Max a signal to stop where she was on the wall next to me.

Holding the Sig by its barrel in my left hand, I tried the knob with my right.

It spun freely.

As quietly as I could, I turned it all the way to one side, then pushed the door inward, just enough that the latch would clear the frame. Then I slowly returned the knob to its starting position.

I glanced over at Max, but she wore a blank, uncaring expression. I couldn't understand that—the hair on my neck was standing on end, and not from the air-conditioning. Reminding myself what the gang had done so far, I raised the Sig, took a deep breath, and pushed the door open with my foot.

At the opposite end of the room, two men sat in rolling chairs, their backs to the door. Both wore heavy headphones over their ears, not unlike the cans I used to wear back in the sound lab, and faced a giant dashboard of sound controls mounted below a window into a darkened recording booth. Although the two men were about equal height, that's where the similarities ended. The one on my left was bald and heavy, a gray sweat-stained T-shirt straining to hold back a roll of fat that desperately wanted to spill over the arms of his chair. The guy on my right had a dark, tightly woven ponytail trailing down to his shoulder blades, and wore a leather vest over a white tee that showed off muscular arms.

I started into the room, tracking along the rear wall. I kept the Sig trained on the muscular one, stopping once I was directly between them. "Turn around, both of you."

The ponytailed man bobbed his head slightly, but otherwise, nothing happened.

Realizing they couldn't hear anything over the cans, I lifted the barrel of the Sig and put a single shot through the middle of the sound-booth window.

Most soundproof glass is made by sandwiching two sheets of regular glass around a layer of soft, sticky lamination. The laminate acts as a shock absorber, dampening the vibrations of sound waves hitting one sheet of glass and keeping them from shaking the glass on the opposite side. Much like a car windshield, the laminate also holds the glass together when it breaks.

That's why, although the bullet I fired was traveling at about fourteen hundred feet per second, it didn't shatter the window. It did, however, leave a nice, tennis ball–size hole surrounded by a spiderweb of cracks. That, plus the muzzle blast, got their attention: .357 Sig rounds are extra loud.

Both men recoiled instinctively at the noise, then spun around. The confusion and terror on the fat man's face when he saw the Sig's barrel made me smile slightly. The ponytailed guy looked nervous, too, but mixed with another expression I wasn't sure I recognized.

As they lifted the headphones away from their ears, I said, "Nice and slow, boys. Put the cans down, then lace your fingers together on top of your head."

"And who exactly are you?" the ponytailed man asked.

"I'm a federal agent, Mr. Garcia. I believe you know this girl."

I could feel Max take a half step out from behind me. When he saw her, Garcia's chin dropped to his chest, and he shook his head.

"Surprised?" I asked.

He glanced back up, wearing a wry smile. "Anything bad ever happens, I can always count on Max to be in the middle of it. I knew she was gonna be the death of me. But I didn't think she was gonna get some Fed to do the job."

"I'm not here to hurt you, Mr. Garcia. Just to talk."

"Oh great. Then put the gun away. Let's go to my office and—"

"Nope. I've had enough surprises already. We're going to stay right here and chat."

Garcia's eyebrows bounced. "She's gotten you nearly killed, too, huh? Sucks, don't it?"

"What're you talking about?"

"Aw, dear old Max hasn't told you? I'm shocked at her lack of concern." Garcia's expression didn't budge.

"Told me what?"

"Go on, Max, explain it. Or are you too strung out again to put the words together?"

"Again?"

"Man, she really been keeping you in the dark, huh? Lemme guess, she's throwing up and shitting all over the place. Can't get out of bed."

I nodded slightly.

Garcia turned to Max. "You back on the Oxy, girl? We worked so hard to get you off that shit. Why you gotta be so stupid and go back to it?"

Clearly, I needed to catch up on the drug history, but that could wait for a moment. "You said she almost got you killed. What are you talking about?"

Garcia rolled his shoulders and looked toward the ceiling. "Man, you wanna talk about a blessing and a curse. Taking her on was the best thing to ever happen to my little piece-of-crap label here. Finally, I got money rolling in, bands fighting to sign with me, 'stead of the other way around." Garcia looked at me, his eyes narrowing. "But I'll tell you, between keeping up with her, dealing with her daddy, I'm surprised I haven't had a heart attack already. And on top of all that, I got people threatenin' to kill me. Not her, *me*! You believe that?"

"What people? What are you talking about?"

Garcia slumped back in his chair. "Before we signed her, man, Otra was one hundred percent Tejano. We had no problems. Then her daddy brings me her tape, and I play it. Like listening to an angel. Look at her"—he nodded in Max's direction—"she got *pop star* written all over her. So I sign her. I train her. Start putting out her songs. She goes platinum, but my listeners, the people who been with me since the beginning, they say I'm sellin' out."

"Selling out?"

"Sayin' I'm a traitor. Sayin' I think white kids' money is greener, and why can't I just play Tejano." Garcia shook his head. "Tejano's dyin', man. Don't nobody 'round here want to hear that, but it's true. All those people, they know where to find me. This place, where I live. Pretty soon, I start getting notes slipped under the door. Someone throws a brick through my window at night. Slashes my tires. Someone killed my dog, man. My dog!" Garcia's eyes were welling up now.

He shuddered, trying to keep it inside, but finally a hand came off his head. Stabbing a finger at Max, he started to stand. "And it's all her fault. None of this shit would've—"

I took a half step forward, the Sig pointed directly at his chest. "Sit. Back. Down."

Garcia plopped back into the seat, sniffling and snorting, blinking the tears out of his eyes.

"So Max is a pain in the ass, and your fans are all riled up. What'd you do about it?"

"Do?" Garcia chuffed. "What can I do? Contract says I got to release the next album. Then I'm free. That's why I been wanting her in here, recording, 'stead of running all over the place. Sooner we get that shit laid down, sooner I can drop her ass and move on."

"Wait, you're planning to get rid of her?"

"Yeah, man."

"What about the money? You're willing to throw that all away?"

Garcia grunted again. "Money don't make up for the stress, man. Just dealing with her is a full-time job—now I gotta worry about who's gonna jump me in the dark. I used to get by on a lot less than I got now, you know? I built this label up from nothin'; I can do it again. I get rid of her, get a fresh start? That's all I need. Hell, I would've kicked her ass to the curb already if her daddy the counselor hadn't tied my hands."

"I thought her contract expires in a couple of weeks. On her birthday."

Garcia's wry smile returned. "Yeah, for her. Her daddy rigged it so he can pull her anytime after she's seventeen. Me, I gotta deliver four albums before I'm done. I only done three, so that means I gotta do one more."

"What do you know about the Second Guerrilla Army of the Poor?"

"Never heard of them. What do they play?"

"They don't play. They're a gang."

"Whoa, man." Garcia shook his head slowly side to side, keeping his eyes locked on mine. "I got nothing to do with no gangs. Everybody knows that."

"C'mon, Charlie, you don't have connections? Your brothers, one of their friends? Maybe you wanted some help eliminating your little problem over here?" I jerked my head backward at Max. "Figure you make one last big score off her name, push out some tribute albums and greatest hits?"

His voice calm and steady, Garcia said, "I swear on Jesus Christ, I got no idea what you're talking about, some go-rilla gang. Everything I got here, I got fair and square. No gangs. No crooks. Only crook I ever dealt with is her daddy. 'Sides, I ain't got no rights to her stuff. Her daddy got that all tied up. I can't release shit if he don't let me."

I tried to think it through. Max and I had both guessed that Garcia had hired the Second Guerrillas, albeit for different reasons. But if he were telling the truth about all this . . . "You got the threatening notes? The contract? Proof of everything you just told me?"

Garcia nodded. "In my office."

Before I could order him to stand, a metallic plunking started.

Softly at first. Then louder.

My first thought was hail, hitting the metal roof. Summer-afternoon thunderstorm.

But the racket wasn't coming from above us. More like in front.

The side of the building.

That's when I realized: machine-gun fire.

I'd just put it together when the back wall of the recording booth exploded in a hot, white fireball.

CHAPTER 17

The blast knocked me backward, on top of Max. My first worry was flying glass, but I didn't feel or see any—the soundproofing laminate must have kept the window from shattering.

Rolling onto my side, then up to one knee, I searched for something, anything, to aim at. Ghostly white afterimages of the explosion floated in my way. Although I squeezed my eyes shut and rapidly blinked to clear them, everything remained hazy and obscured.

I couldn't focus on the gun sights, let alone anything downrange.

My hearing was fuzzy, too, ears ringing from the blast. I still heard gunfire, though. Short, staccato bursts ripping through the air. Louder than before. And then I could almost feel the bullets as they struck around the room.

The Second Guerrillas were storming in, I realized, through whatever hole they'd just ripped in the building's outer wall.

Glancing around for Max, I couldn't see her, either. About the only thing I could make out was the dark outline of the door frame to the hallway. I stood and sprinted to it for cover.

In the hallway, my eyes began to overcome the afterimages of the explosion. As details started reappearing, I turned and leaned back into the room.

Garcia and his sound tech both looked dead. While the window had mostly held together, a couple of large, jagged shards had been blown inward, impaling Bruce in the back, Garcia in the chest. Garcia's white shirt was already almost completely red with blood.

Max lay on the floor near them, apparently unconscious.

I started for her, but a string of bullets shredded the carpet directly in front of my foot. Recovering behind the door frame, I took a breath, then tried to spin outward to return fire.

This time, shots cracked against the wooden frame, showering me with splinters and driving me back again.

Stepping out perpendicularly from the wall, I got a sharp-angled view into the room. Two men with tattooed faces were now bending over Max, reaching for her. I fired at one, hitting his knee and crumpling him. But his partner lifted his automatic, and it was all I could do to dive away before his shots ripped the spot where I'd stood.

I scrambled back to my feet and made one last attempt to get into the room, but bullets kept pouring through the doorway.

I had to try something different.

Turning, I sprinted back the way we'd entered, twisting through the switchback and nearly falling out the glass doors at the entrance. I made for the right-hand corner of the building, taking cover for a moment before peeking out over my Sig.

The Second Guerrillas had pulled two SUVs up to the side of the building, one behind the other in a wide *V* pattern. Several men were pressed against the charred outline of the hole they'd blown through the wall, facing inward. At least three more were visible inside the trucks, whose doors gaped open.

I drew a bead on the rear tire of the closer SUV and fired. It blew with a pop. As that corner sank awkwardly toward the ground, I turned the Sig on the soldiers, firing as many rounds as I could.

I trimmed the nearest man against the wall, and another who tried climbing out of the closer SUV toward me. Two others poured out of the vehicle, driving me back around the corner with more gunfire.

Wedging the Sig between my knees for a moment, I unclipped the sling to free my arm, then reloaded. Between the bursts, I could hear the Guerrillas talking in Mayan. When I stole another peek around the corner, those outside were waving to the men still within.

Several soldiers double-timed it out the jagged hole; a particularly large one had Max draped over his shoulder. I started firing at the ones pinning me down, but they had good cover behind the SUV, and soon another hail of bullets clanked against the corner of the wall.

I waited a beat, then sprinted out, away from the building, to try to improve my angle, but the men had already piled into the lead SUV as it started to roll.

I took three steps after it, firing as I went.

"Max!" I screamed.

The SUV turned in a broad circle away from me, around the rear of the Otra building. I reversed course back toward the entrance, dropping to one knee in front of it, aiming just ahead of the Hyundai and waiting for their vehicle to emerge.

Although I still couldn't see the SUV, its engine roared, and I could hear its tires spitting gravel. To avoid hitting Max, I could only target the driver's head and the two tires facing me.

I took a cleansing breath and lined up the sights.

The Guerillas' truck appeared as a blur of black steel screaming away across gravel.

I squeezed off three quick shots, but before I could even register if they hit, muzzle flashes crackled in the rear windows, and automatic fire began kicking up the stones in front of me. Dropping to my belly, I rolled twice to my left before aiming down the sights again. But by then the SUV had turned, bouncing its way across the grass toward the street in front of the clapboard houses.

I fired two shots to no effect.

Scrambling to my feet, I chased the SUV as fast as I could sprint, emptying the whole magazine.

But it was no use.

Once the SUV hit the pavement, its tires squealed, it zigzagged out to the main street, and sped away.

As the last bit of the SUV disappeared from sight, I stopped in my tracks and doubled over. My shoulder and thigh both throbbed with pain. Although I wanted to yell, I didn't have the air. Hands on knees, I fought desperately to catch my breath. My heart was pounding so hard, I could feel the pulse throbbing in my neck and temples.

Gradually, my chest stopped heaving, but now my throat started to swell shut. My eyes watered. I let out a noise that was nothing intelligible, just a bunch of sounds that had gathered in my belly and forced their way out.

Sirens began wailing vaguely in the distance, but they barely registered.

Oh, Max. Now I've failed you, too . . .

A part of me screamed to get moving as I trudged across the gravel, but the rest couldn't bring itself to hurry.

The loose stones shifted beneath my feet, causing me to stumble across the lot. Other than my heart, still thundering, my insides all felt loose and mangled. As I reinserted my earpiece, the audio player started chattering through the first chapter of an audiobook I'd bought three weeks ago: a new Tesla biography I'd been dying to read. But now the words bounced off my brain like the hailstones I'd originally mistaken the gunfire for.

After wiping my face on my sleeve, I poked around the stranded SUV, then checked the pockets of one of the casualties. Both as empty as I'd expected.

I glanced back across the grass, through the hole that had been blown into the side of Otra. The metal wasn't only charred; it was contorted—bent and twisted over itself like a used piece of chewing gum. They must've used thermite, or something similar, to melt steel like that. That would also explain the bright-white explosion.

"Quite a fucking mess you made," I said out loud. I thought briefly of calling Lavorgna—he'd need an update on all of this, on how royally I'd screwed everything up on my very first case out of the gate.

As would Max's father.

The sirens were growing louder now. The only way to make things worse would be to get tangled up with the police. By the time I'd answered their questions, God knew where the Second Guerrillas would have Max.

Or whatever was left of her.

I wiped my eyes again and moved mechanically to the old Hyundai. Started it, shifted, rolled down the driveway. I began making turns, merging from one lane to another without even thinking about direction.

No matter how I tried to focus on the road or whatever might come next, the main part of my brain kept flashing back to the image of Max, unconscious on the floor. The Second Guerrillas carrying her away. And me, unable to save her.

Had they been watching the studio? Had I walked us right into a trap? What could I possibly do next to get her back?

I needed a plan.

Even more, I needed a place to clear my head. Someplace safe to think. Somewhere without cops, a place to process everything and determine my next move.

Although I'd lived near Dallas for years and had traveled to Texas dozens of times since, at that moment I felt a flash of panic at being landlocked. Since fleeing for California, the ocean had become my refuge. Whenever I needed to remove myself, or gather myself, I'd pull on my wet suit and make for the shoreline. I'd sit in the water, breathe with it, let its rhythm put me back in line. During the few days between

Sarah's funeral and returning to work, I'd spent almost every daylight hour out on the board.

My quick glances out the car window showed no water in sight. Just broad, grassy fields as far as the eye could see, broken only by the harsh angles of man-made structures—houses, garages, stores.

After driving aimlessly for several minutes, I realized I was lost, no idea where in Austin I might be.

I started checking signs. Looking for landmarks.

Nothing helpful. Just generic countryside.

I was about to pull out the burner and hit the GPS when I saw it.

Looming, off to my right. Gleaming in the sun.

Besides the ocean, the only other place familiar enough it might help me recover. And I had to smile at the ridiculousness of my finding my way there by accident.

Being absolutely honest, I'm not big on fate. Predestination is way too hocus-pocus for a math-and-science guy like me. But at that moment, the fact I'd found it seemed like more than mere coincidence.

It just seemed . . . right.

I flipped on the sedan's blinker and took the ramp.

CHAPTER 18

You enter Austin-Bergstrom at the bottom, through baggage claim.

Although the terminal's three stories tall, the windows are up top, meaning precious little natural light spills all the way down. Dim, and built from large blocks of gray stone, baggage claim would have the look of a dungeon if it weren't for the carousels, some of the weirdest I've seen. Shiny chrome, triangular in shape, fed by extralong ramps extending from the wall behind them, they look more like the landing struts of some alien spaceship than a place to retrieve your suitcase.

Since dark and foreboding was the last thing I needed, I maneuvered through the crowds as quickly as I could toward the escalators. Taking the stairs two at a time, I cleared security at the top with a flash of my badge.

Austin bills itself as the "Live Music Capital," and the airport features a stage built right into the terminal, where bands and singers play almost every day. Wandering over, I found a four-man band in cowboy boots and hats playing southern rock. Some wannabe Lynyrd Skynyrd–type song, but a small crowd had gathered, tapping their feet, bouncing their shoulders.

I dropped into an empty chair.

The song ran long, with one of the guitarists moving to the mike and singing. His voice was nasal and flat, but the crowd didn't seem to care. One couple in particular, college kids from the looks of it, weren't even listening: she was sprawled across his lap, their arms wrapped around each other, their mouths locked.

Normally, I'd have looked away, given them their privacy. But their blissful ignorance caught my attention.

I glanced down at the heart on my forearm.

Sarah and I had been like that. So consumed with one another that the world around us seemed to melt away.

Sarah.

The person I'd failed before Max.

Although not the first.

My first failure had been Clarence.

My mentor. My friend.

A man who'd invited me into his home. Made me part of his family. Who'd ended up killing himself . . . because of me.

That was the secret Shirley and my godkids could never know, the one I constantly feared she'd divine. The reason I had so much to make up to the family.

Clarence had treated me like a brother, or a son. He'd genuinely loved me.

Loved me enough that what I did made him want to swallow a bullet.

Sarah had loved me, too.

Not just said the words, but shown it. And all she'd ever asked for was my love in return.

In the end, I'd gotten her killed, too. A fact her family had not let me forget at her memorial.

And now there was Max.

Poor Max. I'd failed her, too. Spectacularly.

Blood on my hands again.

Up onstage, the rock song ended with a flourish. Occupied by my thoughts, I only half noticed the band shifting around. Before I realized what had happened, the nasal, flat singer had moved to a steel guitar. He started a slow, mournful-sounding song, and soon the words were slicing into me.

I might not follow country music, but I recognize Hank Williams's "Your Cheatin' Heart" when I hear it.

My lips began quivering, and tears started to gather in my eyes. But as they filled like cups beneath a faucet, another different feeling came over me.

A pressure, almost.

A squeezing tightness, like a cramp, down deep in my gut.

But it didn't stay there. It spread. Up though my chest. Down my good arm.

My hand clenched into a fist, my arm actually trembling from the strength of it. The hair on my arms and neck flared up.

Max wasn't dead yet. Not like the others.

And she didn't have to be.

Unless I let her.

As I shot to my feet, my chair clattered over behind me, but I didn't pay attention. I was already several steps away, stalking past the lip-locked kids, heading for other parts of the terminal.

I strode to the far end of the airport, then reversed course and slowed my pace. Told myself to be in the moment. To let the ideas flow from whatever surrounded me.

No bolts of inspiration struck.

Each person I passed, I checked up and down, looking for something—anything—I could glean from them. Asking myself what they might be subconsciously telling me. Every time, the only sound I heard was silence.

It was like staring at the blank pages of my pad. Where ideas used to seem to spring from my hand onto the paper, now there was nothing.

I'd nearly reached security again, and in the distance I could see the stage.

My steps slowed even more.

I was passing the food court, a cluster of barbecue and Tex-Mex places with a small collection of tables spread out in front of them. The seating area was separated from the terminal by a waist-high wall, and I drew up to it, leaning my good shoulder against a column that rose to the vaulted ceiling overhead.

The combined smell of rich, grilling meat and sweet, tangy sauce stuck in my nose. My mouth watered and my stomach grumbled, both realizing they couldn't remember the last time I'd eaten. But as part of my brain started cataloging the best-tasting brisket I'd ever had, my eyes landed on something else.

A large family—parents, plus four or five kids—had pushed two tables together. Everyone was seated except the father, who hovered around the family, delivering food he'd retrieved. The kids were impatient, nearly climbing over each other to reach the fries.

What struck me, though, was the mother.

When the father placed a tray in front of her, she eyed the food for a minute, then glanced up at him with a cockeyed expression.

"This is not what I wanted," she said.

The father's chin dropped to his chest. But it was her words that stuck with me . . .

Not what I wanted.

So simple. Yet they cut right to the bone.

Not what I wanted.

Since the start, I'd wondered why the gang wanted to kill Max. They'd massacred the agents at LAX. Attacked my house. Tried to shoot us out of the sky. All, I'd assumed, in an extreme effort to put at least one bullet into Max's head. That's what they'd promised in the threatening notes to Max and her father, so I had always believed that was their goal.

The fact they hadn't accomplished it was something I'd chalked up to a combination of dumb luck and a tiny bit of skill on my part.

But.

At Otra, Max had been motionless on the floor, out cold. You couldn't have asked for an easier target. Trapped outside in the hallway, I certainly wasn't stopping them: easiest thing in the world to cap her on the ground.

My mind flashed to LAX, how the gunmen had done exactly that to the wounded FBI agent. Quick trigger pull, three-shot burst. The agent's head turned into pulp.

But they hadn't done that to Max.

They'd *taken* her.

Why?

Why not just shoot her and be done with it?

Pushing myself off the column, I started walking again. Like the drive to the airport, it was all reflexes, simply putting one foot in front of the other while my brain processed things.

Was Max's body some kind of trophy? Did they need it to prove they'd finished the job?

Even if that were the case, why not kill her when it was easy and efficient, then haul her body away? Live hostages are a hassle—they struggle, they cry out. Why endure that?

Unless.

Unless that was exactly what the gang had been wanting this whole time.

Thinking back over it, recalling each of the confrontations, the gang could just as easily have been trying to *capture* Max as to kill her. Even the dogfight with Jerry Norgard's plane—the Second Guerrillas hadn't shot at us until we took off and gave them no choice.

My brain was clicking now, starting to spin with questions prompted by this new angle. And there seemed to be only one place to get them answered.

I pulled out the burner and opened the map. All the addresses I'd entered recently were still in there.

And Max's house was only fifteen minutes away.

CHAPTER 19

A few quick turns put me back on Highway 360, which the map showed looping northward along the western edge of the city.

Finally, all the "hill country" comments made sense: Out here, the road was split, a grassy median separating the two sides as they undulated in parallel over a series of gentle rises and dips. In places, the earth had been cut away for the road, creating steep walls of striped, sedimentary rock. The trees grew thicker here, too, fringing the hilltops and filling the valleys. The sun, finally relinquishing its hold on the day, bathed the scenery in orange light.

I turned onto Westlake Drive, a quiet suburban street that looked like the kind you could find almost anywhere. Gradually, though, it dropped down into a dark, lush valley where twilight had firmly taken hold. As the road rose, fell, and twisted, you never had a sense of what would be coming next. Fewer and fewer houses were visible, only driveways that disappeared back into the shadows, punctuated by closed gates in earthen tones that seemed like a Texas twist on what I'd seen in Malibu.

The GPS said I was tracking the riverbank, drawing ever closer to Max's house. If the gang had wanted to watch the place, they wouldn't have had an easy time: the road was narrow, with no shoulder or parking places other than the driveways themselves.

Without streetlights, house numbers became harder to read in the gathering dusk. I slowed the car to a crawl, lowering my window to get a better view. The cool breeze rushing in and the soft hiss of my tires against the asphalt were the only sounds disturbing the oncoming night.

Finally, I found the number I needed, mounted on a wrought-iron gate drawn between two columns of stacked shale. A call box peeked out from hedges next to the columns. I rolled up to it, pressed the button, and heard a deep squelch, followed by electronic beeping. Although I expected to hear the voice of Marta, Max's father answered after several beeps. "Yes?"

"It's Seth Walker, Mr. Drew."

Without another word, the gate swung open, and I started inside.

Small, hanging lamps outlined the driveway, which snaked up and around several terraced levels of earth. Although the thick oaks lining the property blocked any residual daylight, they were tall and mature enough not to obstruct the view of the house. From the bottom of the hill, it looked like some kind of majestically lit mission: wings bracketing a central section, all built from sandy-colored stone and topped with a dark tile roof.

By the time I reached the summit, Drew was already waiting in the front doorway, backlit by interior lights. As I parked and exited the sedan, he stalked across the cobblestone courtyard. "Mr. Walker. I'm so glad you finally came to your senses and brought Max home."

"She's not with me," I said, closing the door with a dull thud.

Drew had drawn close enough that I could see his expression harden even in the dim light. "What the hell does that mean?"

"It means I need you to start being straight with me."

"I don't know what you're—"

"Spare me the bullshit. The Second Guerrillas took Max—"

"They have her?" Drew's chest swelled, his hands rising as if he wanted to strangle me. "How could you let that happen?"

Although I considered drawing the Sig, I didn't bother. Even as roughed up as I was, I could take down an old pretty boy like Drew without it. "I didn't have a whole lot of choice, you know, pinned down inside Otra Records by their machine guns."

"You . . ." Drew's hands dropped. "You were at Otra? You saw Charlie?"

"Before the Second Guerrillas killed him, yeah."

"Charlie's dead." Drew glanced off into the distance for a moment, then turned. "Come on. Let's . . . let's go talk in the house."

Drew led me inside, where an open staircase descended into a broad, two-story living room. The floors and walls were done in some kind of stone—granite, marble, I couldn't tell—but the rear wall consisted of full-height, arched windows, gazing across a stone patio and lit pool to darkened trees and what I assumed was the river beyond them.

As we walked, Drew again used his finger to unlock his phone and check something. Apparently the work of the "brand" never stopped, even when its namesake had been kidnapped.

At the bottom of the stairs, Drew waved me to a sofa, then sat on another across a small cocktail table. Elbows on knees, he tucked the phone back inside his jacket before speaking. "I . . . I'm sorry I got upset outside. I didn't mean any offense. Did you . . . Were you able to get information from Charlie before—"

I shook my head. "Not much."

Drew's hands went to his mouth, which was trembling. "I'm sorry. It's just . . . Max is my little girl . . ."

Although it didn't redeem him completely, the concern on Drew's face sparked a pang of guilt in my gut. My godkids weren't much younger than Max—if anything ever happened to them . . . "I understand, sir. And I promise I will do everything in my power to get her back safely. But that's why I need you to start being honest with me. You know exactly who the Second Guerrillas are, don't you?"

Closing his eyes, Drew nodded.

"You faked the death threats to get her protection. You knew they wanted to kidnap her. Why?"

Drew slumped back onto the couch. "They want what everyone wants. Money."

"But why target you, of all people? It is *you* they're targeting, isn't it, not her?"

He glanced up to the ceiling. "You have to understand, everything Max needs—vocal coaches, acting coaches, tutors—it's all very expensive. And I don't know if you know the record business, but it takes a vise to squeeze a nickel out of those bastards. Garcia owes us so much in royalties . . ." Drew took a deep breath, then raised his eyebrows. "Anyway, I needed capital. So I borrowed—"

"Why not go to a bank?"

Drew grunted. "I don't know what banks you deal with, Mr. Walker, but the current lending climate is not, shall we say, friendly. And a man with my history—single father, defaulted on my law-school loans, no W-2—I'm not considered the world's best investment."

He took a deep breath before continuing. "I heard about a private 'investment group'"—he mimed quotation marks with his fingers—"here in town. Charlie recommended them."

"Charlie turned you on to the Second Guerrillas?"

Drew nodded again, solemnly. Then, as if he heard my thoughts, he added, "Don't get me wrong—I'm not suggesting he set us up with them on purpose. They seemed perfectly reputable at first. Certainly not like what they eventually turned out to be."

"How much did you borrow?"

"Seven hundred and fifty thousand dollars."

"And how much did they ask for?"

"Fifteen million dollars."

A nice twenty-*x* multiplier. "And since you were having trouble getting money out of Garcia in the first place—"

Drew chuckled nervously. "Yeah, never quite got there. And at this point, even if I paid—"

"They'd just come back for more."

He nodded, then stared at me silently for several moments. "What do we do next? How do we rescue Max?"

"I've got to find them first," I said. "I don't suppose you have a way . . ."

Drew shook his head. "They make contact when they want to make contact."

"Have you heard from them today or tonight?"

"No."

I realized we might not be alone. Dropping my voice to a whisper, I asked, "Is Marta here?"

"No. With Max away, I gave her some time off."

"She's in with them somehow. Voluntarily, or through coercion, I'm not sure which." When Drew didn't react, I asked, "Does that surprise you?"

He blinked several times and did something with his tongue in his mouth, like he was fiddling with his teeth. "I certainly didn't know that until you just said it. But now that you do say it, no, I can't say I'm shocked."

"Marta leaked to them where Max and I were—that's how they caught up with us. But I'm guessing she's probably been leaking a lot of information to them. I also think the drugs were part of their plan, to keep Max vulnerable and—"

Drew's voice rose now. "Wait, drugs? What drugs?"

"You didn't know Max was taking prescription medication?"

For the first time since we'd come inside, anger flared across his face. "I have absolutely no idea what you're talking about. What drugs?"

"Garcia said Oxycontin."

"My God," Drew said quietly. His eyes dropped to the floor. "Right under my nose."

"Max was desperate to get back here. I think she was running out—or ran out—of her supply. Do you know where she would have gotten that stuff?"

"My first guess would have been Charlie."

I shook my head. "I don't think so. He mentioned trying to get her clean. What about Marta?"

"I can't imagine her having anything to do with drugs. Especially not giving them to Max. Brad Civins, on the other hand . . ."

"The bodyguard you fired?"

"He has all kinds of shadowy connections from his time in the military. And afterward. Who knows what he could get his hands on."

"Do you think he was working for the Second Guerrillas, too?"

Drew raised his eyebrows. "Now that you say that, I think it's possible. Probable, even. If they had Marta and Brad in their pocket, they'd know virtually everything we did." After a pause, he asked me, "Will you go after Civins?"

"He and Marta are the only ties we have."

"I really think Brad's much more likely to be the source of the drugs than Marta."

The papers Lavorgna had given me at the supermarket were still wedged in my pocket. I pulled them out and flipped through them quickly. "Looks like Civins has an address here in Austin."

"You'll need to be careful. He's a tough customer."

Folding the papers back up, I stood. "I'm not worried about that. I'm just worried about Max."

Drew's face blanched. "You think they'll . . ."

"No. She's alive, and there's no leverage over you if they kill her. But she was sick from the withdrawal, and I have no idea how they'll deal with that." I looked Drew in the eye. "I'll find Civins, and I'll find Max. If the gang contacts you in the meantime, let me know immediately. All right?"

As he took down the burner number, Drew nodded slightly, his mouth drawing into a nervous but firm line.

"We'll get her back, Mr. Drew. I promise."

CHAPTER 20

Darkness had fallen completely by the time I left Drew. The papers Lavorgna had given me said Civins was using his GI bill to get started on a psychology degree over at UT. The map showed Civins's address on the opposite side of the city, a short distance from campus.

The street number belonged to a sprawling apartment complex wedged along a busy thoroughfare between two strip malls filled with taco shops and tattoo parlors. As I drew closer, I could see it was one of those student ghettos you found in every state-college town: three stories of shoddy clapboard-and-concrete construction bearing a faded "Welcome Students" banner.

I turned at the next cross street and parked two blocks in. Returning to the complex on foot, I found it ringed by a six-foot-high metal fence that any other time I'd have been happy to scale but couldn't possibly clear with my bad arm.

Instead, I circled the perimeter. Barely a third of the parking spots inside the fence were occupied. No signs of life. I guessed 8:00 p.m. meant students were out studying or drinking or something. Along one side of the lot, a rolling gate blocked the lone driveway. It looked to be triggered by some kind of radio remote control—they likely handed out clickers to anyone who moved in. With no way to spoof that frequency or trigger the capacitance sensor that would open the gate from the inside, I kept going.

Around front, I found a pedestrian gate, but it, too, was secured, this time by an intercom call box not unlike the one that had been mounted on Nancy Irvine's house. This one didn't have a guard monitoring it, though; from the keypad, you could look up residents' names and dial whomever you were visiting so they could buzz you in by pressing a button on their phones.

If I'd had even a pocketknife, I could have defeated the call box easily. Although the circuit inside would respond only to the proper dualtone multifrequency sound played through the speaker line—preventing someone from simply holding a cell phone up to the microphone and trying different buttons to gain access—I could have spliced the wires over to the burner and fooled it. Without any tools, though, that wasn't an option, either.

I'd have to go low-tech on this one. Fortunately, a pizza place across the street had its telephone number written in neon.

Sixteen minutes after placing the call, I spotted what I was looking for: a thin guy in a stiff-brimmed trucker's hat, jogging across the street with a pizza box balanced on his upturned palm.

I'd moved several yards down the sidewalk to wait, but now started back toward the gate. Timing it right, I arrived just as the delivery guy said into the call box, "Hey, 602's not picking up. Can you buzz me in?"

A loud beep burst from the speaker, followed by an electronic hum at the gate. As the delivery guy pulled the metal door open, I offered to hold it for him.

Civins's apartment sat around back. Located on the ground floor, a wooden partition shielded its sliding glass door from anyone trying to peer directly inside. Fortunately, it was dark enough that I could creep up to the partition without being seen.

Unlike most of the units—closed up tight, air conditioners humming—Civins's had the slider open with the screen drawn across it. Lights were on inside, but the place was Spartan: bare walls, just a few pieces of particleboard furniture. No TV, no computer; the stack of textbooks next to the couch seemed to be his most valuable possession.

When a dark shape appeared at the periphery of the room and started toward the door, I retreated around the screen and out to the parking lot, pausing next to a car. A minute later, a man I guessed was Civins emerged from behind the screen dressed only in running shorts and sneakers.

As he stood for a moment, stretching, I got to see what I was up against. Civins's file said he'd spent eight years in Force Recon, the marines' answer to the Navy SEALs, and he looked the part: a good inch or two taller than I was, he sported a high-and-tight haircut, several tattoos, and muscles seemingly cut from granite. Even if I were at full strength, there was little doubt he could take me, and I was nowhere near that.

As he jogged off into the darkness, I tried to come up with a plan for exactly where I could hide to ambush him.

◆ ◆ ◆

"Evening, Brad."

The words startled Civins, and I couldn't really blame him. Finding my Sig trained on you as you stepped from the shower must be a nasty surprise.

Whatever sense of alarm he felt quickly disappeared, however, as one corner of his mouth turned up in a slight grin. "Mind if I throw on some pants?" His file said he was born in Mobile, Alabama, and he still had the accent to match.

"Yeah, I kind of do." After creeping out from the coat closet once I'd heard the water start, I'd deliberately sat on the toilet to disguise my height and obtain a little cover from the sink. "I prefer knowing you're not armed."

"May I, uh . . . ?" Civins nodded downward.

"Nope. I like your hands right where they are, holding that towel up there on your head. But don't worry, I prefer blonds."

The grin spread across the remainder of Civins's face as he squared his feet and shoulders toward me. "Buddy, if you're out to rob somebody, you picked the wrong guy. I don't have anything worth taking."

"I'm not here to rob you," I said. "I need to ask you some questions about one of your former clients."

"Didn't wanna make an appointment?"

"Max Magic's been kidnapped."

Civins's smile disappeared. "Maxie—kidnapped? What happened?"

"That's what I need you to tell me. Let's start with the drugs—what was she taking?"

"When I left, she was on Oxy. But there might have been other stuff in there, too."

"C'mon, Brad, I don't have time for games."

"That's all I know—"

"You were her goddamn connection," I growled. "And let me guess, it was Petén and the Second Guerrillas who put you up to it, right?"

"Whoa," Civins said, "back up a second. I don't know what all you're talking about."

"*Bullshit.*" My face flashed white-hot, and I couldn't tell which was louder, my heartbeat or the clock ticking in my head at how long this was taking. I bounced to my feet. "You stole from Max's father, you were dealing her drugs, and so help me if you don't tell me where I can find the Second Guerrillas right fucking now . . ."

My chest heaved and I was acutely aware of the tension in the trigger against my finger. Part of me worried I'd moved too close to Civins—the bathroom was narrow enough, he could get to me if he lunged.

But he didn't.

After looking at me and looking at my hand on the Sig, he actually took a step backward.

"Take it easy, hoss. I don't know what exactly you've heard, or who you've talked to, but absolutely none of what you just said is right."

My pulse slowed, just a little. "So tell me everything you know," I said. "And, so help me, it had better all be true."

Civins nodded slowly. "I started working Max's security detail right after New Year's. Couple of months in, the head of her label comes to me and says he thinks she's doing drugs. Oxy. I'd known some guys who'd gotten hooked on stuff like that in the corps, so I started paying attention, and then I saw the signs, too. Her mood changing on a dime. Superattentive one minute, supertired the next. She'd scratch at her arms, like she couldn't stop. All stuff I'd just chalked up to her being a teenager, until I really focused on it."

Apparently I wasn't the only one stupid enough to miss the signs. "Why'd Garcia bring it up with you? Why not tell her family?"

A shrug. "Charlie and Drew ain't exactly best buddies. Maybe he figured I'd be more likely to listen."

"Keep going."

"I went back to Charlie, told him I agreed about the Oxy. He said he had a plan to get Max clean."

"And?"

"And I took it to Drew."

"You told Max's father she was doing drugs?"

Civins nodded.

Now things were getting interesting. "So what'd he do?"

"Said thanks. Two days later, he fired me."

"For stealing."

Civins grunted like he found it funny.

"What?" I asked. "Was he wrong?"

"Not technically."

"What the hell does that mean?"

Rolling his eyes, Civins said, "I took a few little things of Max's and auctioned them on eBay. A hairbrush, a toothbrush. Stuff like that. Nothing sensitive. Nothing Max couldn't live without. I'm pretty sure she knew I was doing it."

"How much did you make selling her stuff?"

"Little bit. Like fifteen grand."

"What'd you do with the cash? You certainly didn't spend it on this place."

"I was going to give it to charity."

Now it was my turn to laugh. "Charity. Right."

"I'm serious." His muscles flexed. "You know how many guys like me have killed themselves since coming back? There's one unit alone that's lost fourteen guys. Fourteen. Not to the enemy, here at home. It's just wrong. That's what I'm studying for—so guys like me will have someone to talk to who's been there. Who knows what they've seen and done."

When I'd entered the apartment and looked for a hiding place, I'd seen one of those fancy triathlon racing bikes parked just inside the door. Shiny and new. "C'mon, man. I saw the ride you got out there. That must've cost a grand, easy."

He shook his head. "Everything I got here, I paid for myself. I don't need much to live on, and I banked some pretty good coin doing personal security after getting out."

"All right, but you said you were *going* to give the money away. What happened?"

"I—I did give some of it."

"How much?"

"Three grand. I got the receipts out there." Civins gestured out the bathroom door with his head, but the thought of walking him out into the darkened bedroom to confirm it didn't make me particularly comfortable.

"What about the other twelve?"

"I . . . had some setbacks."

"Like what?"

Civins's gaze drifted off to the side.

"You want me to believe you, I need to know. What happened to the other twelve grand you made selling Max's stuff?"

His head snapped back, eyes locked on me. "I lost it, okay?"

"Lost it how? It fell out of your pocket?"

"No! I . . . I wanted to grow the money into something bigger. So I . . . invested it. But things didn't go exactly like I planned."

"What'd you invest in?"

Civins kept glaring at me but said nothing.

"Tell me. What did you invest in?"

"In myself."

I raised my eyebrows and cocked my head.

"It was my bankroll for a poker tournament. Ten thousand bought my seat, and I was going to donate whatever I won."

"I gather it didn't go well."

Wincing, Civins shook his head. "Out the first day."

"What about the last two thousand? Where'd that go?"

"I spent it trying to make back the ten."

I sighed. "Anyone ever tell you, you have a gambling problem?"

"Poker isn't gambling," he said quickly. "It's a game of skill—"

"Doesn't sound like you're all that skilled, then."

Civins's lips pulled back, showing clenched teeth. "I'm good. You just—"

"Back to where we started. When I spoke to Drew, he fingered you as Max's connection—"

"That lying—"

I raised a hand. "Well, if it wasn't you, who was it? Because that's the person who's got the best chance of leading me to Max."

"Roosevelt," Civins said. "It's gotta be."

"Who's that?"

"Max's doctor. He's got an office out on MoPac."

I remembered what Max had said about her pediatrician, and recalled seeing that name on the map. "Did you take her to him?"

"I went along. Usually Marta scheduled the appointments."

Marta. Of course. "Did you see Marta and this Roosevelt guy together?"

Civins shook his head. "I wouldn't go inside the exam room, not with Max getting undressed and all. I'd wait outside."

"But you know the office, know the doctor?"

He nodded. "Yeah."

"Good, you can take me over there and introduce me."

"What? No way. I got a shift to get to—besides, it's not like they're open this time of night."

"Doesn't matter," I said. "Clock's ticking. If Roosevelt's in with the gang that took Max—and I'm guessing he is, since he apparently got Max back on the Oxy after Charlie got her clean—then he's our best hope of finding out where they're holding her."

"Great. I'll draw you a map. You can say hi to Maxie for me when you rescue her."

I shook my head. "I need an extra pair of hands. So you're gonna come along and help."

Civins's expression hardened, and again I felt a pang of concern about what might happen if he decided to try to take the Sig from me.

I brandished the gun again, my eyes wide. Finally, his shoulders slumped.

"Fine," he said. "I'll go with you. But at least let me call into work so I don't lose my job."

"Sure," I said. "We've got one other stop to make, anyway."

CHAPTER 21

Civins knew a gun store that was still open, despite the hour.

God bless Texas.

From there, we steered down the MoPac Expressway. I made Civins drive while I rode behind him, keeping him covered with the Sig in my bad hand while loading my new purchases into the shotgun with my good one. At this point, he seemed trustworthy enough, but I couldn't afford any surprises.

After a series of undulating hills, Civins turned into the driveway of a modern-looking office complex. Sunk several feet below the road, a group of identical glass-and-metal buildings sat in a tight huddle around a parking lot landscaped to feature trees and a small pond in the middle. We parked near the woodsy centerpiece, the car hidden in long shadows cast by the trees.

As we got out, I carried the shotgun under my arm. It felt more than a bit like we were going hunting.

Civins pointed silently to a building on our left, then started that way. For such a big guy, he was noticeably light on his feet, making no sound as he walked. I followed a few steps behind.

When we reached the entrance to the building, glass double doors revealed a deserted lobby and one of those magnetic locks up at the top of the door frame, holding them shut. From the outside, you could only beep in using an access card, but on the inside, a motion detector was mounted up at the magnet to release the lock for anyone approaching.

I could see a thin crack of light peeking out through the seam between the doors and feel a slight rush of air against my palm emanating from it. Checking the gap at the bottom, it was wider.

Hopefully wide enough.

I hurried back to the pond, ripped off several long cattail stalks, and returned to hand them to Civins. It took several tries, but eventually he managed to slip the bushy end of one cattail under the bottom lip of the doors and then gradually ease the narrower stem up through the seam between them. Once the stem was about eye level, I motioned for him to wiggle the stalk up and down. Inside, the fuzzy spike of the cattail bounced and waved until it triggered the motion sensor, and a metallic thunk sounded.

The door pulled open.

Civins raised three fingers and pointed toward a bank of elevators, but I steered us to the fire stairs instead. After a quick climb to the third floor, we emerged at one end of a hallway. A door marked with bright colors and big letters stood at the opposite end, while all the additional doors along the sides of the hall had been decorated over with shrink-wrapped pictures of superheroes and Disney princesses.

I had to give it to the Second Guerrillas: if this was their doing, it sure made a nice front. No one would ever suspect a drug dealer worked out of a place like this.

The main entrance bore a much heavier knob and lock than the others. More likely to be alarmed, too, although I guessed it might ring to Roosevelt or the Second Guerrillas rather than the police. So I picked a door halfway down the hall, where Spider-Man was swinging on a web. Pointing the shotgun barrel at the lock from maybe six inches away, I fired.

Shotguns are always tricky to handle one-handed, and this breaching round packed a huge kick. But it did its job: the powdered iron slug popped the lock right out of the door.

I motioned for Civins to go first. He nudged the door open with his foot, then proceeded inside. I followed, and found we were in an examination room, cabinets and sink on one side, paper-covered table on the other. Cartoonish jungle animals were painted on the walls.

A door on the far side of the exam room led into the heart of the office, where a set of central cubicles were surrounded by a ring of doors. Each of the rooms around the circle turned out to be a mirror image of the one through which we'd entered, albeit decorated in a different theme: space, pirates, princesses, trains.

I figured Roosevelt wouldn't keep anything sensitive out in the open. The information I needed ought to be locked up somewhere.

Eventually I found it: a door tucked into a shadowy corner past the X-ray room. Buried at the very end of a hallway, it struck you as unimportant, plus the radiation symbol probably tended to keep people away. But it was the only door in the entire office whose handle bore a numeric keypad lock.

The lock took two breaching rounds to dislodge. As the door swung open, I saw a windowless room smaller than I would have expected from the outside, empty except for a desk and chair, pushed against the far wall. The only light inside came from a computer monitor on the desk, running one of those screen savers of endlessly snaking colors. Next to the monitor stood a desktop computer with a small wireless router box perched on top.

Civins stepped into the room first, which made sense because I'd been forcing him to go ahead of me, but in doing so he blocked my view of the computer, and something told me the setup wasn't quite right.

I pushed my way in past him, quickly glancing over everything again.

Not the monitor, that was fine.

The desktop was nothing special, just a big metal shell with disk-drive doors on the front and cords streaming out the back.

The wireless router's antennas pointed to the ceiling while lights blinked across its face, exactly as they should.

What struck me was the wiring.

A bank of electrical outlets stood next to the desk. All three power cords were plugged in. A single Cat5 cable also ran from a jack in the wall to the back of the computer.

But that meant the router wasn't plugged in to the network.

As I realized it was a fake, another thought occurred to me: this box wasn't designed to broadcast a wireless signal.

It was designed to *receive* one.

Dropping the shotgun, I grabbed the router and ripped it away from the wall, unplugging its power cord in the process. I wedged it against the top of the desk with my bad arm and broke the antennas off with my good one.

Heart still fluttering, I took a deep breath before gingerly setting the little box on the floor by itself in a corner.

"What the hell was that?" Civins asked.

"Booby trap," I said. Then, looking back at the door, I spotted the camera: hanging down from the ceiling like a spider. Almost invisible in the darkness, it pointed directly at the desk.

I stepped back into its field of vision, pointing at my own chest, then at the computer monitor.

Hoping that message was clear enough, I drew the Sig and put a bullet right through the security camera's lens. Then I picked up the shotgun and handed it to Civins.

"You're going to need this," I said. "Whoever's watching that video is either on their way to join us, or is running for the hills. If it's the former, I'm guessing we've got about five minutes till they get here."

CHAPTER 22

In the end, it was easier than I'd thought.

Civins and I hid in one of the nearby exam rooms, waiting to see who'd show up. Although my eyes were well adjusted to the dark, my heart drummed steadily in my ears as seemingly endless seconds ticked by.

Ultimately, though, it was just one man. Tall, thin. Older than I'd expected, maybe sixty.

He entered the office slowly, carefully. Leaving the lights off, he took baby steps and did lots of little checks in each direction. In his right hand, he carried a pistol, something small, like a .22. But he toted it up by his ear, where it wouldn't be much help. That, plus the way he was squeezing the grip for dear life, told me he was no marksman.

By the time he'd advanced halfway into the office, the man seemed satisfied he was alone and made a beeline for the room with the computer.

He was so intent on checking it, hunched over the desk, he didn't hear us sneaking up behind him until just before I brought the butt of the Sig down against his skull.

The man moaned as he began to stir. The Dixie cup of water I had Civins dump on his face helped wake him but didn't improve his mood.

"What the fuck—" He rocked side to side in the chair, only then realizing his hands, feet, and chest were bound to it with packing tape we'd found in a supply room.

"How are you tonight, Dr. Roosevelt?" I'd reclined the seat backward, so he had no choice but to stare upward. "Nice of you to join us."

He struggled some more, but didn't answer. Beneath once-blond hair that had almost gone completely white, his face was short and squat with narrow eyes. Deep laugh lines and dimples framed a broad mouth. As he gritted his teeth with effort, you could imagine him smiling—he had the kind of face kids would probably trust.

"You can keep struggling, Doc," I said, "but I don't think you're gonna get through that tape."

His pale face had grown increasingly red, and now sweat dotted his brow. "Who the fuck are you?"

"Two guys who realized the little drug-running operation you've got going here. Let me guess, you write prescriptions for fake patients, then sell them on the side."

Roosevelt shook his head. "Not even close."

"Explain it to us, then."

"Why should I tell you anything? You're just a couple of criminals who broke into my office."

I leaned down, my face closer to his. "Wrong on that one, Doc. He's former special forces and probably knows ten ways to kill you with that paper cup. Me, I'm a federal agent, and all this"—I waved my hand back toward the computer—"is going to be a case of intent to distribute for my friends at the FBI."

"A cop?" He laughed out loud. "Even better. Where's your warrant, cop? You don't have one, and everything in here is inadmissible." His eyes gleamed. "I know my rights."

I nodded. "So then you know all about the exigent circumstances exception to the warrant requirement, right?"

Roosevelt's smile didn't completely disappear, but his brow furrowed.

"That's right, you don't need a warrant to perform a search if there are 'exigent circumstances.'"

Before I'd started my new gig as liaison and investigator, Lavorgna had forced me to attend a weeklong law-for-law-enforcement class taught by the federal prosecutors at LA's Spring Street courthouse. I hadn't really wanted to attend, but I'd learned a few things. I glanced over at Civins. "I'd say looking for a kidnapped minor counts as an emergency, wouldn't you?"

"Damn straight."

"Kidnapped?" Roosevelt was stammering now. "What're you—"

"One of your patients. Max Magic. You know, the sixteen-year-old pop star you had hooked on pills? His former client?" I nodded over at Civins, who took another step closer to Roosevelt; the doctor's eyes darted between us. "The Second Guerrillas took her. I'm guessing they neglected to warn you before they did that."

Roosevelt didn't say anything, but his face gave it away.

"That is who you work for, right? The Second Guerrillas? Don't tell me you set up all this cloak-and-dagger stuff yourself."

"I'm not telling you shit." He spat the words. "I want my lawyer."

"I had a feeling you might say that. Thing is, we don't have time for lawyers."

"So, what? You're gonna beat me up?" Glancing back and forth between Civins and me, he snorted, then looked off toward a corner of the room. "I'm not scared of you."

"You should be scared of my friend here," I said, nodding at Civins again. "But you are scared of Petén, right?"

Roosevelt's eyes jerked back in my direction.

"I get it. Most sane people are. But you know what's even scarier than Petén? The new thermite jockstrap I gave you while you were unconscious."

Roosevelt's eyelids peeled back enough, I could see white all around the irises, even in the dim light. He struggled to look down to his belly, but couldn't, given the angle of the chair.

I leaned in closer, pressing the box against his crotch, making sure the metal edges dug into his thighs. "Feel that? That's right, it's the cute little router box you had on top of the computer. Lucky I figured it out in time."

The muscles in Roosevelt's face had started twitching.

"I gotta admit, you had me for a second. When I first saw it, I thought it might be some kind of bomb. But then I realized, even a bomb might leave the disk drives readable. You couldn't risk that."

Roosevelt's Adam's apple bobbed.

"You needed to make sure the drives would be nothing but slag, and I've seen the Second Guerrillas use thermite before." A metallic mix, thermite shoots up to twenty-five hundred degrees once you get it burning: hot enough to slice through the metal walls at Otra and more than enough to melt right through the cover on the desktop. "So you mounted the thermite on top of the computer and figured if you ever saw someone on your little security camera, you'd ignite it with the remote trigger.

"Of course, the only reason to do that is if the computer has all your illegal transactions on it, right? How many pills went to whom. How much money you've been kicking back to the Second Guerrillas. You couldn't risk anyone getting a look at that, right, Doc?"

Although Roosevelt tried to stay defiant, his expression said I was correct.

"You know," I said, "I've seen some Internet videos of thermite. It burns so white-hot, it's almost too bright for the camera."

With that, I pressed myself back up straight, using the router box for leverage.

Roosevelt struggled against the tape again, then strained to see down past his stomach. His face looked like he'd dunked it in a bucket of ice water.

"Pretty easy to ignite, too. A regular old cigarette lighter ought to light the magnesium strips you've got in there, and they'll set off the rest." I held up a lighter I'd found out in a receptionist's desk and started flicking it on and off. As I did, Civins retreated a step.

Now panting, Roosevelt said, "I don't know anything about them taking the girl!"

"Oh, I know that," I said. "But you do know lots of other things that could be helpful. Let's start simple. What kind of pills were you selling Max?"

Roosevelt's eyes were pointed away from me.

I flicked on the lighter and moved forward. "If we can't even get through that question . . ."

"All right, all right. Adderall and Oxycontin."

"Why those?"

"They're what the kids like. Adderall's an upper—speed, basically. Makes you feel good. Helps you focus. Then the Oxy's for relaxing. Taking the pain away."

In the corner of my eye, I could see Civins's face harden. If I'd feared he might betray me, I needn't have worried—not now that Roosevelt was spilling his guts.

"That shit you gave Max is super addictive," Civins said.

Roosevelt snorted. "Of course it is—that's the goddamn point." After a pause, he shook his head. "I could have made a lot of money off a rich bitch like her."

"You didn't?" I asked.

"Had to give them to her for free. That's what they wanted."

"Who's 'they'?"

"The—uh—the folks you mentioned." Roosevelt's eyes were wandering all over the room now to avoid my face.

"The Second Guerrillas."

He nodded once.

"How'd you get in with them?"

"What's it matter?"

"It doesn't, really," I said. "I'm just curious. This seems like a nice little practice you've got here—why risk it all for people like them?"

Roosevelt's head flopped back against the chair. "It's stupid. I'd been married a long time to the same woman. I wanted to try something different. Feel that thrill of the chase again. But guys my age, we don't exactly go cruising the bars on Sixth Street. So I called one of those agencies in the phone book. Got set up with a beautiful woman, took her to a nice dinner, then to a hotel. I didn't realize they'd rigged the whole place with cameras."

"They blackmailed you."

He looked away for a moment. "Yep. They offered me this plan. Seemed simple enough."

"How do you get the extra pills? If you're not faking patients . . ."

"That was the angle they came up with," he said. "I don't really do anything different—just prescribe what I'd normally prescribe. Adderall for ADHD, Oxy for pain. But I volunteer to fill the prescriptions. Saves them or their parents the run to the pharmacy, plus I get to walk them through the meds myself. Parents like that. It's totally legal—none of the pharmacies question it. But I prescribe more than I instruct them to take, and I skim the rest."

"Why Max?" Civins asked. "Why'd they ask you to get her hooked?"

Roosevelt shook his head. "I don't know. Keep her under control, I guess." He shook his shoulders, trying to break free again. "I've answered your questions—now get that thermite off me!"

"We're not done yet," I said. "Where can I find them, the Second Guerrillas?"

"You really don't want to do that."

"Assume I do."

"I don't know. I just work for—"

"Baloney." I got down in his face again, holding the lighter flame right near his eye. "You have to have seen some place, some kind of local headquarters, something. You tell me where it is, and everything about it, or I swear to Christ I'll light this thing and let it melt you." I leaned on the router box again, putting as much weight on it as I could.

All of Roosevelt's muscles clenched, and his eyes squeezed tightly shut. "Okay. Okay. There's a ranch, east of town. They had me out there a couple of times."

"Great," I said. "Tell me all about it."

Once Roosevelt had told me everything he could, he said, "Now what?"

I was pulling the burner from my pocket as he asked the question. "Now, I have a little planning to do before I go see your friend Petén."

"What about the thermite? Get it off me!" Sweat had soaked through the neck of Roosevelt's shirt, while his face had gone pale as a sheet.

"Don't worry," I said, picking up the router. "It's not going to hurt you."

"How do you know? That stuff's volatile."

"Because," I said, popping the bottom panel open, "I took the thermite out."

CHAPTER 23

Tuesday, July 21

Even though Civins offered to handle the cops as they processed Roosevelt, by the time I dropped them off, got my own plan straight, and left Lavorgna a voice mail about it, it was approaching five in the morning. Max had been gone almost twelve hours. No word from Drew. No contact from the Second Guerrillas. Part of me wondered what they were waiting for, but mostly I hoped I could beat them to whatever it was.

The eastern sky had begun to brighten, a thin stripe of robin's-egg blue against the remaining navy of nighttime. After weaving my way through downtown, I pointed the sedan toward the burgeoning light.

The address Roosevelt had given me sat sixty-eight miles outside the city, according to the map on the burner's GPS. Civilization fell away rapidly, replaced by the same kind of flat prairie I'd encountered on the drive from Dallas. No hills out here, only fields of grass and clusters of trees.

Cruising along the narrow roads, I passed signs marking little towns with colorful names like McDade and Dime Box, but they proved to be little more than small breaks in otherwise endless stretches of barbed-wire ranch fencing. Buildings grew fewer and farther between; I saw far more cows than cars.

As the miles flew by, I tried to focus on the details Roosevelt had provided about the Guerrillas and their headquarters, but it was no use.

I couldn't shift my mind off Max. She'd been so weak before the explosion. Had she suffered any injuries? Would the Guerrillas be taking care of her? She was their leverage against Drew, so presumably they would if they could. The setup at Roosevelt's confirmed they knew technology . . . would they have a doctor on hand?

Answerless questions like these had me squeezing the wheel and shifting in my seat nearly the entire ride. Forty-five minutes after leaving the city, though, the burner said I was getting close.

Although the sun still hadn't hit the horizon yet, the entire sky had brightened to a deep royal blue. A part of me wanted to press the pedal to the floor, but I reminded myself of the plan and backed off the gas: I'd need to time this exactly right.

Five minutes later, coming around a slight bend, I saw it, ahead on the left. The Second Guerrillas' compound was unmistakable once you knew what you were looking for.

The ranch fencing that had continued for miles stopped abruptly, replaced by a stone wall ringing a large tract of land. Constructed from large blocks of sun-bleached stone cemented together, the wall looked almost decorative, not unlike the walls in Max's ritzy neighborhood. But little details confirmed this wall was far more functional. It stood taller than any person. Clusters of dark metal spikes adorned the top of the wall, and as I drew closer, I could see they were razor sharp. Security cameras were mounted at various intervals, peering down to cover wide swaths of the ground between the wall and road.

I needed nearly two more minutes to reach the wall's midpoint, where metal gates blocked the only apparent entrance to the compound. I couldn't get too much of a glimpse of what lay behind their silver bars, but I did spot several guards inside.

Continuing onward, I drove as far as I figured I needed to so no one at the gate could see the car anymore. Then I pulled to the shoulder. Unsure whether any cameras could see me, I steered as far off the road as possible, parking behind a tree.

Once the engine was silent, I inhaled deeply several times, trying to overcome the shallow breaths I'd been taking. Not knowing exactly when—it had to be *when*, right?—I would return, I checked to ensure the shotgun and breaching ammo were hidden beneath the rear seat. Then, despite a sharp pang in my chest, I wedged the Sig and its magazines into the glove compartment and locked it.

Before leaving the sedan, I yanked out my earpiece and tucked it down into the pocket holding the audio player. Then I made sure I had the burner. Those two had to come with me, and they'd need to be enough.

I checked the time: 5:50 a.m.

As I started back toward the gate on foot, I stuck to my side of the road, trudging through the grass, kicking up dust. When I finally drew parallel with the gate several minutes later, I raised my good arm and crossed the road. Several men appeared just inside the gates, which were bound together by a heavy chain. All the men were muscular, with tattooed faces. Two leveled M16 barrels at my chest from their positions inside.

"Don't shoot," I called before I'd even crossed the double yellow line. "I'm not armed." Placing my fingers on top of my head, I took slow, deliberate steps the rest of the way across the road. When I'd drawn within a few feet of the bars, I said, "I need to see Petén. Roosevelt, the doctor, sent me with a message."

One of the guards produced a walkie-talkie, then disappeared behind the wall. He returned several seconds later. "Who are you?"

"I told you, I need to see—"

"Petén doesn't see anyone. What's your name?"

The gunmen on either side of the talker looked fidgety. "My name is Walker."

"What's Roosevelt's message, Walker?"

"I can't tell you. Only Petén."

"Then we'll just shoot you now and be done with it," the walkie-talkie man said, raising his own weapon and staring down the sights at me.

Ignoring the pounding in my chest, I shrugged. "If you want. But then you can explain to Petén why Roosevelt's gone. And why all the money from Roosevelt's drugs has disappeared with him."

He hesitated.

"Look," I said, arms wide, hands open, "I'm unarmed. Frisk me, do whatever you need to. But I need to talk to Petén."

The standoff lasted another full minute, the gunmen aiming at me while I tried to stay as cool as I could.

The talker dropped his weapon and let it hang at his side. He spoke to the others in the now-familiar pops and clicks, then stepped to the chain. After unlocking it, he stepped out with me while the others covered him.

He patted me down thoroughly, confiscating the burner and audio player from my pockets. Then, circling around me again, he asked, "What's wrong with your arm?"

"I dislocated my shoulder."

"Can you move it?"

Although he was hidden behind me now, I didn't dare turn and look. "A little."

"Good." Yanking the strap up and over my head, he dragged the sling all the way off. Then he reached around and grabbed my left elbow, twisting the arm back behind me.

The sudden movement lit my shoulder on fire. I tried not to wince too noticeably, gritting my teeth against the pain.

He pulled my good arm back to join the bad one, then clicked handcuffs down onto my wrists so hard they bit into the skin. I started to wonder what would come next, but before I could finish the thought, something hard struck the back of my head, and the whole world flashed white.

CHAPTER 24

I felt the pain first.

A sharp, stabbing feeling at the base of my skull. The burning in my shoulder. My arms aching from being twisted behind me.

My eyelids parted slowly, uncertainly. The soft, natural light was gone, replaced by harsh, artificial fluorescents that rendered everything bright and blurry. Cool air massaged the skin on my arms, but that wasn't all—something cold pressed against my cheek. Something smooth. Gradually it came into focus: a linoleum floor.

I blinked rapidly and moved to sit up to get my bearings. As I did, something threw off my balance. I heard it before recognizing it: a low-toned clanking noise coming from the several feet of thick chain that linked my cuffs to a metal post.

Struggling to my feet, I followed the post upward with my eyes to find it belonged to the heavy frame of an old-fashioned bed. Tucked beneath coarse-looking blankets, looking pale but otherwise intact, was Max. Her hands, too, were cuffed, to the sides of the bed frame rather than each other, while an IV bag hung above one arm, dripping clear liquid into her. A gray-haired woman stood over her, dabbing at her forehead with a cloth.

I dropped to my knees at the side of her mattress. "Max?"

Her head lolled over to my side of the bed, blonde hair strewn across her face, eyes landing on me almost by accident. They lacked any sparkle, any energy. Her facial muscles were totally limp, her expression dull. "Seth," was all she said.

I looked up at the woman tending to her. "Was she hurt in the explosion? Will she be all right?"

Before she could respond, an accented voice sounded behind me. "Your friend requires several more days of rest and fluids before the medications will be completely eliminated from her system."

As I turned to find the voice's owner, the gray-haired woman stepped away from the bed and said something in Spanish.

A curt answer came from a dark-skinned woman standing just inside the lone doorway at the far end of the room. Dressed in an egg-plant-colored blouse over clingy khaki pants, her black hair descended in ringlets that bounced as she started toward us.

The older woman spoke again, more heatedly this time.

But the other woman was having none of it. She snapped again in Spanish, giving the older woman a glare that sent her scurrying from the room with only a quick glance back at Max in the bed.

As the younger woman approached Max and me, I realized I hadn't fully gauged our surroundings. We were at one end of a long, narrow room that seemed to be some sort of makeshift building, with flimsy-looking walls supporting a corrugated-metal roof. The linoleum was a black-and-white checkerboard pattern that could have come from any one of the elementary schools I'd attended. Each of the walls bore windows, but their glass was frosted, letting in light but no scenery. They didn't look like they opened, either, although one on each side had been removed in favor of air-conditioning units that contributed a droning hum to the space.

While Max's bed had been pushed lengthwise against the wall behind me, three other matching mattresses extended from the wall on my left. All empty. Between them stood chairs and various pieces of medical equipment—monitors, other stuff I didn't exactly recognize. The opposite wall was lined with modular shelves containing all types of neatly organized supplies: canned goods, chemicals, automotive parts, and large car batteries.

The burner phone and my audio player sat next to each other on the farthest bed.

That was fortunate.

When the younger woman stopped in front of the shelves several feet away, I said, "I'm guessing that was Marta."

"*Sí.* Like you, she cares very much about the girl."

"So who are you?"

"You should know. You asked to see me." Despite the way she had dismissed the old woman, her voice now sounded even and calm. Almost amused.

"I asked to see Petén."

"And that is what they call me."

"You're Petén? You're the one behind all this?"

"*Sí.*" Her mouth turned down into a scowl. "And you are Seth Walker, the man who keeps turning my men's wives into widows."

The comment made my stomach twist. "I'm sorry," I said. "About your men. But I didn't kill anyone who didn't try to kill me first."

One of her eyebrows arched sharply, etching deep lines in her forehead. "We are engaged in a war, Señor Walker. My men understand the stakes, as do I. But that does not mean I do not take their losses personally."

I lowered my eyes and nodded.

"I have been told you are carrying a message for me from Roosevelt, the doctor?"

"That's right."

A gold-faced watch hung at her wrist, and I stole a glance at it, trying to read the time upside down: nearly six thirty, meaning I'd only been out for a few minutes.

"What is the message?"

"The message is for Petén. I'm only telling him."

The woman shifted her weight from one foot to the other. "And why do you assume Petén must be a man?"

"Because that's how the people who know about Petén referred to him."

She snorted through her broad, prominent nose. "And what, exactly, did these 'experts' know about Petén? Did they tell you what he looked like?"

"No."

"What, then?"

"That he gets his name from a certain region of Guatemala."

"That much is true. I am from Flores. Anything else?"

"They didn't know exactly. Some people think he was a soldier, some don't." After a beat, I added, "But everyone knows Petén is in charge and has turned the Second Guerrillas into a force to be reckoned with."

The woman smiled, and I saw that her mouth was painted with a shade of lipstick so subtle you could barely detect it. "Very nice try, Señor Walker. Flattery will get you almost anywhere." She moved her head, shimmying her hair so it hung behind her. "What else do the police have to say about me?"

"That you—or whoever Petén is—can be brutal."

The smile changed, and she took a half step forward, leaning down toward me. "Do you need me to be brutal to prove my identity?"

"No," I said. "But something would be nice."

"Fine." Straightening, she stalked back to the door and pounded a fist on it. "Cirilio!"

Metallic clunking noises sounded, and the door opened. A burly soldier stepped sideways through it, then closed it behind him. Dressed in black fatigues, he bore the same kind of facial tattoos as the Second Guerrillas I'd seen before.

"Cirilio?" she said again. Although he towered over her, the woman's voice was firm, authoritative. She didn't look at him; she stared directly at me.

"*Sí.*" He kept his eyes on the ground as he addressed her.

"*¿Cómo te llamas?*"

"Petén."

"*Gracias. Saca tu cuchillo.*"

With his right hand, the soldier reached into his belt and withdrew a large knife, straight edged on one side, serrated on the other.

"*Córtate en el brazo.*"

Without hesitating, the soldier extended his left arm, jabbed the tip of the knife into the muscle, up by the elbow, and started drawing it down toward his wrist.

The woman continued glaring at me for another moment, before finally turning back to the soldier. Putting her hands gently on his shoulder and arm, she changed tones altogether, saying some quiet words to him I couldn't make out.

She led the man, bleeding, to the space between two of the beds. There, she used some supplies from a drawer to clean and field-dress the wound until he began flexing it and nodding. Then she said some final words, and he stalked back outside, the door clunking closed behind him.

Petén turned back to me and smiled. "Satisfied?"

"Yes," I said.

"Good. I expect such skepticism when dealing with the cartels, but I am always surprised when I encounter it in America. It happens more than you would think."

She seized two metal chairs from between the beds and carried them effortlessly to our end of the room. Stopping in front of the shelves again, she slid one chair across the linoleum toward me with a kick of her foot, then sat in the other herself, crossing her legs and folding her arms.

"Now, what is this message you carry from Roosevelt?" she asked.

I sat in the chair as best I could, given the way my hands remained chained. "That he really doesn't want to talk to the cops."

Petén blinked at me. "I am not certain I understand."

"I have him stashed. Someplace safe. If I walk out of here with her"—I jerked my head in Max's direction—"in the next thirty minutes, he goes free, and you can do whatever you want with him. But if I don't walk out of here, or if she isn't with me, then Roosevelt ends up with the FBI." After a moment, I added, "And you know him, he'll end up telling them everything."

She shifted her weight back in the chair. Staring at me, she remained silent for several moments before speaking again. "You place me in a difficult position, having to choose between the girl and Roosevelt."

Still trying to get comfortable with my arms pinned behind me, I smiled. "That was kind of the idea, yeah."

"I can appreciate the cleverness of your plan, just as I can appreciate the skill you demonstrated against my men."

I felt another pinch in my gut.

"The problem is, I think you have underestimated the girl's value to our organization."

"Surely Roosevelt is worth more to you in the long run . . ."

Petén pursed her lips in a disapproving way. "It is much easier to find someone like the doctor than someone like her."

"With respect, that's not the point," I said. "The doctor knows too much. He told me about you, about this place. He can give all that up to the police."

"You would be mistaken to assume that either of those things is irreplaceable. This facility is convenient. But we have others. And I am just one woman in an army, Señor Walker. If something happens to me, the fight will continue."

"But you're not just a soldier. You're their leader. And you're a businesswoman."

She gave the slightest nod.

"So then you have to see, Roosevelt can earn the money Drew owes you in what, a couple of weeks, months?" My eyes flicked downward to Petén's arm: the minute hand on her watch had crept past the eight, almost to the nine. "Isn't that kind of ongoing revenue worth a lot more to you than just a single debt?"

"*Sí*, we require resources. As they say, bullets win wars, so someone must buy the bullets." Her eyes narrowed. "But that is exactly why we went into business with Señor Drew in the first place."

"So you're just going to blackmail him over and over again? He doesn't—Max doesn't have that kind of money—"

"I think you misunderstand our arrangement."

"Drew told me about the money you loaned him. And about the . . . interest you're charging on the debt. I know you view her as the collateral to collect what you're owed. But—"

Petén's gaze had drifted away from me gradually, and now she looked down, shaking her head and smiling.

"What?"

"Drew has misled you. Not that I am completely surprised." Her eyes locked on mine. "We never loaned Drew money. Every dollar my organization takes in, we require for the battles we wage against those who oppress us. I would not risk what little we have by giving it to someone like him."

"Didn't Garcia introduce you?"

"The record producer? No." She smiled slightly. "Contrary to what some in your country may think, not everyone who speaks Spanish is related. Drew approached us. We did not approach him."

"What was he proposing?"

"He worried that others were turning her against him. That she"— Petén nodded toward Max's bed—"would leave him. So we assisted him, in exchange for a percentage of her earnings."

"Assisted?"

"We removed the threat."

"Who was this . . . threat?"

"A man."

"Who?"

Petén shrugged. "He was merely a name Drew provided. That is all I know."

"Okay, so Drew gave you a cut of her earnings to do some dirty work for him. That still doesn't explain why you'd put her on the drugs. You were risking your own investment—"

Petén's mouth opened for a moment before she spoke. "You believe the drugs were *my* idea?"

"Of course," I said. "Roosevelt works for you."

"*Sí*, but I could not have made that decision alone."

Still pounding from the blow outside, my head tried to make sense of what she was saying. There was only one person who could have made the decision along with her. "You're saying Drew agreed to put Max on drugs."

"Not just agreed," Petén said. "It was his idea."

"Wait, what?" I blinked several times, then turned in my chair to glance at Max. Her face remained expressionless.

"*Sí*. He believed the medications would render her more compliant. He requested the drugs, and we connected them with Roosevelt. After instructing Roosevelt to keep the drugs within certain bounds, of course. I am familiar with their side effects from my life before all of this."

As Petén gestured around us with her hand, my eyes didn't follow. I was remembering Drew's expression, his tone of voice, when we'd talked the previous night. I had believed him. Civins had contradicted him, but still—the idea that Drew had personally requested the drugs, for his own daughter?

"You care about the girl," Petén said. "That is obvious. So you should understand, her circumstances will improve markedly now that we are fully in command of the situation."

"How's that?"

"Has she not told you? The conditions her father maintains?"

"Not much."

"Drew thinks we know little of what goes on, but he discounts our intelligence." The inflection she placed on the final word was subtle, but there was definitely a double entendre there. "Drew works the girl constantly. Once we are fully in charge, however"—Petén shook her head—"there will be no more need for this. She is to be the symbol of our movement."

Although Petén's eyes shone with enthusiasm, I wasn't so sure—who was going to wage a war for Max Magic? "How do you figure?"

"Are you familiar with the *narcocorridos*?"

I shook my head.

"*Corridos* are folk songs about the lives of the people. A form of oral history that has existed for centuries. Only now, like so many things, the cartels have taken the *corridos* and made them their own. *Narcocorridos*. Songs glorifying the lives of the drug traffickers."

"So what does that have to do with Max?"

"Do you not see? The girl is young and beautiful. Her voice, like an angel's. She will be the perfect anti-*narcocorridista*: an innocent face singing the praises of the true heroes of our movement, so that the people understand what we are fighting for."

"And, what, you'll just force her to do it? At gunpoint or something?"

Petén shook her head, and a smile crept across her face. "There will be no need. Once we free her from her addiction and liberate her from her father, I think she will gladly volunteer."

"But even if she's willing, Drew won't exactly be pleased with the idea of you taking her away from him," I said.

She shrugged. "Drew is powerless. He continues to live only because I allow it. And, in any event, I do not concern myself with the feelings of those who would have their own children murdered. Señor Drew and I are quite different in that regard."

I felt like I'd been hit in the head again. "What did you just say?"

"Did you not know that, either?" Petén sighed. "After we initially provided the medications to her through Roosevelt, Max decided on her own to reject them."

"Charlie Garcia helped get her clean."

"*Sí*. When that happened, Drew returned to us, worried he was losing control. He wished to renegotiate our original agreement. His new request was that we eliminate her." Petén's face grew serious as she glanced over my shoulder at Max. "But I have seen too many children die. I will not kill them myself."

Petén waited for my reaction, but I was still trying to absorb what she'd just said: Drew wanted to have Max *killed*?

Why?

Petén had mentioned *control* several times—could it really be that simple? If Drew couldn't control Max, he wouldn't let anyone else?

I looked back over my shoulder, and what I saw disturbed me even more than Petén's words.

The look on Max's face wasn't shock. Or dismay.

Not even disappointment.

Although tears had begun trickling from her eyes, her face hadn't changed expression. She remained calm and relaxed, shackled hands open next to her lap. There were no signs of anger or sadness.

Merely resignation.

I hated myself in that moment. Max had bad-mouthed Drew, but I'd never followed up. I hadn't pressed her, or him, for better answers. About anything. I'd just happily wallowed in my own assumptions— about both of them.

Some investigator.

All this time, I thought I'd been saving Max, and here I'd actually been fighting to return her to a life of drug-addled service to a man who despised her enough to use her up and throw her away.

As I stared at her pale cheeks, blonde hair scattered across them, all I could think was that she deserved better.

So much better.

But despite wanting to plan what I would do to Drew when we got out of here—*if* we got out of here—a glance back at Petén's watch showed that it wasn't quite 6:50 a.m. I found her still staring at me. "You don't have the . . ." I circled my face with my index finger.

She raised an eyebrow. "Tattoos? No. In my culture, men do that as a sign of their bond and commitment to the family. A woman's commitment"—she took a long breath—"is understood."

I let the silence linger as long as I could. But then, before she could speak again, I asked, "Now what? It doesn't sound like you're taking my deal for Roosevelt."

"I am afraid I cannot."

"So, you're just going to kill me?"

"I could," she said. "And, if I am forced to, I will. There is a long line of people within my organization who would readily volunteer, including all the wives of the men you have slain. Women make better torturers than men, believe me.

"But if we kill you," she continued, "then we lose Roosevelt for certain. As you say, I am a businesswoman. I prefer to win." She brushed her hands backward across her shoulders, sweeping her hair behind her. "Roosevelt has his problems, but he represents a steady stream of income we require. Therefore, the only way we get everything we want is if I convince you to return Roosevelt without taking the girl in exchange."

"That's your proposal? I return Roosevelt and leave Max with you?"

"*Sí.*"

"What's in it for me?"

236

"Your life. Knowing the girl will be safe."

"How can I possibly trust that Max will be safe with you?"

"I have told you, I do not harm children." Petén shrugged. "But even if you choose to ignore my words, we have given you no indication we would harm her. We have cared for her. And there are other signs of my good faith. I could have killed you outright, but I did not. I suspected that you did not know the entire situation with Drew, so I have shared those details with you."

"Now you're putting *me* in a difficult position." Although I cracked a slight smile when repeating her line, Petén's expression didn't change. "In this scenario you're envisioning, I do what? Just walk away?"

She nodded. "Walk away."

After stealing one last glance at her watch, I inhaled deeply through my nose. "That's my problem," I said. "I've never been very good at that."

I expected her face to grow angry or disappointed at that moment, something. But no emotion registered. Instead, in a flat tone, Petén said, "Fine. Have it your way."

Petén stood, her chair squeaking against the linoleum as it slid behind her. From behind her back, she drew a pistol. A Glock, exactly like Shen's.

She pointed it directly at my face.

CHAPTER 25

"Your last chance, Señor Walker," Petén said, cocking the hammer. "Just walk away."

I took a deep breath and slumped my shoulders, as if resigning myself to concede. But before I could exhale, a loud explosion erupted outside.

Finally.

When Petén's head turned, that was all the break I needed.

I sprang out of the chair toward Max, my only instinct to cover her, but I couldn't resist peeking back at Petén. Although her expression had changed only slightly—small furrowing of her brow, visible tension in her jaw—the difference in emotion was stark.

She was angry now.

I looked back to Max's bed, only a couple of steps away.

And that's when I realized, I had to turn around.

At this range, the .40 caliber slugs in Petén's Glock would pass through me like I was a loaf of bread. Every shot at me would be a shot at Max, and that magazine held fifteen rounds.

Planting my left foot, I spun as best I could with my hands cuffed behind me and lunged in the opposite direction, aiming for the nearest empty bed. If I could slide beneath it, maybe the metal frame would offer some sort of protection once Petén pulled the trigger.

I was just starting to consider how to slide, trying to remember what my Little League coaches used to say, when my arms and torso suddenly yanked me backward.

It felt like a firecracker had gone off in my left shoulder. I'd reached the end of my chain and landed squarely on my ass.

My eyes returned to Petén, her face a mask of grim determination as she trained the Glock on me.

I shut my eyes until I heard shots thundering even louder than I'd expected.

But when no impact came, I reopened them to find Petén doubled over and writhing.

Sunlight forced its way through new holes in the wall behind her, and at first I assumed she'd been hit by bullets.

Until she straightened up. Although there was no blood, something had happened to her skin. Like it had liquefied and begun spilling off her.

As Petén dashed for the door, I checked the shelves lining the wall. Sure enough, several car batteries and containers had been shattered by gunfire, splashing her with some mix of sulfuric acid and other chemicals.

Across the room, Petén pounded on the door, each effort weaker than the last, until it popped open with a metallic thunk. When she disappeared through it, I sighed with relief.

Until the big guy—the one Petén had called Cirilio—appeared.

He stepped into the room and started in my direction. Stopping a few paces from me, an ugly, angry look spread across his face as he tucked his pistol away. He crossed the remaining distance between us, seized my shirt in one hand, and hauled me up to my feet as if I weighed nothing.

Once I was upright, his face twisted into a perverse smile. I had only a split second to wonder why before I caught a glimpse of his fist looping through the air.

When it connected with my bad shoulder, I thought he might have knocked the arm clean off: I couldn't feel it anymore. Only the pain, which was so intense it turned everything white. Although my legs had gone limp, Cirilio still supported me. Two hard uppercuts to my stomach lifted my feet off the ground and left me hacking and sputtering for breath.

Finally, he tossed me back against the wall. I barely noticed the impact as I crumpled to a heap at the base of it. My vision had cleared just enough to see Cirilio racking the slide of his pistol to chamber the round that would finish me off.

I'd lucked out getting past Petén, but this would be it.

That's when a four-shot burst rang out. It spun Cirilio around and dropped him to the floor. His tattooed face ended up just inches from mine, and I watched as the last bit of life slipped away from his dark eyes.

A shadow moved over me at that moment. I looked up to find a familiar face blocking the light: Salvador Peña, Grayson's gang-unit colleague from Dallas.

"You're . . . ," I sputtered, "*late.*"

Peña smirked. "C'mon, man. We were watching you the whole time from the drone. Looked like you had 'em right where you wanted 'em."

CHAPTER 26

The next few minutes went by in a blur.

Peña hadn't come alone. A group of what looked like soldiers filed in behind him, and soon Max and I were being carried out.

Although I hadn't gotten to see the interior of the Second Guerrillas' compound on the way in, as we were leaving, it looked like a war zone. Explosions and gunfire echoed and flashed all around; the sky overhead was clouded with smoke.

The soldiers ferried us through a giant hole that had been blown through the compound wall, out to a neighboring field where several helicopters were waiting. Although I didn't realize it immediately, they loaded Max and me into different copters. I'd have complained if I'd known. Or had the ability.

Though uncuffed now, I lay on my good side, vision cloudy, electric crackles of pain spreading from my injured shoulder down into my chest every time I breathed or moved.

One face in particular appeared in front of me. A man in a helmet. Just inches away, I tried to focus on his features: the few, distinct white hairs in his otherwise dark mustache, the weary rings around his eyes. His mouth was moving. Talking, or asking questions, I couldn't tell. The pain had fogged up my brain almost as much as my eyes.

Soon I could feel him doing something to my arm. Moving it around somehow.

He must have known the same trick Enjeti used that night back in Silver Lake, because with no warning at all, almost all the pain disappeared in a flash.

It felt like emerging from a pool after nearly running out of air: suddenly I could breathe again. All my senses came flooding back.

The deafening hum of the rotors.

My tongue, swollen and seemingly grafted to the roof of my mouth, which was bone-dry.

My skin, slick with sweat, from both the ordeal and the intense heat inside the aircraft.

I barely had time to process it all before the helicopter jolted.

I shifted upright, my immediate thought being that we were under attack. But a quick glance around showed the soldiers rising and filing to the chopper's hatch to disembark.

We'd landed.

Somewhere.

Peña appeared next to me, helped me to my feet, and led me off the copter. We were standing on some rooftop. With the sun up now, heat rippled off the tar, and the downdraft from the rotors felt like the blast from a convection oven.

"Where are we?" I tried to yell, but my voice croaked after the first word.

"Hospital," Peña shouted back. He pressed something smooth and metallic into my hands, and I looked down to find the burner and my audio player.

Despite the din, I immediately plugged the earpiece in; just feeling the hard plastic in my ear was a relief. As I tried to shove the player and phone into my pockets, Peña ushered me toward a set of double doors.

Inside, cool, antiseptic air seemed to suck the heat off my scalp, and my hearing began to return. Before I could say anything more, Peña started walking. Although I was exhausted, I had no choice but to follow him down the pastel-colored hallways.

"Where are you going?"

Peña turned but kept moving. "Debriefing. Don't worry, it'll only take a couple of minutes. Then the medics can finish with your shoulder."

"There's no time for any of that. I've got to arrest Max's dad. And where *is* she? I need to talk to her."

"Her chopper landed before ours—I'm sure she's getting checked out. But don't worry about Drew. My guys have been on him at the house, just like you asked. I'll call out there and have them pick him up."

"No," I said. "I want to do it myself. After I talk to Max." Given everything she'd been through, everything she'd heard from Petén, I thought she deserved that much.

Peña stopped. "Look, the docs ain't gonna let you see Max before they examine her, and that's gonna take a few. Drew isn't getting away, not from my guys. And the task force needs to hear what you heard and saw out there with the Second Guerrillas. Besides, we're here."

He opened the door next to us without knocking. I followed him into a large, rectangular conference room. One long wall supported a series of portraits—famous doctors, I guessed, since all were wearing white coats—while the opposite wall was all glass, overlooking a green, grass-covered hillside. All but two of the dozen chairs around the oval table were taken by serious-looking men. But, despite the collection of shoulder holsters and crew cuts, the room seemed thick with joy as they laughed and joked with one another.

Peña led us to the empty seats. As I sat, I was surprised to find I recognized the man sitting next to me.

Franklin, from JFK.

He wore a broad smile. "Quite a haul you handed us, Walker."

Before I could ask what he meant, the man at the head of the table cleared his throat and leaned forward. "Thanks, everyone, for coming," he said. "I know we all have work to get back to, but I thought it would be worth taking a moment to discuss what we accomplished today.

"For the benefit of our distinguished guest"—the man paused and, to my surprise, raised a large, gnarled hand in my direction—"I'm Russell Ainsworth, DEA, and head of this little band of merry men." He flashed a quick smile, teeth gleaming against his dark skin. "We are the TTFD, which most people think means 'Texas Task Force—Drugs,' but those of us in here know really means 'Talk, Talk for Days.'"

The joke drew snickers from around the table. Just from his looks—thick ropes of muscle protruding from his collar, his face all lean, sharp features—Ainsworth appeared to be the furthest thing from a paper pusher, a man whose hands did a lot more than typing.

"Today, thanks to a bit of fortuitous timing"—he nodded at me again—"months of investigation and police work culminated in a raid against the Second Guerrilla Army."

I listened as Ainsworth briefly detailed the operation. Apparently, plans to strike the Guerrillas had been in the works for weeks—my call to Peña from Roosevelt's office had given them an excuse and some of the final details they'd been looking for. They hadn't been counting on having to deal with civilian hostages like Max, though, so my volunteering to go in first had provided them with a view inside.

Ainsworth went around the table, crediting and complimenting the work of at least five different agencies. Between that, the soldiers, helicopters, even a drone with infrared, I suddenly realized what a large-scale operation this was.

Leaning over to Franklin, I started to whisper, "So you were—"

He nodded. "Yep. We'd connected Drew to the Second Guerrillas and were using him as an angle to gather intel."

"The commercial flight . . . that was to draw them out?"

"Sorry I couldn't warn you."

"You ever find the leak?"

"Turns out, it was a cleaning woman in the New York Field Office. She was reading memos people dropped in the shred bin."

Ainsworth continued, cataloging the number of Second Guerrilla soldiers they'd captured, the stockpiles they'd commandeered. With each passing statistic, the hoots from various people and knocks on the tabletop grew louder and more boisterous.

"Where's Petén?" I asked.

Ainsworth, who'd been flashing his smile around the table, turned to me. "What?"

"Petén. Did you capture her? Or kill her?"

"Petén's a *her*?" someone interjected from the side.

"Yeah," I said. "I was hoping you were gonna tell me you've got her locked away."

Ainsworth shot a serious look at two men across the table, who immediately rose and ran out the door. Then he turned back to me. "Why don't you tell us exactly what happened to you and the girl."

I recounted the entire story from the beginning. Just as I was describing how Petén had been injured, the two men returned. Ainsworth's eyes darted in their direction, only to find them shaking their heads.

"So, what? She escaped?" I asked.

When no one answered, I rose from my chair. "I've got to go find Max." Peña started after me.

"She's on the sixth floor," Ainsworth said. "We can call down—"

"Tell them I'll be there in a second." I was almost out the door already.

"Don't worry," Franklin said, "we've got guards stationed outside her room—"

I glanced back at him. "Because that's helped so much in the past."

CHAPTER 27

When we hit the hallway, Peña took the lead, winding us through several corridors to a door marked "Stairs."

"She's gonna be fine," he said once we were inside, his voice echoing off the cinder-block walls. Nevertheless, Peña started moving faster, bouncing down two steps at a time. "Petén's gonna care more about getting the hell away . . ."

Nearly tripping trying to copy his trick, I decided to just move my feet double time. "I hope you're right."

The sixth-floor stairwell door clattered against the wall as Peña burst through it, and I dashed behind him before it could slam closed. Three more quick turns and we reached a room with two bulky guards standing outside.

They turned and saw us coming. Like those upstairs, these two had serious faces, but younger. So clean-shaven they might not show stubble for three days. Although I knew it wasn't possible, when I looked at them, all I could see were members of the LAX detail.

"Has anyone tried—"

But before I could even finish the question, the guard on the left answered, "Nobody. Only ones in and out have been the medical team."

Reaching them now, I stared directly into the eyes of the one who'd talked. "Listen, the head of the enemy is a woman, okay? Dark hair, hurt a little bit. Don't assume everyone in scrubs or a mask is a doctor or nurse. You got me?"

He gave me a confident nod.

"Good." Before I could decide whether I needed to worry about who might've gotten past them already, I got a glimpse through the window of Max in her bed. Without saying another word, I headed inside.

She lay in one of those adjustable hospital beds, the upper half elevated so she could sit up or watch television.

Instead, she was curled on her side. Crying.

I dashed to the bed and wrapped my good arm around her shoulders. "Thank God," I said.

Opening her eyes, she recognized me and nearly burst off the mattress, throwing her arms around my neck.

"Sh." I rubbed her back gently. "It's all right."

Still clutching herself to me, her breathing grew heavier, and she started shaking. "I tried—I asked—to see you—but they wouldn't—"

"It's okay," I said, keeping my voice as even as I could. "I'm here now. I just had a quick meeting with the police who rescued us."

Max pulled away slightly, until our faces were inches apart. Lines of fatigue were etched all over her skin; her hair was a knotted jumble. Her eyes were red and bloodshot as tears spilled from them while mucus dripped from her nose. "They don't—understand—have to—"

I moved my hand to her shoulders and squeezed it. "It's all right. Let's take a couple of deep breaths."

I took them with her, and by the end of the third one, she'd stopped panting, although she still trembled slightly.

"You're safe," I said. "We're safe. There's police everywhere, including two big guards outside. And I'm gonna stay right here with you. Everything'll be fine."

Her head started swinging back and forth. "No, Seth. We—I—"

"I know you're upset. You're scared. But they've captured or killed most of the gang. Petén got away, but she's not going to be bothering—"

"It's not Petén!" After yelling at me, she started sobbing again.

"What do you mean, it's not Petén?"

Drawing a deep breath in through her nose, Max coughed and sputtered. "That's not who I'm afraid of. Everyone thinks I'm scared Petén's gonna come for me, but that's not it. Not at all!"

"Then what is it, sweetie? Who are you scared of?"

"My father! We have to—"

"Oh, sh. Don't worry about him. The police are watching him, and we can arrest him whenever we want. I was thinking you'd want me to do it, but I can call them right now—"

Her eyes flared as wide as I'd seen them. "No! No, no, no, you can't arrest him. You *can't!*" Max seemed to lose all muscle tone, sliding slowly from my arms back down onto the mattress, where she curled up into an even tighter ball than before.

"After what he's done to you, what he tried to do? We have to arrest him. He has to be punished."

A single sob burst from her mouth, like a belch or a hiccup. But it quickly led to another. And then another.

I tried to soothe her, rubbing her arm and her shoulder. Nothing seemed to work. Crouching down, I got my face as close to hers as I could. "Listen, I know it must be scary. But this isn't going to all happen overnight. First, we'll finish getting you clean. After that, we can get you some help. Maybe there's some relative you like. Or, you're probably old enough, we could find some sort of guardian to help you live on your own—"

"No," she said. "You don't understand."

"Understand what?"

"He owns *everything*. All my music—everything I've ever recorded—he made me sign all the rights over. If I leave, he'll keep everything and I'll have nothing . . ."

"I'm no lawyer, but after what's happened, I've gotta think you can challenge all that. We can figure that part out. But even if he gets to keep it all, that stuff's not worth hanging on for. We're talking about a man who tried to have you—his own daughter—killed. He has to go away for that, Max. He has to."

She kept shaking her head, mumbling, "Can't, won't work," again and again. I started to worry she was locked in some kind of mental loop when suddenly, the crying stopped. Max's eyes locked on mine, and for the first time in a long while, they were completely clear. Focused.

"There's something else. Something no one else knows about. And they can't . . . they can't know about it. No one. I'll tell you, but I can't trust anybody else."

I rubbed her shoulder again. "What are you talking about? What else?"

"There's something I need to do, Seth. Before he gets desperate and knows I've turned against him."

"What's that?"

"There's a tape. I have to find it. Please. Please promise me you won't arrest him until I find the tape."

My shoulders relaxed a bit, and I slid back onto my heels. "Max, listen. I know he worked you like a dog, but again, you've got your whole career ahead of you. You can re-record any song you want . . ."

Max shook her head slowly and deliberately. In a hoarse whisper, she said, "I'm not talking about that kind of tape."

I squinted at her, still not understanding.

After a long pause, she said, "It's a videotape. A sex tape."

CHAPTER 28

"What did you just say?"

Max squeezed her eyes shut, and I noticed tiny droplets leaking out the corners. "It's a *sex* tape," she whispered.

"But you're only . . . how does he . . . ?"

"He's got it, and he's threatened me with it. He said if I ever left him, he'd put it on the Internet, and now if he gets desperate, I know that's what he'll do. I *know* it!" Her face contorted, every muscle beneath it seeming to contract. And then she shuddered, letting out a low wail that droned on even after I pulled her in close.

Although questions were still swirling through my mind, I didn't even try to speak for a while. I just held her and let her cry: pure pain, pouring out of her in a torrent.

When it finally seemed like she might be slowing down, I said softly, "Listen, I don't know how he got this thing, but plenty of celebrities have had . . . embarrassing stuff come out. This might be a little different because you're underage, but—"

Pulling back from me, she said, "This is *totally* different."

"What do you mean? How?"

I could feel all the muscles inside her clench.

"We can figure this out, Max," I said. "We can fix it. I can help. But I've got to know exactly what we're up against."

She swung her head side to side. "I can't. I—"

"Start at the beginning if it's easier. Tell me the whole thing. But you've gotta tell me."

Max inhaled deeply, and then descended into a long series of coughs. I passed her a handful of tissues from a box nearby, and she cleared her nose and mouth, then wiped her face. Finally, after setting her fragile-looking jaw and staring at the mattress for a moment, she began speaking again.

"Before I hit it big, before Charlie, or the label, or any of that, I just liked to sing. I mean, I got a few parts, like, in the school play and stuff, but nothing big. Nothing that made me think I was something special.

"But my dad must've seen it. 'Cause when I turned twelve, I remember he bought this microphone and recorder. He brought it home and said we were going to start making records. I had no idea what he meant. I just sang whatever song he wanted me to into the microphone, and that was that.

"My dad went to Charlie the next year. I guess from what I've heard he actually went a few times before that, but Charlie blew him off. Anyway, something about the song I sang that time caught his ear." Max glanced up at me, and for a moment her face brightened. "Maybe you know it. ''Til There Was You'? From *The Music Man*?"

I shook my head.

She smiled briefly, then looked down again, as if remembering a dear friend who'd died. "It's a hard song—the original is all this high-register, vibrato stuff—but I just sang it straight. Anyway, Charlie liked it, and brought me in. He had me record six or seven test songs, and we all agreed 'Love Takes Time' was the best one. So that was my first single.

"Looking back, I guess I should have figured out something was wrong way before I did. My dad started saying things about Charlie.

Bad things, like, Charlie didn't know what he was talking about. At home, my dad would be pushing me to record different songs from what Charlie was having me do. And then I'd have to go into the studio, and Charlie would get mad, 'cause my voice wouldn't always hold up. So I'd be singing whatever he'd picked out, and I'd have trouble, and my father would be right there trying to play this other thing, saying it was better."

"Did they fight?"

She nodded. "A lot. I didn't always know why, but I knew they weren't getting along.

"Then things started taking off, you know? I got some radio time. I got invites to sing on shows and stuff. That was another sign: my dad would never let me travel to do TV. It pissed me off, 'cause I wanted to go to New York for the *Today Show*, or *Good Morning America*, but he always made me do it remotely. I didn't understand—what was the point of being famous if you couldn't see all these cool places? He said I wasn't old enough.

"So the older I got, the more I pressed him. Eventually, he didn't have a choice, and started bringing me places. New York, LA. But it was always weird, you know? Each time I was supposed to do an appearance, it would fall through at the last minute. A few times it was we got 'bumped.' But after you've heard that three or four times, you're like, 'What's the deal?'"

I nodded.

"The movie was going to be different."

"The movie with Nancy Irvine?" I asked.

Max nodded again. "They contacted me through Charlie, instead of my dad. He thought it was awesome, and when he told me, I was so excited. With Charlie on my side, I figured I had more leverage, so I went to my dad, and I made him promise. Made him swear I could do it. He tried to talk me out of it, but I wasn't going to let him. I didn't even need Charlie, I had my mind so set on that. And I think my dad realized, so he said yes."

"But then that fell through, too," I said.

"Yeah. Irvine was so mean, I just bought into everything my dad was saying. That it was her fault. That it was Hollywood. They were trying to screw us on the money."

"Do you know why he didn't want you in the movie?"

"Because he worried it would make me too big a star."

"Maybe," I said. "But that's not all of it. He wanted to control the money." I told her quickly about the Coogan accounts Irvine had explained to me.

Max blinked several times as she listened, but her expression didn't change. "When the movie fell through, that was the first time I really thought to myself, 'I need to be on my own.' I started thinking about leaving."

"Leaving your dad?"

"Yeah. He was saying we should leave Charlie, and I just thought, 'Why don't I leave him, too?' I didn't tell you that part in California, I'm sorry."

I shrugged.

"I looked up the emancipation laws and stuff, though. Texas makes it really hard."

"You ever think that might be why your dad moved you here in the first place?"

"I hadn't thought of that. I guess that makes sense." Max paused, furrowing her brow, as if struggling to remember where she'd left off. "Anyway, after the movie thing, Charlie and my dad really weren't getting along. My dad was pushing for all these extra songs and endorsements and photo shoots."

"You mean like the swimsuit ones?"

"It started with those. But he kept wanting it to go further. He said fans needed to be able to think of me as a grown-up, as a woman. He wanted the photos to be sexier and stuff."

"Did you tell him no?"

Max nodded gently. "I kept saying, 'Let's just finish this album—we're so close.' But then he'd go off about how awful Charlie was, how we were going to leave him."

"So then what happened?"

"Turns out, Charlie had been putting together a tour for me. He told me the day we wrapped the second album. Twenty dates, cross-country."

"Which was gonna mean going to New York and California again," I said.

She nodded. "I did three dates before my dad pulled me off the road. Just tiny little clubs, tune-ups for the big arenas. And then he canceled the whole thing." Her eyes squeezed shut for a moment, and tears spilled out the sides. "I just started screaming at him. Right there in the dressing room, when he told me after the show. Touring's where the money is now, you know, and so I just couldn't understand why he was blocking me from it. It seemed so . . . stupid."

Max took a deep breath. "When we came back home, that's when I started seeing Dr. Roosevelt."

"That's when you started the Oxy."

She nodded silently.

"Did you know your dad was behind that before Petén told us?"

She shook her head. "The doctor said to take them, so I figured they were good for me. They made me feel good. And for a while, everything seemed okay. Until later, when Charlie noticed I was acting different.

"One day, we're in the studio, and it was like he just saw me and knew, you know? Like he could see right through me. He ripped me a new one. He was trying to help, I guess, but my dad had told me so many bad things about him. I couldn't listen. I was just so tired of being controlled, I couldn't take it anymore. I—"

Her eyes flooded again. "I didn't quite see, at Otra. Is he . . . is Charlie . . . ?"

I shook my head.

Max's chin dropped to her chest.

"Go back—what happened after you started taking the Oxy?"

"The second album was doing good, even with the tour getting canceled. My dad started pressing again about the photo shoots, saying this was the perfect time. He had this thing in mind, a shoot where I was with a man. He said not to worry, nothing would really happen. Like on TV, it would just look like it."

"What did you say?"

"I told him no. And I dodged it. I'd pretend to be sick, stuff like that. But he was so insistent. So we had this big fight. I remember, it was right before Thanksgiving. I screamed at him, and screamed at him. And finally, I . . ."

"What, Max?"

"I said . . . I told him . . ."

"What did you tell him?"

Max's neck muscles clenched as she swallowed. "I told him if he didn't drop it, I would get rid of him just like we were gonna get rid of Charlie."

"How'd he react?"

She raised her eyebrows. "Different. I figured he'd do something horrible. Normally, if we were fighting, he'd yell back at me, make threats. But that time, he just let me go. It's fuzzy if I think about it now, but I think . . . I thought I won." Max looked up, the corners of her mouth curling into the slightest smile. "Stupid me."

"You scared him," I said.

"Next thing I know, he tells me we're off to the Caribbean." Max rolled from her side onto her back so that she was staring up at the ceiling.

When she didn't speak for several seconds, I said, "Okay."

"I was sort of excited, you know? I mean, I was still pissed about the tour and everything, but . . . the islands? Finally, I was gonna get to go somewhere.

"We left home early in the morning. Connected in Dallas. But to a private jet. It was so different—I'd never traveled that way before. There were these waiters on the plane. I'd had alcohol before, you know, at parties and things. But never in front of my dad. I didn't think he even knew. During the flight, though, he's ordering the waiters to give me these blended-up margaritas. They were so soft and sweet, like Slushees, almost. I can still remember him with the pitcher, refilling my cup.

"I'd never drunk hard alcohol before, just like, wine and champagne. I don't know how much I had, but it must've mixed with the drugs, 'cause I got so wasted. I mean, everything was spinning, and all I could think was, 'Hey, maybe my dad's turning cool.' You know, like, after the fight, he . . . maybe he respected me more or something."

"Where'd you go?"

"I passed out before we landed. Later, I found out it was Saint Lucia. But that's when . . ."

"When what?"

Max didn't speak for several seconds. Her chin trembled.

"What happened when you woke up?"

When she finally spoke again, it was almost in a whisper. "I was really out of it. So wasted, so hungover, it was hard to wake up. My head was pounding. I remember feeling cold, which I thought was weird, 'cause it was supposed to be so hot there . . ."

"What else, Max?"

"It took me a second to figure stuff out. I was in some house, some . . . bedroom I didn't recognize. It was bright. The cold was because I wasn't wearing a shirt. And there was this guy, standing behind me. He had his . . . hands on me."

"Your dad went through with the shoot?"

Max nodded slowly. "I was so confused. Scared. And that's when I heard his voice."

"Whose voice?"

"My dad's. He was . . . directing. Telling the cameraman where to stand. Telling the guy . . . what to do."

"Oh God."

"And that's . . . that's when it got bad."

"What do you mean?"

"My dad called *cut*. Like they should stop. The shoot was over. But they . . . they didn't listen."

"Max," I said, "you don't have to tell me the rest." In truth, I knew I didn't want to hear it.

She didn't hear me. Her eyes had turned glassy, her arms tightening around her sides as she kept telling the story.

"The guy behind me stripped off the rest of my clothes. Then he . . . he forced me down onto my knees. They were laughing." Tears began pouring from her eyes.

"Didn't your dad—"

"When they didn't listen to him at first, he tried to stop them. Sort of. I guess. But when it kept going, I looked up . . ."

"What? What did you see?"

Max's eyes grew distant, her voice falling into a near monotone. "I saw him. My dad. He was just . . . standing there. His arms crossed like . . . like it was no big deal."

My mind was racing and I shivered, literally. It seemed like every hair on my arms and neck was standing straight up.

Max rolled toward me and threw her head onto my shoulder. She was bawling, spasming. I wrapped my arms around her as tightly as I could, feeling her chest shuddering beneath them as it all came spilling out.

I don't know how long she cried or how long I held her. But when Max finally grew quiet, I asked, "So he has this tape?"

Raising her head took visible effort, but she nodded. "After . . . after it was over, he made me watch it. He was trying to tell me it was a good thing. Like, we could cut it a little here or there, and . . ."

"What did you say?"

"I just . . . lost it. I went after him, punching and kicking. I'd never been in a fight before, I don't know how to do any of that. But I just . . . I was so . . ."

Max sucked air through her nose. "He kept pushing me away, but I was still screaming at him, and then . . . then, he got all weird. He pointed at the screen, told me to take a real good look. He said if I ever tried to leave him, everyone would see the video."

Her eyes were bloodshot, nearly totally pink, but that wasn't the worst part. The blue irises had gone gray and looked hollow. As if whatever energy inside her normally gave them their color had all been sucked away.

"It was against your will," I said. "That's a crime, plain and simple. Plus, you're only sixteen. What he did, filming you, that's a crime, too. We already have him for attempted murder, and now this—"

"No," she said.

"No, what?"

"It's not a crime."

"What do you mean? Of course it is."

Max's mouth had drawn into a narrow line. "When he showed me the tape, he showed me papers, too. I'd signed them. I don't know whether he got me to do it while I was wasted, or he copied my signature or what. But they say I"—Max's voice cracked and trembled—"consented."

"That's bullshit," I said. "You're only sixteen. You can't agree to any of that. Child pornography is never legal."

Max looked up at me, her eyes locking on mine. "That's why he flew us to Saint Lucia."

All my confidence, all the bravery and strength I was trying to transfer to Max immediately evaporated. The hospital air felt frigid against my skin. "Let me guess, he'd researched the laws . . ."

She nodded slowly. "He told me it was all legal there. Even though I was only sixteen, it was perfectly fine."

"My God, Max. I'm—" I took a breath to try and think, but even by the end of it, my brain couldn't summon another word, and my mouth stopped moving. For several long moments, I sat there, next to her, silent, as I tried to think of some way through the maze Drew had erected. "Where does he keep it, the tape? At your house? Is there a safe, or—"

"No, it's not here. He left it over there someplace, hidden. That's the thing—I have to go look for it. I *have* to—"

"Hang on," I said. "He told you this? What exactly did he say?"

"He said, 'I've got copies hidden overseas. You'll never find them all.'"

Multiple copies.

While some parts of my brain were still reeling over the story Max had just recounted, I tried to focus on the tape. Multiple backups made sense. For something this important, you wouldn't risk something happening to your only copy.

Copies. Did Drew mean hard copies, like on disk? Or digital copies? In the cloud, even. Could be either. Or both.

Hiding it abroad also made sense. After all his trouble to ensure the tape was made legally, Drew wouldn't have undermined himself by bringing it back here. Besides, at every turn—with Irvine, with Garcia—Drew's game was always the same: he wanted to outsmart everybody else. The only way to do that was to keep the tape legal.

How big was Saint Lucia? I wondered. It was just an island, right? But there'd still be a million places to look. Safe-deposit boxes. Storage units. Airport lockers—

No.

That wasn't right. He would never risk being thousands of miles away and having the tape inaccessible. For the tape to be a credible threat, he had to be able to reach it quickly.

Remotely.

Which meant he'd likely gone electronic.

There were still plenty of options. Memory was so cheap these days, networking solid and reliable. Commercial cloud services would let you buy a block of online storage. But even if Drew didn't feel comfortable putting this kind of file on a commercial site, it'd be easy enough to do it privately.

"Have you seen him check on it?" I asked Max.

"What do you mean?"

"The file, the video. Does your father check on it, to make sure it's safe? Has he ever said anything to make you think he's monitoring it?"

"Yeah, I guess."

"What did he say? What, exactly?"

Max shrugged. "I don't know. He's taunted me with it. Like, 'It's still right where I put it, don't you forget.' Something like that."

I thought back to each of the times I'd seen Drew. That's when I put it together. And when I figured out how to solve it.

I grinned at Max, and now the confidence in my voice wasn't just for show. "I know what we're going to do. I need to call Shen and check on something. And I need to get a couple of things together real quick—a laptop and a thumb drive. But it's all going to be okay."

"I don't believe you," she said. "I want to. But I don't."

Looking her right in the eyes, I said, "Trust me. We're going to fix this, Max. All of it."

"Emma," she said.

I was already pulling out the burner, doing math on the time difference to LA. A big question was whether I could get Peña to cooperate with what I had in mind. Then I heard what Max had said and did a double take. "Huh?"

"Emma. My real name is Emma."

CHAPTER 29

By the time I had everything I needed, the cops watching Max's house reported that Drew was on the move. Driving his black 328i, but not hightailing it. Just steering the Beemer like he was out for a leisurely cruise. The route he was taking—out of their ritzy neighborhood and onto 360—would place him right by the airport.

Peña promised that his pickup truck was fast. I hoped he was right but didn't necessarily believe him until Max and I were belted into the thing, barreling down 35. The speedometer said eighty, and the diesel was growling, asking for more.

We pulled into Austin-Bergstrom's parking lot in seven minutes. Well ahead of Drew, who—according to the surveillance units—was still ten minutes out. A couple of badge flashes got us into the central security office, which, like JFK's, was hidden down a hallway behind a nondescript door.

The TSA shift manager, a hefty African American woman named Janelle Thomson, had large, bright eyes and an easy smile. Once I'd explained what we needed, she led us farther down the hall, to a matched set of doors. "This one's the observation room," she said, pointing at the nearer of the pair, "and that's where we'll put him for questioning."

"Thanks so much," I said.

"Anything else you need, sugar?"

"Is the room videotaped?"

"Yes, sir, video and audio. Controls are in the observation room."

Peña started to lead Max through the first door.

"Be there in a sec," I said. "I just need to check something."

Poking my head into the interrogation room, I ignored the standard-issue furniture and one-way mirror and instead checked the corners of the ceiling. As I suspected, the eye-in-the-sky camera sat nestled in the corner between the door and the mirror. If Drew sat at the table facing the mirror, the camera would be looking down at him from above and slightly to the left of his head.

When I joined the others in the observation room, Max sat sprawled across a chair, chewing her nails, while Peña stood by the mirror.

"How you wanna play this?" he asked.

I nodded down at my sling. "I might need an extra pair of hands, but otherwise, I think I got it." Then I turned to Max. "You don't have to watch."

Her eyes locked on me, and the fingers slipped away from her mouth. "Yes, I do."

I nodded and turned back to the window to wait.

Several minutes later, two blue-shirted TSA agents walked Drew into the interrogation room. Dressed in his usual blazer and T-shirt, he wore crisp blue jeans this time. Although he was visibly annoyed, his hair was perfectly combed, his face smoothly shaven. The skin around his eyes suggested he hadn't missed even a minute of sleep.

After depositing his bags in the corner, Drew sat in the witness chair facing the mirror. He set his tickets to his left on the table, then withdrew his cell phone from inside the jacket and set it off to his right. Finally, he folded his hands in front of him.

Double-checking the printout I'd stuck into a manila folder and the hard piece of plastic in my pocket, I said, "Here we go."

After thanking and ushering the agents out of the interrogation room, I set the closed folder on the desk and asked, "How are you, Mr. Drew?"

If he was surprised to see me, Drew didn't let it show. "Okay. Except now I'm slightly worried I might miss my flight."

"Good point. Where are you going, anyway?" Without awaiting his answer, I stepped to the table and spun his ticket jacket around. The topmost boarding pass said DFW, but underneath were additional cards for Los Angeles and Beijing. I whistled. "China, huh? There much demand for Max's music over there?"

Drew smiled. "Not yet."

"So it's a business trip, then. Nothing to do with the lack of an extradition treaty."

"I have absolutely no idea what you're talking about."

"When I left you, I asked you to keep an ear out for any contact from the Second Guerrillas."

"And I did that. But you went off to track down Brad Civins. I had no idea when you'd return, if at all. This trip has been planned for quite a while. I couldn't risk canceling it."

I gave him a nod. "Calling off Max's nationwide tour was no big deal, but this trip needs to happen?"

Drew made a face. "Did you ever find him, by the way? Civins?"

"Oh yeah. Civins. Dr. Roosevelt. Even Petén. I saw her, and the barrel of the Glock she had pointed at my face."

Drew cocked his head. "And yet, here you are. You must be a very lucky man, Mr. Walker."

I crossed my arms. "Not nearly as lucky as you."

"How do you figure that?"

"You hire Petén and the Second Guerrillas to get rid of Max. When they don't, you call in the FBI, hoping they'll take down the Second

Guerrillas. I come along, you send me after Civins, figuring one of us will take out the other. Everyone does all the dirty work for you, and you ride off into the sunset."

"What on earth do you mean, 'get rid of Max'? I—"

I rolled my eyes. "Spare me, Counselor. Petén explained your whole agreement to me. There was no debt—you approached them. And not to kidnap Max, but to hook her on drugs, and when even that didn't work, to kill her. Except they screwed things up by trying to double-cross you."

Drew leaned forward, eyes narrowing. "She told you that? Petén? And you believed I could actually do something like that to my own—"

"Oh, I'm not the only one she told."

Slowly, subtly, Drew recoiled in his chair. "What—what do you mean?"

"Max was there, too. Petén was actually working to take her off the drugs you and Dr. Roosevelt had her hooked on."

"Max heard these lies about me? Where . . . where is she? Where's my baby? Is she safe?"

"It's so interesting to me that you waited until now to ask that question."

Drew's face twisted into a sneer. "I have no idea why you've chosen to believe the extortionist head of a criminal organization over a father who's been worried sick over his daughter—"

I nodded. "You do look worried now."

Drew paused and adjusted his face. Then he continued, "—but I'll tell you, I'm about this close to calling my lawyer and ending this little conversation."

"I thought you hadn't done anything wrong."

"I certainly haven't. But I know when I'm being railroaded. You seem convinced—"

"I'm convinced an awful lot of the things you did to Max are perfectly legal. Keeping her from working in New York and California to avoid Coogan accounts and all the other child protections they have? Legal. Moving here to Texas, a state where it's hard for a minor to become emancipated? Another good legal move, Counselor."

"I've told you before," he growled, "I'm not a lawyer."

"Oh, I know. But you really should be. The way you thought of all that. The way you made sure Max assigned everything to you. The way you banked hundreds of hours of Max's material so, just on the off chance something unfortunate ever happened, you'd be standing at the ready with tribute albums and greatest hits and never-before-released recordings? I mean, that's thinking. That's being a shrewd businessman. But you know what your greatest legal achievement was?"

Blinking at me, Drew didn't say anything.

"By far, it was Saint Lucia."

His eyes widened, stretching out the skin that had gathered at their corners.

"Oh yeah. Max told me all about that. And I did a little legal research online."

"Every sovereign state is entitled to its laws."

"So you don't deny it?"

Drew slid his hands to the edge of the table, then leaned back in the chair and smiled. "Deny what? You know about the video, obviously. But you also appear to understand that it was a consensual act, the filming of it consistent with local standards. It remains where it was made, where it is perfectly legal. So I don't see why I would need to deny anything."

My stomach muscles tensed, and although my left arm was immobilized in the sling, my right fist balled up. Nothing would have made me happier than to knock the sonofabitch's head right off.

But there was something better I could do.

Looking to the mirror, I jerked my head to signal Peña I needed him. When he entered the room, I introduced him to Drew.

"Always good to meet one of the people who work so hard to keep us safe," Drew said. "Thank you for your service."

Peña crossed his arms and remained stoic as I stepped to the table and retrieved Drew's phone from across it. "Wonderful little piece of machinery, isn't it?"

"It truly is." Drew nodded, still not betraying any nerves whatso-ever. "I don't know what's more impressive, honestly: all the things it can do, or the fact it's locked with such strong encryption, no one can hack into it." He smiled again.

Now it was my turn to grin. "Encryption can be a wonderful thing. Except when a user does something completely idiotic to undermine it. Stick out your right thumb, Mr. Drew."

"I don't have to do that."

"Yes, actually, you do. *US v. Arnold*, Counselor. I'm surprised you're not fresh on that one—it's one of the Air Marshal Service's favorites. This"—I gestured around the room—"is considered a border of the United States. I don't need a warrant to search you here, and I'm allowed to inspect your electronic files. Now please, give me your thumb, or I'll have Agent Peña help you give it to me."

Drew glanced at Peña, licked his lips, then grudgingly presented his thumb. I touched the phone's little sensor to it, and the screen sprang to life.

"I have no idea what you think you're going to find on there." For the first time, Drew's voice didn't drip with confidence. "Certainly nothing illegal. Nothing but e-mail and my calendar and address book."

"We'll see." I opened the browser and selected the Internet history. Sure enough, mixed between visits to Forbes.com and the *New York Times* were several long, strange URLs. "I started thinking to myself, if I wanted to keep tabs on an electronic file I didn't want anyone else to know about, how exactly would I do it? And you know, I wouldn't use some commercial cloud service. I think what I'd do is rent a space on some private server rack somewhere. That way, I could log on to it over the Internet, but no one else would know where to look."

I glanced over at Drew. Small dots of perspiration on his brow told me everything I needed to know. So I hit the first of the weird-looking links. A log-in screen appeared on the phone.

"Of course, if you did that," Drew said, "you'd put some security on it. That way, even if someone did figure out where to look, they'd still need to know a username and password to access the site. Otherwise, all they get to see is an empty web page."

Sure enough, the navy-blue page on the screen held two empty white boxes where you could type in your access credentials. With the company's name printed down at the bottom with a couple of other links, it looked like cheap, commercially available software. But that was still enough to do the trick.

I glanced at Drew as my thumbs started typing.

His lips spread even wider, showing off his perfect teeth.

"Go ahead, Mr. Walker. Try every combination you like. But I warn you, after ten tries, the web page will lock, and you'll never be able to access it from there again."

I glanced over at the mirror, imagining Max behind it, crumpling into her chair at her father's words. Then I looked down at the screen again, moving back and forth between the browser and Drew's e-mail.

Drew's history contained three of the mysterious links, and it took me several minutes to visit each one. As time ticked by, I felt Peña staring at me, too. I moved my fingers even faster, but Drew seemed to be emboldened by each passing second. "Come on, Mr. Walker. How long is it going to take you to realize you've lost? You can check all the sites; they're all the same. You'll never break into any of them."

Lacing his fingers behind his head, Drew leaned back so the front feet of his chair lifted up off the ground. His eyes gleamed.

Once I'd visited all three sites, I scrolled farther back through the history, checking to make sure I hadn't missed any. Then I clicked the phone off and flipped it at Drew, hitting him in the paunch that pro-truded over his belt.

"Finally gave up, huh?" Drew asked. He picked up the phone and ran his thumb over the sensor. "Don't feel bad, Mr. Walker. I may have dropped out of law school, but you're certainly not the only one I've outsmarted in this life."

"I'll give it to you," I said. "You're pretty damn smart. But you forgot about one little detail."

Drew looked up from the screen, eyes piercing into me. "What do you mean?"

"The password reset."

I could see he was confused, and I glanced at Peña, only to find the same reaction.

"The software you used—it's designed for setting up commer-cial web pages. They figure you want to have customers come and go. Customers who might, say, forget their password."

Peña's eyebrows rose. "So you—"

"I told it I forgot my password and asked it to send me a temporary one in e-mail. Since I had access to Mr. Drew's e-mail, I grabbed the temp password, then went back over and used it to log on."

"So you deleted the file?" Peña asked.

"Nope, it wouldn't let me." I jerked my head toward Drew. "He set it so the file couldn't be deleted. But, he didn't change any of the administrator settings on the website. So I created a new, twenty-six-character password for the account, changed the recovery e-mail to one of my addresses, and turned off the reset option. Now"—I turned back to Drew—"I'm the only one who can get in there."

The color had blanched from Drew's face, rendering his deep tan an odd, almost greenish color.

"You hear that, Max?" I said, moving to the mirror. I spoke loudly, just in case the microphones hadn't caught the whole thing. "You're free. Nobody's ever gonna see the video sitting on those servers. And someday, when their rent expires, the owners will come along and erase them to rent them again." I wished I could see her expression.

"You're pretty proud of yourself," Drew said. "But I still own the rights to all her songs. When I walk out of here—"

"I don't know that I'd jump the gun on that just yet," I said.

Drew stared at me. Still defiant, but now the slightest bit uncertain.

"I talked to a lawyer friend of mine." Scrunching my face, I nodded. "Unlike you, he's an actual lawyer. Anyway, he told me copyright assignments by minors are only valid if they're made for the benefit of the minor. I don't think a court's going to look at the documents Max's child-pornographer-rapist father forced her to sign and think those were for her benefit."

Drew shook his head. "You're missing the point, Mr. Walker. Rape? Child pornography? Those are *legal* concepts, defined by statute. I haven't done anything that would fall under those definitions. What I did was legal—you admitted that yourself."

"To be fair, I actually said what you did in Saint Lucia was legal. There's still the tiny matter of hiring the Second Guerrillas to have Max killed. That's conspiracy, attempted murder, and murder for hire. Federal charges, federal prison."

"And how do you plan to prove that, exactly? With your hearsay testimony about a supposed confession from the head of an international crime ring? Once a jury hears how you went off the reservation, kidnapping my daughter and dragging her all over the country, I don't think they're going to be too sympathetic."

"There's Max."

"You'll put her on the stand? Oh, good luck with that. By the time she gets cross-examined about her drug use and behavior, no one's going to be looking to do her any favors." Drew gave me a fake pout. "If that's the best you've got, I'll take my chances."

The truth was, I'd thought through all that, too, and Drew was right. The odds of getting him convicted for attempted murder on either Petén's word or Max's were pretty long. I turned to Peña. "You think if he was into kiddie porn in the Caribbean, he was into it here, too?"

Peña shrugged. "I've always heard pervs like that, they can't help themselves."

"That's what I've heard, too." I dug into my pocket as I circled the table to the corner where Drew's suitcases stood. Taking the soft computer case off the top, I brought it around so I was standing at the corner of the table to Drew's left. Peña and the camera were directly behind me. "Let's see what we've got in here." I unzipped the bag. "Laptop, power cord." I set each one on the table. Then I turned the bag over, letting pens and other supplies pour out of the pockets.

A small plastic thumb drive hit the table and clattered to a stop.

"What have we here?" I asked, picking it up and turning to show Peña.

Drew exploded out of his seat. "That's not mine! I've never seen that before!"

"That's what every tweaker says, too, when you find the dope in their car," Peña said.

I handed him the USB drive. "You wanna go check it?"

"Sure."

After he'd left, I turned back to Drew.

He was shaking his head. "You'll never get away with this, Walker. I'll prove that wasn't mine, and then you'll burn."

"Maybe," I said. "But if you're wrong, and if a jury doesn't like whatever's on that memory stick and concludes it belongs to you, that prison stay of yours is gonna be a helluva lot worse than it would be for murder."

Drew blinked at me, his cheek starting to twitch.

I stared him right in the eyes and stepped closer. Close enough that he could hear me even as I dropped my voice to a low hiss next to his ear. "I loaded that thing with the most disgusting filth I could find in the bowels of the Internet. You get one parent on that jury, and you're toast."

He grunted. "That's how you think this is gonna go?"

I nodded. "The only questions are how long you go away for, and what your cellmates are gonna do to you while you're in there."

Drew's chin dropped toward his chest, and he shook his head slightly. "You really think you're so smart. You think you have it all figured out. But you don't know anything."

Here was the moment. I'd gotten him out on the limb—would he jump? "Oh really? Enlighten me, then."

His head rose again, his eyes locking on me. "You don't just need one juror, Mr. Walker. You need all of them. *I* need one—just one to acquit. One poor schlub who's suffered through the same kinds of things that I have."

"You've suffered?"

"Oh, you have no idea what those bitches did to me—Max and her mother and Petén. They're all the goddamn same, really. You think I can't find one guy on a jury who feels screwed over by the women in his life?"

"I think you're going to have an awfully hard time finding anyone sympathetic to setting up the rape of your sixteen-year-old daughter."

"For chrissake, will you stop calling it rape? It was *legal!* And it was never even supposed to go that far. If she'd just listened to me in the first place . . ." Drew's hands balled into fists, and his muscles all clenched the same way they had when I'd arrived at his house that night. Then, suddenly, he relaxed. His voice softened. "Why can't you see—I'm really not the bad guy here. I'm the *victim.*"

Now it was my turn to shake my head.

Drew looked past me, to the corner of the ceiling where the camera was mounted, and started approaching it. "You want to hear it? The truth? I might as well tell you since the authorities here are going to try and frame me. I might as well tell you everything, so you know my side before you hear the stories made up by that . . . that juvenile delinquent."

"That 'delinquent' is your daughter." I really didn't like the way he was speaking to the camera instead of me.

Drew whipped around. As soon as his back was to the camera, his eyes lit up, and his lips spread into a smile. "Funny you should say that," he whispered. "Goes to show how little you know."

CHAPTER 30

Drew spun on his heel again to face the eye in the sky.

"I wanted to be a lawyer from the time I was seven years old. My father worked in a Missouri steel mill, and I saw him come home dirty and exhausted every night. I told myself that when I grew up, I'd build a better life for myself and my family than that.

"But a funny thing happened on the way to law school: I met a woman. A beautiful, beautiful woman who stole my heart. Her name was Deborah, and we got married the week after we both graduated from Mizzou.

"Now, as much as I wanted to be a lawyer, that's how much Deborah wanted to be a mother. She absolutely adored children—she'd studied to be a kindergarten teacher. So, even though everyone politely warned us that law school wasn't the best time to start a family, in between the first and second years, we found out we were pregnant. Max came along just before spring exams."

Drew had started pacing back and forth, gesturing as he talked.

"Now, the second summer of law school is an important time. That's when most students apprentice at whatever firm they're hoping to join after graduation. I was fortunate enough to make the law review, and I had a summer job at one of St. Louis's biggest firms. Needless to say, juggling work with a newborn wasn't easy. But as hard as it was on me, it took an even larger toll on Deborah. We didn't know as much about postpartum depression back in those days; they called it the 'baby blues,' and she had a particularly bad case. I would come home from work each night in my suit to find her lying on the couch, crying. Max's diapers hadn't been changed; sometimes she hadn't been fed.

"Although I got my job offer at the end of that summer, when we went back to school, it was clear things weren't right with Deborah. The doctors had prescribed her pills to help her sleep, but she'd started taking more than she should. Eventually, she left us."

Drew's voice cracked on that last part, and I wondered whether it was real, or just for effect.

"That left me in a precarious situation," he continued. "I tried to keep going—the school and the firm were both extremely gracious—but I just couldn't figure out a way to be a single dad to a six-month-old and a full-time law student. I dropped out of school, took a job. Not the one I wanted, mind you, the one I'd dreamed about, but one that paid the bills. And I settled in to an even more important role: being Max's father.

"I'm sure many people watching this know how difficult—and expensive—it is to raise a child these days. We certainly had plenty of bills, including paying back the loans I'd taken to go to law school. Without the law-firm salary I was expecting, it was almost impossible to make ends meet. Ultimately, I had to default on the loans and declare bankruptcy. My credit was ruined."

I didn't know if Drew had practiced this or was just winging it, but he hit every beat, every pause, exactly right to maximize the solemnity of it all.

"Then one day, something magical happened. A tiny glimmer of hope. I came home from work and there's Max, playing on the floor and singing. I think to myself, 'Hey, that sounds pretty good.' I start thinking, 'Maybe this could be a way out. Maybe I'm not the one who's destined to succeed after all.'

"Encouraging Max's talent wasn't easy. Or cheap. Little girls are easily distracted. And there were lessons. Recording sessions. I spent every night researching what I could do to help her make it in show business. I booked her small gigs. I found Charlie Garcia, a well-known producer here in Austin, and persuaded him to listen to her. When she finally broke through, I dropped everything in Missouri, the only place I'd ever lived, and moved us here so she could chase her dream."

Drew took a long, deep breath, then sighed it out heavily.

"They warn you show business can be a dangerous place, but nothing really prepares you. Record producers, movie producers. Everyone looks to make money off your child, and no one wants to pay a cent more than they have to. Max was lucky in some ways—with the things I'd learned in law school, I was able to protect her. Stand up for her rights. Keep her from being cheated.

"Through it all, my only goal was her long-term success. I mean, in the short term, sure, I wanted to recoup the money we'd invested in her. And make no mistake, we had a pretty deep hole to dig ourselves out of. But I knew, as long as I could look out for her, manage her brand, get her exposure and endorsements to augment her recording career, I knew our debts were just a speed bump.

"What I didn't know was that, as soon as we'd had just our first sniff of success, a man would come calling. A man named Jed Cooper. He showed up on my doorstep one night a year and a half ago, claiming to be Max's biological father."

My eyes darted to the one-way glass, wondering what Max's reaction was behind it. Cooper must have been the man Petén mentioned. But Max's real father?

Drew continued talking. "I'm sure you can imagine how that rocked me to my core. It impacted me so much, in fact, that I did a very stupid thing." He paused here and turned directly to the camera. "When Cooper asked for money, I paid him."

"I didn't believe him, mind you. I figured Cooper was just some kind of con man, looking to capitalize on Max's success. But Max and I'd had a tough enough time since her mom left. The last thing I wanted, the last thing I thought I could afford, was planting any seed of doubt in her head that I was her father. Because I honestly believed I was.

"Now, why do I say paying Cooper was a mistake? Because if you pay a man like that once, he's going to come back for more. And that's exactly what Cooper did. This time, though, I thought I was better prepared. When he knocked on the door again a few months later, I told him he could shove off, and went to slam it right in his face. But Cooper surprised me. He handed me a sealed envelope. He said a paternity test inside would prove he was Max's father. He said he'd release it to the world unless I paid him an ungodly sum of money.

"Now, I shoved that envelope inside a drawer and swore to never look at it again. I still didn't believe him. But I knew I had a real problem. Even if I was correct, if Cooper went to court, they might take Max away from me while custody was decided. I might lose the one thing I had left.

"I brought all this to Max's producer, Charlie Garcia. I figured he might have dealt with something like this before. He listened and told me not to worry. He told me he knew someone who could help.

"And that, ladies and gentlemen, is how I got involved with the Second Guerrilla Army of the Poor. Garcia introduced me to their leader, a woman named Petén. In exchange for a percentage of Max's earnings, she promised to scare Cooper away. Not hurt him, mind you—I insisted on that—but just scare him away, so we would never see him again."

"You know," I said, "you spin a pretty good story." I meant it, too: Drew had built up so much momentum, anybody watching might easily have believed him about all of it. "But I don't think it quite happened that way. I think *you* found Petén, not Garcia. But even after you got her to eliminate Cooper, there was still one small thing you couldn't control."

Drew had turned away from the camera to face me. Now he put his hands on his hips. "What's that?"

"Max," I said with a little shrug. "She wanted to live it up, to go on tour. But you couldn't have that, so you got her hooked on the drugs."

Drew shook his head. "The drugs were all Petén's idea."

"You know, Petén's one convincing woman. She sees all the angles—she even tried to make me a deal. So maybe she suggested the drugs. But, ultimately, you said yes to them. You agreed to get your own daughter hooked on Oxy, just so she'd be more pliable."

Drew spun back to the camera. "I had nothing to do with that. Absolutely nothing. "

"Even on the drugs, though, you still couldn't control Max the way you wanted, right? She wouldn't do your sexy photo shoots, she wouldn't listen to you."

"Anyone who's a parent out there knows teenagers have minds of their own. They always think they know best. That's why it was so important that Max stay with me, so I could guide her, and keep her safe—"

"But she would have given anything just to get away from you," I said to the back of Drew's head. "She even told you that. Boy, that must've hurt. Your 'big investment,' the kid you'd sacrificed your career for—one day, she announces she's going to cast you off, just like her mom did."

Slowly this time, Drew turned to face me. I could see the rage burning in his eyes.

"Is that when it happened, Mr. Drew? Is that when you decided you could sacrifice your own flesh and blood for a couple of bucks?"

"You don't know anything," he said in a low, controlled voice.

"Oh, Max told me exactly how she threatened to get rid of you."

"There was a time," he said, glancing back over his shoulder at the camera, "when I hit rock bottom emotionally. Thanksgiving, last year. I was worried I was losing my daughter to all these outside influences. In a fit of depression, I pulled out that envelope I said I'd never open."

Drew's face contorted into something sorrowful, something pathetic, and then he turned back around to the camera, his hands upturned.

"And when I looked at that paper and I learned Max wasn't mine, you know what I discovered?" He was talking through tears now, having seemingly produced them on cue. "I discovered it really didn't matter. She wasn't my blood, but I loved her just the same."

"Oh, I don't think that paternity test made you all lovey-dovey," I said. "Just the opposite—I think it liberated you. You could finally hate Max for what her mother had done."

Drew pointed a finger back at me, and told the camera, "That's a lie!"

"Is it? Why else wouldn't you stop those men in Saint Lucia? Why would you let them assault your daughter?"

"That's not—"

"Because there was a piece of you that *enjoyed* it. That's why." Now my voice was peaking. "You stood by, and you let them take advantage of her because you wanted Max to suffer. And then, once you had that tape, you figured it would bind her to you forever."

"No, I—"

"But it didn't work, did it? You showed it to her and realized Max was already gone. That's why, when you got back, you ran to Petén, hoping she'd do your dirty work again, just like she had with Cooper."

Drew stood with his shoulders perpendicular to me and the camera. "I'm telling you, killing Max was Petén's idea. Not mine. Was I angry at Max? Sure. Was I sad? Absolutely. But I'd never hurt—"

"See," I said, shaking my head, "again, maybe Petén suggested it. Maybe she realized how fragile you were and decided you just needed the tiniest little push to tumble over the edge. But Petén didn't actually want Max dead—she wanted her *alive*. Alive and willing to help the Second Guerrillas. The best way to do that was to be the open arms Max would run into to get away from *you*."

Drew set his jaw. "Baloney. Petén's been the one shooting at Max all this time, not me. If I'd wanted Max dead, I wouldn't have hired Brad Civins as her personal bodyguard."

"One man? You knew one man wasn't going to stop the Second Guerrillas. Civins was cover."

"But it wasn't just him. I brought Max to the FBI."

"That's right, the FBI," I said. "You contacted them in April." I started inching back toward the table, where I'd left the manila folder.

"Exactly. After I had to fire that thief Civins in March, I knew Max was vulnerable."

Picking up the folder, I extracted the single page of paper inside. "So then why did you file this paperwork with the Texas Secretary of State in December?"

Drew's face contorted. "What are you talking about?"

"Remember that lawyer friend I told you about? He's a really smart guy, and he explained a couple of things to me. Like how Texas is one of the few states where you can assign the rights to a celebrity's likeness after they die."

Drew's eyes widened just a bit.

"They call it the Buddy Holly Bill. The protection lasts fifty years—that's why no one could use Buddy Holly's picture until 2009 without getting permission: his family owned all the rights."

He swallowed hard.

I held the paper up toward the camera. "So before you ever thought Max was in danger, you just happened to file papers to ensure you'd own her image after she died. What a coincidence."

His mouth opened, but nothing came out.

"In fact," I said, pulling the paper down and double-checking the date, "you filed this on December 20. You and Max returned from the Caribbean on the eighteenth, isn't that right?"

He continued to stammer.

I walked over and got right in Drew's face. "You *knew*. After Saint Lucia, you knew everything you'd tried to control Max had failed. And so it was just a matter of time till she left you." I paused a beat. "Just like your wife did."

Drew's cheek was almost vibrating now, and I could see his temples flexing.

"When you brought Max to the FBI in April, it wasn't because you thought Petén was going to kill Max. After four months, you'd finally figured out she *wasn't* going to kill Max. Petén had double-crossed you—and if Petén wanted Max alive, that meant she didn't need you. Going to the FBI was you trying to save *you*."

Leaving my eyes locked on Drew's, I called toward the mirror. "You get all that, Chava?"

Peña's voice sounded over a loudspeaker. "Clear as a bell."

I leaned forward onto the balls of my feet, and Drew shrank in response. Then I turned and stalked out of the room.

When I reentered the control room, my eyes went immediately to Max. She was almost prone in her chair, crying. But when she saw me, she exploded from it. As she collided with me, arms wrapping around my chest, her momentum almost knocked me over.

"It's okay," I said, rubbing her back. "It's all okay now." Over her shoulder, I looked at Peña, who was grinning.

"Nice work, chief," he said.

"That'll stick, right?"

He nodded emphatically. "Oh yeah. Guy talks a good game, but you nailed him. Nobody's going to lose any sleep about taking him off the streets."

I took a deep breath. Finally, maybe, it was over.

Peña held up the memory stick between two fingers. "I gotta ask. Is there really—"

I nodded. "Don't go plugging that into your work computer."

Peña's lips pushed up toward his nose, and he nodded. "You're a bad motherfucker, Walker. Remind me never, ever to cross you."

I looked down at Max. "C'mon. Let's get you back to the hospital."

CHAPTER 31

Saturday, August 22

Max—no, *Emma* . . . I needed to keep reminding myself of that—had her fingers at her mouth. I could hear each click as her teeth bit through the nails.

"You've got nothing to worry about," I said. Although traffic on 30 was light, at this rate she wouldn't have any enamel left by the time we reached Fort Worth.

"I can't help it."

"It's just for the afternoon. And they're going to love you, trust me."

"How do you know?"

"I just do."

Twenty minutes later, I pulled us up to the curb, and Emma took in the small house at the top of the flagstone walkway.

"Hey," I said, and she spun back toward me. "It's gonna be fine. Michael is nine, and Rachael is five. They both listen to you on the radio. They love your songs. And I can guarantee you're the first pop star that's ever stopped by their house."

Emma smiled back, but barely. "I just . . . I hope I'm . . ."

"You're ready," I said. "Four weeks cooped up is plenty. The Center must've thought some fresh air would help, otherwise they wouldn't have given you the pass."

She closed her eyes and nodded.

I followed Emma up the walk. She wore the pink Chuck Taylors and denim shorts again, although this pair extended to midthigh. A tank top matching the sneakers revealed the freckles on the tops of her shoulders, but not much else. She kept her arms straight as she walked, hands balled into tight fists pulled up toward the outside of her arms. Despite all the nerves, she seemed bouncier. More energetic. Her long hair, highlights brightened by the summer sun, hung in a thick rope of a braid that danced between her shoulder blades.

At the screen door, I stepped around her and rang the bell, a deep two-note chime: ding-dong.

"Stay behind me," I said.

The sound of feet scrambling against wood was audible inside, as if a pack of dogs were charging the door. But then the locks clicked free, and two smiling faces appeared against the screen.

"Uncle Seth! Uncle Seth!"

Michael stood nearly up to my elbow now—he seemed to grow inches between my visits. He had long, scruffy brown hair that had doubtlessly been combed that morning, not that you could tell, and his mom's big green eyes. He'd gotten glasses before my last visit, and he wore them now, wire frames supporting rectangular lenses. Rachael was much shorter, obviously, with hair so curly it tended to frizz. A smear of freckles dotted her nose, and her two front teeth showed a sizable gap. Braces probably weren't that far away, I realized.

"Uncle Seth," Michael said, "Mom told us last night you were coming, and Rachael didn't sleep at all!"

"Did, too! Uncle Seth, wait till you see the painting I did for you at school."

The two continued talking over each other, even as a taller silhouette approached slowly from inside. "Kids, why don't you let the poor man inside the house?" Shirley's face appeared, eyes sparkling. She'd always been thin—not so much you worried for her health, just enough you thought she was lucky, or wondered how she found the time to exercise. "I think he may have a surprise for you."

"A surprise? Whatisit, whatisit?" Their eyes darted back and forth between Shirley and me.

"Come on outside," I said. "I brought someone with me."

The screen door creaked open, and as the kids emerged onto the walk, I stepped to the side.

"This is my friend Emma. That's her real name, at least. You two probably know her better as Max Magic . . ."

Before I could even finish the sentence, Michael's jaw had dropped, and Rachael was squealing.

"Uh, hey, guys." Emma gave them a meek little wave.

Rachael charged her, throwing her tiny arms around Emma's leg. Emma giggled. "Hey there," she said, looking down. Then she glanced up at Michael. "Are you more the shaking-hands type? 'Cause you can give me a hug, too."

His mouth remained wide open but turned up into a wide smile as he stepped forward and she wrapped an arm around his shoulders.

"Do you two like to play?" she asked.

Two hours later, I rocked in a chair on the back porch of the house. The kids were still going, although they'd moved to the pool to cool off. That's when Shirley and I had retreated to the shade.

"Thanks again," I said, "for letting me bring her out here."

"Don't be silly. It's not every day the kids get to meet one of their idols from the radio."

"Yeah, but after everything that happened, I wouldn't have blamed you if you didn't want her around them. I think it's really good for her, though. The doctors say the more she can readjust to being a normal teenager, the better the rehab'll take."

"How much longer does she have?"

"She's officially halfway. The real trick will come when the program's over."

"Will she just live on her own?"

"No," I said. "I found an in-home caretaker she can use until she turns eighteen. Hopefully by then she'll be ready to figure out what she wants to do with the rest of her life."

Off in the water, Emma swept her arm in a wide circle, showering Michael and Rachael with spray. Their giggles carried across the yard easily despite the thick afternoon heat.

"Seems like they're digging the pool," I said.

"They're in the water every day. You can see how good Rachael's gotten, and Michael's been asking about joining a swim team, if you can believe it." Shirley paused. "They won't remember to say *thank you*, so I'll do it for them."

I just shook my head. Back when their father, my mentor, Clarence, had first bought this house, he'd talked about putting a pool in the yard once they were old enough to enjoy it.

The kids switched to Marco Polo. Emma had her eyes closed, trying to catch up to the little ones as they splashed away from her.

"Looks like she's doing pretty well to me," Shirley said. "I read about that facility you said she's at. Best in the state?"

"Something like that."

"And let me guess who's footing the bill?"

"Her assets are all frozen over the trouble with her dad. When she gets straightened out, if she can pay me back, great. Otherwise . . ."

I could see Shirley smiling from the corner of my eye. "How are you doing with all of this?"

Although the words sounded light and airy, they dripped with curiosity. And while I knew Shirley was probably just trying to mother me, hearing those kinds of questions from her always made my skin crawl. It wouldn't take much for her to steer the topic to Clarence, and once we were there, how long would it take for her to ask about the subject I'd dodged all these years? Without looking at her, I said, "Me? I'm fine."

I rotated my shoulder a bit. Enjeti's work on it had left it feeling strong and sturdy. At least that was something you could repair.

A light, grazing touch tickled my forearm, and I glanced down to find Shirley's fingernails trailing back and forth over the *SA* tattoo.

"This one's new," she said. "A heart, huh? That have something to do with that woman you were seeing over in Dallas?"

Knowing the lump in my throat would cause my voice to crack, I nodded.

"You were coming down here quite a bit there for a while—we enjoyed seeing you so much. When you stopped, though, I didn't want to pry. I guess it . . . didn't work out?"

I swallowed hard, forcing the lump as far down as I could. "No. It didn't work out."

Shirley clucked her tongue. "I'm sorry, hon. She must've been pretty special to make the Arm of Fame."

Even I had to chuckle at that.

"Are you sure it's over?"

Pursing my lips, I nodded.

"Well, then, there'll be another one. You're too good a man for there not to be."

As always, Shirley knew exactly what to say to make me feel like I'd been stabbed in the heart.

◆　◆　◆

The afternoon slowly evaporated like the puddles that had spilled from the pool onto the concrete deck surrounding it. Shirley insisted we stay

for dinner—"Emma looks like she could use a home-cooked meal"—
and the kids had her read their bedtime stories. She even sang each of
them a lullaby, the first and second time I'd ever heard her sing in person.

We made our way out to the car then, so the kids would have some
hope of going to sleep. Evening had taken hold, and in the distance you
could see fireflies flashing.

"Thank you so much for today, ma'am," Emma said. "I had a lot
of fun."

"You are most welcome. You come back anytime you like. The
children absolutely adored you. And you, Mister"—Shirley turned and
poked me in the chest—"when will we be graced by your presence
again?"

"Soon, I hope. But we'll see what the Service has in mind for my
next assignment."

Shirley put her arms around my neck and kissed my cheek. "Take
care of yourself." As she pulled away, she patted my chest. "I mean that."

On the ride back to Dallas, Emma was quiet. Darkness had fallen
enough that I could only catch glimpses of her face when oncoming
headlights flashed over it for a moment.

"Whatcha thinking?" I asked.

"That today was just about perfect. Thank you."

"No problem. A few more weeks, you can start having days like
that every day."

"I'm gonna have to get back to real life, though, too." We passed a
semi, and I saw her head turn toward the window.

"You scared?"

"Yeah," she said.

"That's good. You'd be crazy if you weren't."

"Will you . . ."

"Of course. And I'll help any way I can. You know that."

"Thanks, I . . . you're . . . well. You know." Then she turned to face me. "You do know, right?"

"Yes, I do. And I feel the exact same way."

◆　◆　◆

After I got Emma checked back into the Center, I headed to the hotel. My flight wasn't until ten the next morning, so I flopped onto the bed and switched on the television. I flipped through the channels with the remote twice, but found nothing to watch.

Turning it off, though, I had an idea.

I'd stayed at so many hotels like this one. Each one received a different set of channels, though, and even when some channels were the same, they were always in a different place on the dial, assigned a different number. There seemed to be no way to avoid having to spin through all of them at least once.

Unless.

What if you had a remote control you brought from home? One that knew the channels you liked, or which television shows. One that could interface with a TV anywhere, and guide you directly to the channels or shows you wanted?

I got up off the bed and went to the desk. I'd fished a mechanical pencil from my bag before remembering I didn't have any paper with me.

Returning to the bed, I found a small notepad on the nightstand. Manila-colored stationery, barely bigger than a postcard, bearing the hotel's insignia. It'd have to do. I clicked out some lead and started drawing.

By the time it was done, the schematic stretched across nine of the little pages. I smiled at it, even as I had to mark the corners to remember which way they fit together. Shen wouldn't want to receive a mess like this, but I could redraft it once I got home.

He'd need the drawing to start a new file for me.

ACKNOWLEDGMENTS

While writing a novel can be an incredibly individual enterprise at times, it also requires guidance and assistance from countless people. In addition to the unwavering support of my family, I could not have written this book without input from: Tom Millikan on all things technical; real-life pilots including my father, Shelly Irvine, and Mike Voie; and various Texas friends including Alan Albright, Conor Civins, and Bradley Coburn. Beta readers—all wonderful writers in their own right—including Jennifer Sarja, Rachael Martin, Anjali Enjeti, Jaime Olin, Taline Manassian, and Michele Cavin provided feedback on various drafts and lent a sympathetic ear whenever one was needed.

As hard as writing a novel is, publishing one is even harder, so I am forever indebted to those who helped *Takeoff* along the way. The entire team at Thomas & Mercer supported this project in countless ways, particularly my editor, Liz Pearsons, who pushed the book to be better at every turn. My agent, Cynthia Manson, believed in the manuscript (and me!) when no one else did, and showed incredible determination to perfect and sell it. And Ed Stackler, a fantastic editor and even better friend, was the Sherpa without whom I would still be out lost on the mountain.

ABOUT THE AUTHOR

Photo © 2017 Makela Reid

The son of a navy helicopter pilot, Joseph Reid chased great white sharks as a marine biologist before becoming a patent lawyer who litigates multimillion-dollar cases for high-tech companies. He has flown millions of miles on commercial aircraft and has spent countless hours in airports around the world. Although published in both his academic disciplines, *Takeoff* is his debut novel. A graduate of Duke University and the University of Notre Dame, he lives in San Diego with his wife and children.